THE

In the softly diff
moment to focu
the room was p
opied bed. The
room, on which were two
glasses, and standing beyond the table with his back to the door was a man.

For a moment as she looked at him she felt her heart contract with fear. It was not Lord Ravenscar. He was too tall. Then he turned round. Her lips parted, but no sound came from them.

It was Peter who stood there!

Arrow Books by Barbara Cartland

Autobiography

I Search for Rainbows
We Danced All Night

Polly: the Story of My Wonderful Mother
Josephine Empress of France

Romantic Novels

1 *Sweet Punishment*
2 *The Black Panther*
3 *Stolen Halo*
4 *Open Wings*
5 *The Leaping Flame*
6 *To Mend a Heart*
7 *Towards the Stars*
8 *Armour Against Love*
9 *Out of Reach*
10 *The Hidden Heart*
11 *Against the Stream*
12 *Again This Rapture*
13 *The Dream Within*
14 *Where is Love?*
15 *No Heart is Free*
16 *A Hazard of Hearts*
17 *The Enchanted Moment*
18 *A Duel of Hearts*
19 *The Knave of Hearts*
20 *The Little Pretender*
21 *A Ghost in Monte Carlo*
22 *Love is an Eagle*
23 *Love is the Enemy*
24 *Cupid Rides Pillion*
25 *Love Me For Ever*
26 *Elizabethan Lover*
27 *Desire of the Heart*
28 *Love is Mine*
29 *The Passionate Pilgrim*
30 *Blue Heather*
31 *Wings on my Heart*
32 *The Kiss of Paris*
33 *Love Forbidden*
34 *Danger by the Nile*
35 *Lights of Love*
36 *A Light to the Heart*
37 *Love is Dangerous*
38 *Love on the Run*
39 *Theft of a Heart*
40 *The Enchanted Waltz*
41 *The Kiss of the Devil*
42 *The Captive Heart*
43 *The Coin of Love*
44 *Stars in my Heart*
45 *Sweet Adventure*
46 *The Golden Gondola*
47 *Love in Hiding*
48 *The Smuggled Heart*
49 *Love Under Fire*
50 *Messenger of Love*
51 *The Wings of Love*
52 *The Hidden Evil*
53 *The Fire of Love*
54 *The Unpredictable Bride*
55 *Love Holds the Cards*
56 *A Virgin in Paris*
57 *Love to the Rescue*
58 *Love is Contraband*
59 *The Enchanting Evil*
60 *The Unknown Heart*
61 *The Reluctant Bride*
62 *A Halo for the Devil*
63 *The Secret Fear*
64 *The Irresistible Buck*
65 *The Odious Duke*
66 *The Pretty Horsebreakers*
67 *The Daring Deception*
68 *The Audacious Adventuress*
69 *Lessons in Love*
70 *The Complacent Wife*
71 *The Little Adventure*
72 *Journey to Paradise*
73 *The Wicked Marquis*
74 *A Heart is Broken*

Barbara Cartland

THE WINGS OF LOVE

ARROW BOOKS

ARROW BOOKS LTD
3 Fitzroy Square, London W1

An imprint of the Hutchinson Publishing Group

London Melbourne Sydney Auckland
Wellington Johannesburg Cape Town
and agencies throughout the world

First published by Hutchinson & Co (Publishers) Ltd. 1962
Arrow edition 1967
Second impression 1967
This edition 1975

Made and printed in Great Britain
by The Anchor Press Ltd
Tiptree, Essex

ISBN 0 09 910280 3

1

'Amanda will walk into dinner before Lady Hamilton, will she not, Mama?'

Mrs. Burke looked horrified.

'Really, Harriet, I cannot allow you to soil your lips with that person's name. I hope and pray that Amanda will never be under the same roof as such a woman, and I am sure Lord Ravenscar would not countenance his future wife coming in contact with any lady who does not belong to the "*beau monde*".'

'And she will take precedence over the wives of baronets and knights,' Harriet continued irrepressibly. 'Just think, Amanda, what fun it will be to toss your head at Lady Dunkley. Whenever she sees us with Papa, she always says —"Really, Vicar, I cannot think how your family manages to grow so fast!" As if we were doing something indecent.'

'Harriet, you are not to talk like that,' Mrs. Burke said, but she spoke absent-mindedly as if her mind was not on the conversation of her sixteen-year-old daughter.

She was, in fact, concentrating on turning up the hem of a gown worn by her eldest child. And now, with her mouth full of pins, she said:

'Turn a little to the left, Amanda dearest. This gown is still far too long for you. I cannot think how, when I am quite tall and your father not far off six foot, we should have such a tiny daughter.'

'I am sorry to give you so much trouble, Mama,' Amanda said in her soft voice.

'It is no trouble, my love,' Mrs. Burke replied. 'And I certainly do not want you to feel out of place amongst Lord Ravenscar's friends from London.'

Amanda did not reply. She had a feeling that however she was dressed she would feel shy and gauche amongst the sophisticated ladies and the elegant dandies she had seen two days ago driving in their smart carriages and cabriolets up the drive to the Castle.

The village church and the Vicarage were just inside the park and it had long been an amusement for the Vicar's children to watch the guests arriving for what the villagers spoke of as ' 'is Lordship's wild carry-ons'.

Until a few days ago it was years since they had seen Lord Ravenscar. In fact he had been nothing but a profile flashing by behind the glass of a painted coach, or a figure on horseback galloping across the park with a dozen other riders beside him.

Amanda had not even thought about him very much or wondered about his parties, although Harriet was incessantly preoccupied with them.

'What do you think they do?' she had asked Amanda a few days ago when they were undressing and the windows of the Castle were shining brightly through the trees and were reflected golden and glowing in the lake.

'Eat and drink, talk and perhaps dance, like other people,' Amanda replied.

'There must be more to it than that,' Harriet insisted. 'Everyone is so shocked—more shocked than they are by Lady Hamilton. Some people even forgive her because she has made Lord Nelson happy, but it does not seem as if Lord Ravenscar makes anyone happy.'

'I cannot conceive why he should interest you so greatly,' Amanda smiled.

'Of course I am interested,' Harriet said. 'It is all very well for you, Amanda. You are content with doing the same thing day after day, year after year, and seeing nobody but the villagers. I want to go to London, and somehow I will get there when I am grown up.'

Amanda had laughed, but the questions that Harriet had asked remained in her mind and she had thought of them as she walked up the drive to the Castle the following day to fetch the flowers to decorate the altar in the church. It was traditional that the flowers in the church should come from the hothouses of the Castle.

She slipped into the garden by the side gate and made her way across the lawns towards the greenhouses. Everywhere the daffodils were like golden guineas and she noticed that the azaleas were already showing colour. The spring was late this year, the gales in the Channel had been unprecedentedly rough and the winter had been hard.

Amanda drew a deep breath. Two days of warm weather had wrought a miracle. All around her was the soft, tender green of opening buds and the pink-and-white blossom of the fruit trees. She looked across the gardens to where they sloped abruptly towards the river.

It was not surprising, she thought, that Lord Ravenscar came less often to visit his country seat in the winter time. It could be bitterly cold when the winds from the sea swept round the Castle or when the mist rose, damp and penetrating, from the little river which wound its way through the village into the creek which broke the cliffs to the west of them.

Ravensrye, as the village was called, was mentioned in the Domesday Book, and the Castle had been there before the Norman invaders took it over, improved it and made it one of their strongholds.

Not that it looked very Norman now, Amanda thought, glancing up at it. There was only one old tower left. The rest was a hotchpotch of each succeeding generation, culminating with the new and magnificent Georgian wing built by Lord Ravenscar's father soon after George III came to the throne.

Realising that she was dawdling, Amanda picked her way across the garden and found, as she had expected, Forsythe, the old gardener, cutting the lilies for her in the first greenhouse she came to.

'Good morning, Forsythe! How beautiful the lilies are this year!' Amanda exclaimed.

'Ye said that four years ago in 1800 when Oi first started these yer lilies, Miss Amanda,' he replied. 'An' ye 'ave been a-saying' it every year since. But for once Oi think ye be telling th' truth and not payin' Oi a compliment.'

They laughed at that and with her arms full of lilies Amanda turned to go. She came from the greenhouse to find that the spring sunlight was breaking through the sea mist which had veiled the countryside since dawn. She looked up and her eyes were blinded for a moment so that she did not see anyone approach, and a deep masculine voice made her jump.

'And who have we here?' it asked. 'Are you an angel come to visit us?'

Wide-eyed, she looked round to find a middle-aged man regarding her through his quizzing glass. Even in the first fleeting glance she appreciated the elegance of his closely fitting blue coat with its velvet collar, his white breeches and the polished hessian boots in which she could see her own reflection. To complete the picture he carried a gold-handled malacca cane and had a high beaver hat set at an angle on his dark head.

Just for a moment she hesitated and then she dropped a curtsy.

'I think you . . . must be Lord Ravenscar,' she said a little nervously.

'You know me and I do not know you,' he replied. 'Who are you? If, indeed, you are not an angel.'

Amanda had no idea how lovely she looked with the sun glinting on her fair hair, the lilies filling her arms and her blue eyes fringed with dark lashes raised towards her interrogator.

'I am Amanda Burke, my Lord.'

'Amanda Burke,' he repeated. 'A charming name, though I might have expected you to be called after some goddess. Damme, I have it! You are Persephone, come from the underworld to bring us spring after the darkness of winter.'

A little smile brought Amanda's dimples into prominence.

'I am afraid I have not brought you anything, my Lord,' she replied. 'Instead I have come to fetch from your greenhouses the flowers for the church. We are exceedingly grateful to you for giving them to us for the altar and I assure your Lordship they are much appreciated.'

'For the church,' Lord Ravenscar repeated, and then gave an exclamation. ' 'Pon my soul! Burke! You are the Vicar's daughter.'

'Yes, my Lord. My father has been the Vicar of Ravensrye for near on sixteen years.'

'I perceive that I shall have to leave my cards on him.'

'I am sure my father would be most conscious of the honour your Lordship paid him,' Amanda said primly.

She turned as if to leave, but Lord Ravenscar moved forward beside her.

'Tell me about yourself.'

'There is very little to relate,' Amanda replied.

'What do you do all day?'

'Sometimes I assist my father in the parish,' Amanda answered. 'And I help my mother look after the younger children.'

'I cannot imagine why I have never seen you before,' Lord Ravenscar complained.

'Your Lordship does not often attend the Sunday services,' she replied demurely.

She spoke mischievously, then felt she had been rude and added hastily:

'Your Lordship must not think that I was reproaching you. We quite understand that when you come to the country from the gaieties of St. James's you wish to rest.'

'So that is the excuse is it?' Lord Ravenscar asked with an amused smile.

'But of course,' Amanda replied. 'My father has always explained that you live a very busy and active life in London as a friend of His Royal Highness the Prince of Wales. When you do come to the country, you wish to relax and perhaps make up for the sleep you have lost.'

'I am honoured that you should know so much about my activities,' Lord Ravenscar smiled.

'I do not think we know anything really,' Amanda answered. 'It is just that people in the village talk and my father has always said that scandal can often be averted if people speak frankly and sensibly about what is happening instead of making a mystery of it.'

'I quite see I must be grateful to your father,' Lord Ravenscar said.

They had reached the gate at the end of the garden which led into the park. Amanda stopped, then curtsied once again.

'I usually go this way across the park, my Lord. It is a quicker way to the Vicarage than down the drive.'

'When shall I see you again?' he asked.

She opened her eyes a little at his tone.

'If you care to call on us, my Lord, my mother . . .'

'You know I do not mean that,' Lord Ravenscar said impatiently.

She looked up at him, noting the heavy lines running

from his nose to his mouth, the pouches under his eyes, the somewhat unhealthy pallor of his skin.

'He is not a very nice man,' she thought. But it would be fun to tell Harriet that she had actually talked to the notorious Lord Ravenscar. She could already see the surprise on her sister's face. She had a feeling, however, that there would not only be surprise but concern in the expressions of her father and mother.

'You are very pretty, Amanda!'

She edged a little way towards the gate.

'I . . . I think, your Lordship . . .'

'No, pretty is not the right word,' he went on. 'Lovely! You are lovely, young, unspoilt, innocent. My God! I had forgotten such women existed.'

Holding her lilies with one hand Amanda managed to open the gate with the other.

'I must go now, my Lord.'

'Amanda, look at me!'

The words were a command and instinctively, childishly obedient, she looked up at him. She saw his hand go out towards her, felt his fingers cup her chin, and then realised in a sudden terror as his thick, rather sensuous lips drew nearer to hers that he intended to kiss her.

She gave a little sound that was half a cry, half an expression of anger. And then she was gone, running swifter than the wind itself, and Lord Ravenscar stood watching her go with a heap of white lilies lying in the dust at his feet.

The lilies were returned to the Vicarage an hour later together with a huge bunch of orchids. They were accompanied by a note addressed to Miss Amanda Burke.

'What is this?' Mrs. Burke asked, coming into the hall as a groom in claret-and-gold livery handed over the flowers.

'The flowers are from the Castle, Mama,' Amanda answered.

'Indeed, I thought you went to fetch them!' Mrs. Burke exclaimed. 'And those orchids! How magnificent they are! We have never had orchids before.'

'I expect Forsythe thought we would like a change,' Amanda said quickly.

She took the flowers and hurried down the path towards the church. She did not mean to lie to her mother, but somehow she could not bear to tell anyone of her encounter with Lord Ravenscar. She felt a little sick when she thought about it. She could still feel his fingers on her chin and see the look in his eyes as his face drew nearer to her.

'He is old and horrible!' she told herself; and putting down the flowers in the church porch she opened the note. There were only a few words written on the sheet of crested writing paper.

To Persephone from someone who longs for her loveliness as the winter longs for the spring.

Amanda read it through, tore the paper into a dozen tiny pieces and leaving the flowers in the porch walked across to the rubbish heap. It was in the corner of the churchyard, where the graveyard keeper burned the dead flowers from the graves and the long grass which he cut with his scythe.

A bonfire was still smouldering and Amanda threw the pieces of Lord Ravenscar's letter into the midst of it. Then feeling it was somehow satisfactorily disposed of, she went back to the church. She arranged the lilies on the altar, but the orchids, beautiful though they were, she placed on an obscure window-ledge where few people could see them.

Her task completed, Amanda dropped on her knees in one of the pews and bent her head. She tried to say the prayers she always said—one for her family whom she loved so deeply, another for the people who were sick in the village, and lastly a plea that the war might be over soon and the armies of Napoleon Bonaparte defeated. But somehow today the familiar words and phrases seemed meaningless. Instead she found herself praying wordlessly and not quite coherently that she herself might be saved.

She could not even formulate what she meant or of what she was afraid. She only knew it was there, an instinct which told her she had something to fear. But as she raised her head from her hands and looked at the cross on the altar, shining in the sunlight, she thought how ridiculous she was. There was nothing to be afraid of—nothing.

It was only as she walked back towards the Vicarage and saw a high phaeton with black-and-yellow wheels standing outside the front door, with a groom in claret-and-gold livery at the horses' heads, that she knew why she had felt the need to pray.

Harriet met her in the hall.

'Who do you think is here?' she asked in a whisper, her eyes dancing with excitement.

'Lord Ravenscar,' Amanda answered.

'Oh, then you know!' Harriet exclaimed. 'How disappointing. Did you see him arrive or did you guess?'

'I saw his phaeton outside,' Amanda replied.

'Why do you think he has come?' Harriet enquired.

It was a question Amanda was already asking herself and she did not reply.

'Do you think he has come to ask us to a party at the Castle?' Harriet went on in a low voice resonant with excitement. 'Or do you think he has come to offer Papa another living?'

'Another living?' Amanda questioned in surprise.

'Well, he has got dozens of them,' Harriet answered. 'I have often heard Papa say so. And the Dean of Frackenbury died a month ago.'

'You mean that Lord Ravenscar could appoint Papa to a position like that?'

'Of course he could,' Harriet replied.

'But Papa would not want to leave here.'

'Why not?' Harriet asked fiercely. 'And even if he did not want to, Mama would make him. He has been sixteen years in this mouldy little village with never a rise in salary, never a chance of preferment, when all his contemporaries have become arch-deacons or bishops.'

'I never thought of that,' Amanda murmured.

'It would be wonderful to live in Frackenbury,' Harriet went on. 'Think of the shops and all the friends we could make. Oh, Amanda, keep your fingers crossed!'

Amanda went towards the stairs.

'Where are you going?' Harriet asked. 'Are you not going to wait here and see him when he comes out?'

'No, no, of course not!'

Harriet's words made Amanda run up the stairs to her own bedroom. She sat down on the edge of the bed and looked through the window across the parkland towards the Castle. She had not remembered until now that Lord Ravenscar was the patron of her father's living. He had seemed so much apart from their lives, and yet it seemed that they owed him even the bread they put into their mouths, the clothes that they wore and the house in which they were living.

It was obvious that she must not offend him. At the same time she could not help hoping that she need never see him again.

The door burst open and Harriet came rushing in.

'They want you. They have sent for you,' she said breathlessly. 'Mama says you are to go down at once.'

'Me?' Amanda said. 'Why should Mama want me?'

'Lord Ravenscar is still there. I suppose he wants to see you. Mama did not say I could do so, but do you think I could come in with you?'

'Are you quite certain they asked for me?' Amanda enquired.

'Yes, of course I am,' Harriet said. 'Mama came out into the hall—and, Amanda, she looked strange, almost as if she had been crying or she was going to cry, and yet at the same time she spoke quite sharply. "Go and fetch Amanda and tell her to come here at once," she said. So I flew up the stairs. Oh, Amanda, hurry up! Do not just stand there. Had you not better change your gown? The one with the blue sash is better than that one.'

'No, I will go down as I am,' Amanda answered.

'Then comb your hair,' Harriet wailed, but already Amanda was half way down the stairs.

She moved swiftly until she reached the door of the sitting-room and then she hesitated a moment, her hand shaking as she put it out towards the handle.

She was vividly conscious as she entered that Lord Ravenscar seemed to dominate the room. He was standing with his back to the fireplace and he appeared to tower above her father, who was standing beside him, and over her mother who was seated in one of the worn armchairs which badly needed re-covering.

Just for a moment they all turned to stare at her, and Amanda, having glanced at Lord Ravenscar, looked away from him, afraid of the expression on his face. Her father walked towards her. He took her hand in his and she was astonished to realise that his fingers were trembling. His face was very serious and she knew instinctively that what he had to tell her was bad news.

'What is it, Papa?' she asked in a low voice.

Harriet had been wrong, she thought. Papa was not going to get preferment. Perhaps Lord Ravenscar was going to dismiss him. She felt his hand tighten on hers.

'Amanda,' he said in his quiet, grave voice, 'I have something of great import to tell you.'

'Yes, Papa.'

Whatever it was, she thought to herself, they could face it all together. If they had to leave their home, if they had to go to a smaller and less well-paid living, somehow they would manage. Now that she was eighteen she would be able to help her mother more than she had done in the past. There was always the question of education, of course. That was bound to be expensive, especially for Roland because he was a boy.

'It is something,' her father was saying, 'which has come as a great surprise to your mother and myself. But it is also something on which we cannot make any decision, or indeed take any action, without consulting you first.'

'No, indeed,' Mrs. Burke said from the fireplace.

Amanda looked towards her mother. She understood now what Harriet had meant when she said Mama looked as if she had either been crying or was just going to. There was something else in her face, something Amanda did not understand. She felt a sudden surge of anger towards Lord Ravenscar. Why should he upset her parents like this?

'What is it, Papa?' she asked again.

She felt her father draw a deep breath before he replied:

'Lord Ravenscar, my dear, has done us the honour of asking for your hand in marriage.'

Afterwards it was difficult for Amanda to remember exactly what she had said or done in that first moment of shock. Only at the back of her mind was the knowledge that Lord Ravenscar could, if he wished, promote her father to a better living or even take away the one he had already. She could not seem to take in anything else. She could not seem to understand exactly what they were saying to her.

'There is no hurry,' she heard Lord Ravenscar say. 'I will, of course, wait for my answer.' He raised her fingers to his lips. 'Do not make me wait too long, Persephone,' he murmured so that only she could hear.

And then he had gone, her father showing him to the

front door and bowing to him as he drove away in his yellow-and-black phaeton. But Amanda just stood as if turned to stone while her mother, and Harriet who had been listening at the keyhole, both talked at once.

'Where did you meet him?'

'How has he ever seen you?'

'I cannot believe it is true!'

'It seems utterly incredible!'

'To think you will be Lady Ravenscar, you will be living at the Castle. You will go to London; you will meet the Prince. Amanda, Amanda, 'tis beyond belief!'

Their words were like waves beating on the shore, until her father came back in the room and Amanda moved towards him almost as if she was walking in her sleep and put her hands in his.

'You alone can decide,' he said a little heavily.

'What made him ask for me?' Amanda enquired.

'He said he had seen you in the garden . . .'

'You never told us that,' Harriet interrupted.

'He said,' the Vicar went on, 'that he realised then that you were the wife he had been looking for all his life.'

'It does not seem possible,' Mrs. Burke said. 'Lord Ravenscar! But, Arthur, have you thought . . . ?'

Her eyes met her husband's, and now the tears that she had held in check ran unashamedly down her cheeks.

'It is entirely up to Amanda,' the Vicar repeated.

'What can she know?' Mrs. Burke asked almost as if Amanda were not present.

'But, Mama, think what it would mean to all of us,' Harriet said. 'I could go to a finishing school, Caroline could have a governess—a proper one, not the village teacher—and Roland could go to . . . to Eton and on to a university like Papa. Oh, Mama, is it not wonderful?'

'That sort of consideration does not enter into it,' the Vicar said sharply. 'Amanda must make up her mind whether she can love this man. Of course, she has hardly met him as yet. As I said to Lord Ravenscar, "It is absurd, my Lord, to expect a girl who does not know you to accept your offer without very serious consideration, honoured though she may be by your Lordship's condescension."'

'Condescension?' Mrs. Burke questioned. 'From him!'

'My dear,' the Vicar answered. 'We cannot sit in judgment of a man of whom we know so little. He is, moreover, a member of the aristocracy, a personal friend of the Prince of Wales and, I understand, an intimate of the Prime Minister and many members of the Government.'

'But, Arthur, his reputation!'

'What do we know of him, Margaret?' the Vicar said. 'What really have we heard?—The gossip of a few jealous people in the County, the tittle-tattle of the villagers. Have we ever been to one of his parties at the Castle? Have we ever met his friends? We have got to be fair. At the same time, Amanda shall not commit herself to anything until she is sure, absolutely sure, that this is the man with whom she wishes to spend the rest of her life.'

Mrs. Burke dried her tears.

'Yes, of course you are right, Arthur, and we must give him a fair chance, just as we would give any man who wished to marry one of our girls as fair a chance to show us he was worthy of her.'

'Well, I know what I would say,' Harriet remarked. 'And I should not waste any time about it either. Just think of being Lady Ravenscar!'

'I am afraid, Harriet, I sometimes detect in you a very materialistic streak which is not at all desirable,' the Vicar said sternly. 'This is not a moment to think of the social advantages that such a marriage would bring to Amanda, but whether she could ever feel that this man was meant by God to be her true and rightful spouse.'

'Yes, of course, Papa,' Harriet said in a meek voice, accepting the reproof in a manner which she knew very well would soften her father's heart. Instantly he put out his hand to pat her bent head.

'That is the right spirit, Harriet,' he said. 'And I suggest now that you and I take a little walk together and leave Amanda to talk to her mother.'

'We shall have to do more than talk,' Mrs. Burke said briskly. 'If Amanda is to dine at the Castle with us tonight she will need something to wear.'

'Dine at the Castle tonight!' Harriet cried with a little shriek. 'You did not tell us. May I go too?'

'No, Harriet, you are not invited,' Mrs. Burke replied.

'It is too unfair, it is really,' Harriet wailed. 'Why could he not have seen me in the garden?'

Taking her by the hand the Vicar dragged her away, protesting; and when they returned from their walk they found Amanda being pinned into a gown of her mother's.

'It will never be ready in time, I am sure of it,' Mrs. Burke said. 'And she has nothing else to wear. For goodness' sake, Harriet, stop talking so much and go and press the sash you will find in the top drawer of my chest-of-drawers—and be careful you do not burn it.'

Somehow, Amanda was never quite sure how, they reached the Castle on time. Her mother gave her last-minute admonishments about being careful with the gown because the sash had had to be pinned into place and the hem was only tacked up. Nevertheless the effect was very attractive.

Even so, Amanda felt she compared very unfavourably with the elegantly dressed ladies who were assembled in the big Silver Salon of the Castle. She found it impossible to take in their names or those of the gentlemen to whom she was being presented. She was conscious only of feeling small and very insignificant and of being afraid of looking up into Lord Ravenscar's face for fear she would see that look in his eyes that had haunted her ever since she had seen it for the first time that morning.

It was there, she was sure of it, and her fingers were cold in his and she made no response to the fulsome manner in which he greeted her father, her mother and, lastly, herself.

'Welcome to my home,' he said. 'I do not think you have been here for some years, Vicar. I must show you the new pictures I collected when I was in Italy and the furniture my father imported specially from France—the buhl, I believe, is quite unique of its kind.'

He turned to Amanda:

'And what can I show you, Persephone?' he asked. 'Will the flowers in my conservatory interest you more than anything else?'

She felt as if every word he spoke to her was a trap.

'I should like to see the pictures you are going to show Papa,' she answered.

She caught a sudden glint in Lord Ravenscar's eye as he turned to offer Mrs. Burke a glass of Madeira.

Dinner was a fantastic meal as far as Amanda was concerned. She had never imagined that people lived in such a lavish and opulent style. There were gold ornaments on the table, and they ate off silver plate. Each dish was more exotic and delicious than the last; and the wines in the cut-crystal glasses were superb. It was all something that she had never encountered before in her quiet, austere life.

She was surprised to see that her mother and father were not in the least overawed at being in such company. Mrs. Burke, on the contrary, was talking to a red-faced, middle-aged man of her girlhood in the Shires and how she had hunted with the Quorn and the Pytchley and he was regaling her with his own experiences with the same packs. And the Vicar was discussing pictures and books with an ease and a knowledge which made Amanda proud of him.

It was the women who made her feel shy. One of them, who was seated on Lord Ravenscar's right, wearing enormous diamonds in her ears and round her neck, was obviously sulking about something. Her red lips were pouting and in a voice which contrived to be both sweet and poisonous she made rather rude, unkind remarks which often seemed quite incomprehensible to Amanda.

It was difficult for her to take in everything. There was so much to see, so much to hear, so much to eat, that in the end she gave up the unequal struggle of trying to talk and just sat silent, letting the conversation flow around her, but conscious that a great deal of the time Lord Ravenscar's eyes were on her.

'I will not look at him, I will not,' she told herself. And yet, somehow, as if he were a magnet, she found herself looking towards him unwillingly yet irresistibly.

'He is old,' she thought again. 'He seems even older than Papa. How can I marry someone like that? How could I make him happy? How could I possibly love him?'

Dinner came to an end and the ladies repaired to the Salon.

'Do you really spend the winter here?' the dark lady with the diamonds enquired with a note of sarcasm in her voice.

'Of course. We have work to do,' Mrs. Burke replied, 'apart from the fact that we could not afford to go anywhere else.'

'And your daughters—I understand you have more than

one—how do they spend their time?'

'Up to now they have been busy being educated,' Mrs. Burke replied.

'And now they are grown up,' came the question, 'will you try to marry them to some worthy farmer or will you look further afield?'

The question was intended to be deliberately rude, Amanda could see that.

'If I had my way,' she thought, 'I would never allow such people inside the Castle.' The implication of her own thoughts made her breathless. She would be mistress here—mistress of all this luxury and grandeur. There would be no question of the guests ignoring her or making her feel insignificant.

She could hear Harriet's excited voice, hear her exclaim over the gold and silver plate. She could shut her eyes and imagine Caroline running down the corridors, Roland sliding down the banisters of the grand staircase. How wonderful it would be to send him to Eton, to know that he could be sure of going to Oxford! He would have a horse to ride in the holidays.

She could hear him now complaining, as he did so often: 'Why cannot I have a pony, Mama? Even the farmers' sons have ponies.'

'We cannot afford it, Roland.'

'We cannot afford it. . . . We cannot afford it. . . . We cannot afford it!' Amanda could hear those four words being said over and over again. She had not realised how much they were part of her life, how indivisibly knit into their very existence.

With a start she realised that the men were coming from the dining-room and she had not heard anything the ladies had been saying for the last quarter-of-an-hour. She had been lost in her own thoughts, sitting a little apart, her hands in her lap, her fair head a little bent.

Lord Ravenscar came straight across the room towards her.

'Come, I have something to show you,' he said.

She rose obediently to her feet. He drew aside the curtain and led her through the open window on to the terrace. It was a warm night and she saw that fairy lights had been arranged on the lawns and around the edge of the lake. Twinkling like tiny stars, they were reflected in the water and shimmered amongst the leaves of the bushes and shrubs into which they had been skilfully woven.

'Oh, how lovely!' Amanda exclaimed.

'I thought it would amuse you,' Lord Ravenscar said. 'You are only a child, are you not? And there are so many things I can do to amuse you, so many things I can show you.'

'It is very pretty,' Amanda said. 'It makes the lake look quite different—the garden too.'

'I did it for you,' Lord Ravenscar repeated.

'Thank you. Thank you very much.'

'Is that the only way you are going to thank me?'

His voice was low and deep. She felt his arm go round her shoulders.

'I . . . I think we should go back and . . . and fetch Papa and Mama,' she faltered.

'But why?' he enquired, and she realised that his arm was tightening about her.

'They . . . they would . . . like . . . to s . . . see . . . the . . . l . . . lights,' Amanda stammered.

'There is no hurry,' Lord Ravenscar said. 'We can watch them together and the others can come out later if they wish.'

His arm tightened still further and Amanda felt herself trembling.

'Please . . . please, my Lord.'

'Must you always run away from me, Amanda?' he enquired. 'I am waiting for your answer to my proposal.'

'Yes, I . . . I know, my Lord, but . . . I must wait and have time to think. We do not . . . know each other very well.'

'Is that necessary?' Lord Ravenscar enquired. 'We shall have plenty of time to get to know each other when we are married.'

He drew her very close to him.

'I will teach you to love me, Amanda. You are young and lovely and you excite me as I have forgotten it was possible to be excited. I want to marry you, Amanda. I want to marry you now, at once. Then I can teach you what love is.'

His voice was so hoarse that she could hardly hear what

he said. His breath was coming quickly, his hands were caressing her bare shoulders and moving upwards towards the soft rounded warmness of her white neck. She felt his fingers tighten there and then suddenly his mouth came down on hers.

She gave a little cry; she strove to struggle against him and realised even as she did so how small and ineffectual she was against his strength. She felt a sudden revulsion, an absolute horror of the hot, hard pressure of his lips, of his mouth which seemed to fasten on hers greedily and possessively as if it were a leech which must suck the very life-blood from her.

And then as she struggled, even as she felt almost faint with the horror of what was happening, a sudden shot shattered the silence, followed by a very fusillade of shots, one after the other in quick succession.

Lord Ravenscar released Amanda and stared into the darkness beyond the garden.

'What the devil is happening?' he enquired angrily.

2

For a moment Amanda and Lord Ravenscar stood absolutely still. It was a warm night without a breath of wind and the sound of the shots seemed to echo all around them. Then in the distance they heard men shouting and swearing.

'Good God, Ravenscar! Has the invasion started?' a man asked from the window.

There was a sudden scream as one of the women heard the words and cried out:

''Tis Napoleon! He has landed!'

Amanda woke from the inertia which had held her spellbound. With a lithe movement she turned from Lord Ravenscar's side and ran down the terrace and on to a gravel path which skirted the lawns.

She knew the way so well that she could have traversed it on the darkest night, but at this moment the moon came from behind the clouds and the gardens were flooded with a silver light.

Like a ghost Amanda ran between the dark shadows of the bushes and out into the moonlight, only to disappear a second later beneath another clump of shrubs. The garden began to slope downhill. Built upon high ground, on the west side of it lay the river, widening at this point until it reached the creek which led into the sea.

It was from there that the sound of the shots had come, and as Amanda drew nearer she could hear quite distinctly someone giving orders, men shouting confusedly at each other and a number of full-bodied oaths as one man evidently cursed another for doing something wrong.

She came to a halt at the top of a long flight of steps which led down to the boat-house. There was a wrought-iron gate and she pulled it open. Just as she did so, three men came up the steps in front of her.

In the moonlight she recognised two of them instantly. One was Ned Hart, an ostler at the local inn who was known for being wild and a ne'er-do-well, and the other was Ben Oakes, a young ploughman who had got into bad company because he was so easy-going and ready to do anything that was asked of him.

Both men stared at her apprehensively and she saw that between them they supported a third. He was a man she had never seen before; but the sight of him made her draw in her breath sharply, for blood was pouring down his face from a wound in his forehead.

'What is it, Ned?' Amanda asked. 'What is happening?'

' 'Tis the Dragoons, Miss. They caught us unawares. We got away all right, all but this gen'lemen 'ere.'

The word gentleman made Amanda look again at the man they supported. She saw by his clothes and by the elegant cut of his hair that he was of a very different class from the men who carried him. She was about to say something when Ned turned his head fearfully to look behind him.

'Them be after us, Miss,' he said simply.

Amanda stepped aside from the gateway.

'Get into the maze, Ned,' she commanded. 'You know the secret of it, but strangers will not.'

Ned and Ben with their burden moved forward to obey her, but as they reached the shrubs which bordered the way to the maze she heard Ned ask in a hissing whisper:

'Where shall us take 'im afterwards, Miss? Like as not th' soldiers'll search our 'omes.'

Amanda hesitated. For one moment she was about to say the Vicarage, and then realised that this might implicate her father.

'The Temple, Ned,' she said in a low voice which she hoped would reach no other ears but his. 'Take him to the Temple.'

'Aye, Miss.'

His words had hardly reached her before Amanda could hear heavy breathing and the sound of men's feet coming up the steps from the river. She moved forward to stand in the gateway, and a second later a sergeant appeared, wheezing and sweating, and behind him two Dragoons with their muskets in their hands. When they saw Amanda barring their way, they stopped.

'What is all this noise and commotion?' she asked sternly. She tried to speak calmly; at the same time her heart was beating suffocatingly. She was well aware that she must delay the soldiers so as to give the three men time to get into the very heart of the maze.

'Smugglers, Ma'am,' the sergeant replied. 'You must have seen 'em, for they came this way.'

'I fear you must be mistaken, Sergeant,' Amanda answered. 'I have just this moment come from the Castle and I met no one. There is no other path but this.'

'They must be 'iding in th' garden,' one of the soldiers muttered. 'We saw 'em coming up these steps—three of 'em there were, and one of 'em wounded.'

'Smugglers! Did you say smugglers?' Amanda asked, speaking to the sergeant in tones of intense surprise and ignoring the comment made by the soldier.

'Yes, indeed, Ma'am,' the sergeant replied. 'And a ferocious gang of 'em too. We'd 'av 'ad the lot if one of my men, the stupid idiot, 'adn't fired too soon and warned 'em so that they took to the water in the darkness.'

His voice was rising in indignation when he remembered that he had more important things to do than to explain to a woman what had happened.

'Never you fear, Ma'am,' he said. 'If you'll just stand aside and let us enter the garden we'll catch 'em yet. They can't have gone far—not with a wounded man to slow 'em up.'

He advanced forward as if to pass her and, with a sudden sinking of her heart, Amanda realised how weak and helpless she was beside these armed men. Then to her relief she heard footsteps behind her and saw that Lord Ravenscar was approaching and with him several of his guests.

'Ah, here is his Lordship!' she exclaimed. 'You must ask his permission before you enter the garden.'

'What is all this? What is all this?' Lord Ravenscar asked in tones of extreme irritability. 'Are these men annoying you, Amanda?'

'No, indeed, my Lord,' Amanda answered. 'But it is they who are responsible for the shots that we heard.'

'Dragoons!' Lord Ravenscar exclaimed, staring at the

sergeant. 'What are you doing here, my man?'

'We're after smugglers, m'Lord. With instructions to shoot or take prisoner every man engaged in that nefarious trade. We were told there were some boats coming in 'ere and we'd 'ave caught 'em red 'anded if . . .'

'On whose orders were you sent on to my land without my permission?' Lord Ravenscar interrupted.

The sergeant looked somewhat taken aback.

' 'Tis not usual to ask anyone's permission, m'Lord. The people along the coast are only too glad to co-operate with the coastguards.'

'The people along the coast must do as they please,' Lord Ravenscar replied, 'but I will not have anyone firing on my land and making such a devil of a noise without my permission. Go back to your Commanding Officer and tell him to call on me in the morning.'

'But, my Lord . . .' the sergeant began, 'there are three smugglers . . . hiding in your Lordship's garden.'

'Let them hide,' Lord Ravenscar said. 'Sergeant, you have my instructions. Tell your officer, whoever he may be, that I wish to speak to him. I've never heard such impertinence,' he added, turning to this guests. 'The demmed fellows think they can make one's private garden a rifle-range. The next thing we know they will be walking all over the Castle looking for fugitives. I shall see the Secretary of State for War on my return to London and tell him to keep his troops in order.'

'Good for you, Ravenscar!' someone ejaculated. 'I have heard a lot of people say the soldiers are a nuisance, but nobody has ever complained about the smugglers. Not when they leave a good keg of brandy on the doorstep, eh?'

There was laughter at this and Lord Ravenscar, holding out his arm to Amanda, said:

'Come, Amanda, let me take you back to the Castle. Your father and mother will be wondering what has become of you.'

'Thank you, my Lord,' Amanda answered. 'I am indeed glad you will not consent to further bloodshed.'

'Did you see anything of the fellows, Miss Burke?' a man asked.

'I was so busy listening to the sergeant,' she prevaricated, 'that I had little time for anything else. I suppose there were smugglers, but in the dark it could easily have been a figment of the soldiers' imagination.'

'There are some exceeding rough gangs operating near Dover,' an elderly gentleman remarked, 'and others near Newhaven. But I have never heard of any in this particular area.'

'That is typical,' someone else said. 'The Dragoons dare not challenge the real gangs, they're too frightened of them. They seek out the local smugglers, village lads who make a run across the Channel for the pure devilment of it, and then send a fulsome despatch to Whitehall, hoping to impress the authorities with their brilliance. I saw the last shipload of prisoners sent for transportation and I assure you they were mostly village yokels. There was not a real smuggler amongst them.'

' "An Englishman's home is his castle!" ' Lord Ravenscar quoted. 'And I am not having anyone trespassing on my property without a good reason for it.'

Amanda could not help but feel grateful to him. If he had behaved in any other way the Dragoons might easily have run Ned and his companions to earth. The maze was not a difficult one and, though as a child she had often been terrified that she would not find her way out and would have to stay there all night, it would have been easy, if Lord Ravenscar had been agreeable, to find one of the gardeners who would reveal the secrets of its winding paths and clipped hedges to the searching soldiers.

'Thank you, my Lord,' she said to Lord Ravenscar as he helped her up the steps and on to the terrace, and her gratitude was more fervent than was necessary for mere politeness.

They came back into the drawing-room to find the ladies waiting for them full of excitement and curiosity.

'It was not Boney and his soldiers,' Lord Ravenscar announced, 'but merely a few trespassing and over-enthusiastic Dragoons shooting at the local smugglers. As far as I can ascertain they were such bad shots that the smugglers got away with hardly a scratch.'

Amanda glanced at her father and saw the relief in his face. He was well aware that there was always extra money in the village when the sea was calm; but it was tacitly understood that the Vicar would not interfere. On Sunday after a successful trip the collection would be unexpectedly large or there would be a golden guinea in the wooden offertory box which stood just inside the porch.

'I think it is time we went home,' the Vicar said.

Mrs. Burke rose quickly to her feet.

'Oh, not so soon!' Lord Ravenscar ejaculated. 'I have not had time to show you my pictures. And I am sure there are many things here in which I could interest your daughter.'

He smiled at Amanda as he spoke, but she looked away from him.

'I am, indeed, a little fatigued, Papa,' she said in a low voice to her father.

'We are most grateful for your hospitality, my Lord,' the Vicar said, holding out his hand.

As if he realised that they were determined to leave, Lord Ravenscar made no further protest and escorted them towards the front door. As they left the Salon, Amanda, going last, heard one of the guests say:

'What maggot has got into Ravenscar's brain? A parson to dinner! I could hardly believe my eyes.'

Somebody answered with a remark that Amanda could not catch, but it was followed by a burst of laughter and she guessed that some reference had been made to herself. She felt her cheeks burn; and then, as she reached the hall, she put her hand into Lord Ravenscar's and felt him raise it to his lips.

'You are enchanting, Persephone,' he said softly. 'I will come for my answer tomorrow.'

'No, my Lord . . .' Amanda tried to answer, but already he had turned away and the flunkeys were helping them into the carriage which had been ordered to carry them the short distance to the Vicarage. Mrs. Burke sank back against the cushions.

'I had no idea that Lord Ravenscar could be so charming,' she exclaimed. 'Perhaps, Arthur, we have misjudged him all these years. It is so typical of people to give a man a bad name just because they do not see him or they do not get invited to his house. No one could have been more considerate. Did you see the gold plate?'

'It was certainly a very pleasant evening,' the Vicar said

slowly. 'Did the soldiers apprehend anyone, Amanda? Was anyone hurt?'

Amanda parted her lips to tell him about the stranger whom Ned and Ben had hidden in the maze, but then she decided against it. She felt that her father would forbid her to get involved in any way, but she knew that already it was too late. She was involved. She had sent them to the Temple and that was where, as soon as she could, she must join them.

'The sergeant of the Dragoons said they caught no one,' she answered.

'I am glad of that,' the Vicar said. 'Our village boys will take these risks, but they know the penalties if they get caught.'

'They are so foolish,' Mrs. Burke cried. 'Transportation is too terrible to contemplate and yet they go on risking their lives and their liberty just for the sake of a few guineas. You would think they would find the game was not worth the candle. I really think you ought to speak to them, Arthur.'

'They would only tell me to mind my own business, my dear,' the Vicar said.

The carriage came to a standstill.

'Here we are home again,' he went on. 'And although I have enjoyed the evening out, I must admit that I am ready for bed.'

'And so am I,' Mrs. Burke agreed.

She lit three candles in their silver candlesticks which were placed ready for them on the table by the door.

'Run along to bed, Amanda dear,' she said, 'and try to sleep. I know you have got a lot to think about and a very big decision to make. You must leave it in God's hands to guide you to do the right thing.'

'Yes, Mama,' Amanda answered dutifully.

She kissed her parents and picking up her candle followed them upstairs. She went to her bedchamber but she did not undress. Instead, she searched her chest-of-drawers for the things she needed—a bandage, a bottle of witch-hazel, scissors and a soft towel. She put them all together in a little bag and then thought that the final thing she needed was a bottle of brandy.

Very quietly she opened the door. Her parents were

already in bed. She could hear them talking, but their light was out. Very slowly, taking care to walk where she knew the boards did not creak, Amanda crept down the stairs. She would have waited longer, but the memory of the blood running down the stranger's face gave her a sense of urgency.

She crept into the dining-room and opened the cupboard in the sideboard. As she had hoped, there was a bottle of brandy in it, used only occasionally by the Vicar when someone was ill or when he had a distinguished guest to entertain. There was not much left in the bottle, but it was enough.

Amanda thrust it into her bag and then tiptoeing down the passage let herself out by the garden door. Once again the moonlight made it easy for her to find her way—not that she could not have done so blindfold. She crossed the garden, plunged into the shrubbery at the far end and came through the bushes to a small wood in the centre of which was the Temple.

It had been built at the beginning of the last century by a somewhat eccentric ancestor of Lord Ravenscar who had a predilection for everything that was classical. Legend had it that he sat in the Temple attired in a toga, but after he died no one at the Castle had gone there again. Gradually, because it was far away and on the very boundary of the Vicarage garden, it had become both neglected and ignored.

The Burke children had appropriated it as their own. It became a secret hiding place where no one interfered with them, where they amused themselves on wet days and where they could play all sort of games of pretence without being told to tidy up or to put their things away.

Coming upon the Temple now in the moonlight, Amanda thought what a perfect hiding place it was. The briars, brambles and shrubs had grown so closely round it that it was approachable only from the Vicarage, and even that way it was hidden by the trees and undergrowth. Once inside it was a veritable fortress against the outside world. Its paint was torn and peeling, but the pillars which supported the carved frieze were strong and when the fire was lit the damp on the well-built walls was speedily driven out.

Just for a moment as she approached it Amanda had a sudden qualm of fear. Was she wise to go on with this? Would it not be better to shut her eyes, as her father did his, and not to interfere? And then resolutely she pushed open the door.

For a moment she thought no one was there. The place was in darkness. And then she heard a moan and Ned said:

'Ah, 'tis ye, Miss Amanda. We 'ave been a-sittin' 'ere without a light for fear the soldiers 'ad a-followed us.'

'No, you are safe enough,' Amanda answered. 'His Lordship said he would not have them on his property.'

''E said that!' Ned ejaculated. 'That be the best thing Oi've ever 'eard on 'im.'

'Light a candle,' Amanda said. 'You will find two on the mantelshelf. Ben had better get some wood and we will make a fire.'

She stood still while the men obeyed her; and then as the candle flickered into life, she looked and saw that, as she had expected, they had put the wounded man on the old couch. Just for a moment Amanda felt her heart give a sudden start of fear. He looked so still and the blood on his face was vivid against the pallor of his skin.

'Is he . . . is he dead?' she asked.

'Nay, 'e be alive,' Ned answered. 'We rattled 'im cos we were in an 'urry ter get 'ere. But we couldn't 'ang about could we, Miss? Not with th' blinkin' soldiers after us as if us be Frenchies.'

'No, of course not,' Amanda agreed. 'Hurry up and get the fire going. He must be cold.'

As she spoke she pulled some blankets and a rug from an oak chest which stood by the couch. Last summer Harriet, who had been going through a phase when she wished to commune with Nature, had insisted on sleeping in the Temple and Mrs. Burke had given her blankets and a rug with which to do so. The idea had, however, not been a success. Harriet had declared that the owls kept her awake, but Amanda had thought secretly that she was afraid of the dark and the ghosts which her vivid imagination had invented.

Amanda covered the wounded man and picked up a china bowl from amongst the children's tea things and odd plates which were stacked by the fireplace.

'Fill this with water,' she said to Ned. 'There is a small well behind the Temple. It is not deep, but the water is clear and comes from a spring.'

'Oi knows it, Miss,' Ned answered.

As he went out through the door, he bumped into Ben coming in with an armful of wood.

'Get the fire going quickly, Ben,' Amanda commanded.

She bent forward and touched the injured man's hand. His skin was chill to her fingers and, although the hand was shapely and the skin white, she had a feeling that it was strong, and there was strength, too, in the limp, still body lying on the couch.

Ned brought the water and held it while she started to wipe away some of the blood congealing on the man's forehead and still oozing a little in a dark trickle.

'If there is a bullet in him, what are we going to do?' Amanda asked.

'There be no bullet,' Ned answered. 'If there 'ad been, 'e'd 'ave been dead as an 'erring. Th' shot caught 'im sideways and knocked th' sense out of 'im. Oi 'oisted 'im on me back an' splashed out inter th' rushes. Th' soldiers couldn't see we for 'twas dark.'

'It was brave of you to save him,' Amanda said.

'We didna want ter leave no prisoners be'ind in case they blabbed on us,' Ned said with an impudent grin, but Amanda knew he had not thought of that at the time.

'Hold up the candle so that I can see,' she commanded.

Ned did as he was told, and now she saw that he had been right. The bullet had seared its way across the side of the gentleman's forehead, making a nasty wound and singeing the side of his hair, but it had passed on harmlessly into the air and had not lodged anywhere in his body.

'You were right,' Amanda sighed. 'Thank goodness for that. And now give me the brandy. You will find a bottle in my bag on the table.'

'Brandy!' Ben ejaculated.

'We canna get that down 'is mummer at th' moment, Miss,' Ned said.

'He is not going to drink it,' Amanda explained. 'I am going to get the wound clean. I have always heard that men die because their wounds are dirty and fester. Brandy cleanses—though any wine is good.'

''Tis a waste if ye asks Oi,' Ned quipped.

'I am not asking you,' Amanda said severely. 'Hold the light still. I want to see what I am doing.'

She poured a little brandy over the wound and the pain of it roused the man from his unconsciousness. He started muttering, saying strange words in a hoarse voice, which made Ned exclaim:

''E be delir'ous. 'E 'as th' fever, that's what 'e 'as.'

'He will be all right,' Amanda said soothingly. 'Hand me that bandage.'

She made a little pad of soft linen and placed it on the man's forehead. Then with Ned raising his head a little she managed to get the bandage into place, winding it round and tying it neatly before she tucked the ends away.

'Th' physician 'imself couldna do better,' Ned said admiringly. 'Oi'll know where ter come, Miss, if Oi stops a bullet.'

'And if you do get one, I shall not treat you,' Amanda said sharply. 'You are a fool to risk your life on these dangerous trips. Do you not know what would have happened to you if the soldiers had caught you tonight? You would be in chains and coming up for trial at the Assizes. And you know what the sentence would be?'

'Aye, Oi knows. But all th' same, Miss, 'tis worth it.'

Amanda knew it was hopeless talking to him. At that moment the man with the bandaged head stopped muttering and opened his eyes.

'Where . . . am . . . I?' he asked.

'You are safe,' Amanda answered.

By the light of the candle she looked down into his face and realised that this was the first time she had really looked at him properly and not at his wounded forehead. He was good-looking, she thought. Young, too—he could not be much more than five-and-twenty. He had clear-cut features and dark grey eyes, deep-set beneath strong, dark eyebrows.

There was no doubt that he was, as Ned had said, a gentleman. There was no doubt, too, judging by the quality and cut of his clothes, that he was warm in the pockets. There was a gold ring on his finger; there was a gold fob in his vest pocket which doubtless had an expensive watch at the other end of it.

'What . . . happened?' he asked in a dazed way. 'I . . . I cannot remember. But wait . . . I do now. There was . . . a shot.'

' 'Twere th' soldiers, Sir,' Ned told him. 'They were a-waiting for us. Somebody must 'ave spilt the beans. If Oi could find th' miserable chit 'oo did that, Oi'd choke 'im ter death with these very 'ands.'

'Aye, that's what 'e deserves,' Ben said from the fireplace, where the flames were beginning to leap. 'But 'oo could it 'ave been?'

'I do not suppose it was anyone in the village,' Amanda said quickly, knowing how such rumours and suspicions would cause feuds and unhappiness once they gained ground. 'The sergeant said that the coastguards were reporting places all along the coast and that they had seen boats coming in to the creek.'

'They'll be a-watchin' for we after this,' Ben said. 'A-watchin' all th' time.'

'I expect they will,' Amanda said firmly, 'so that if you have got any sense, you will stay at home and stop smuggling, all of you.'

'Smuggling! Yes . . . that is what . . . they were doing,' the man on the couch said. 'They were . . . smugglers. They gave me a . . . passage.'

His eyes closed wearily as if at the effort of speaking.

'Who is he?' Amanda asked in a low voice.

'Oi dunno, Miss. 'E came when we was a-loadin' an' asked us ter bring 'im back to England. 'E told a rare tale as 'ow 'e'd been swept overboard from a British ship in th' gales. Said some French fishermen kept 'im 'idden and 'e wanted ter get 'ome again before Boney's men put 'im in prison.'

It was a strange story, Amanda thought, and yet it might be true. The only thing was that the gentleman's clothes seemed extraordinarily smart for a man who had been hiding amongst the fishermen on the French coast.

Then he opened his eyes and smiled at her.

'My name is . . . Peter Harvey,' he said. 'I am sorry I cannot rise to . . . to introduce myself.'

She smiled back at him.

'Lie still,' she admonished. 'You have had a nasty wound on your head, and if it was not thanks to Ned here, the

Dragoons would have captured you.'

'I am grateful, Ned,' Peter Harvey said quietly. 'I will see that . . . you do not go unrewarded for this.'

'Oi didna do it for that,' Ned said awkwardly. 'Oi just didna fancy 'em redcoats a-gettin' their dirty 'ands on ye.'

'I want to say . . . thank you all the same,' Peter Harvey said.

He tried to turn his head and winced.

'Lie still,' Amanda commanded. 'You have lost a lot of blood. You are very weak and if you are not careful you will run a fever.'

Peter Harvey's eyes lighted on the bottle of brandy standing on the table. 'Can I have a drink?' he said. 'And then I will try to move.'

'You have got no reason to move,' Amanda said. 'And, indeed, you would be very unwise to do so. The Dragoons are in the village. They will be searching the cottages and questioning everyone. The only place they will not come is here because it is inside Lord Ravenscar's park. He has refused to allow them on his property. Ned and Ben must both stay here too; and then in the morning they can go off to their work as if nothing had happened.'

She looked at the men to see that they had taken in her instructions, and went on:

'But you must not be seen. They know someone has been injured. They will be lying in wait for him. You will have to stay here until we are certain there is no danger.'

She poured the stranger some brandy while she was talking. He drank it quickly and she saw a little colour come back into his face and knew that he must have been feeling faint.

'I will do as you say,' he said. 'I do not seem to have much alternative.'

'I will bring you some food in the morning,' Amanda told him.

She started to gather her things together and put them back in her bag. For a moment she hesitated over the brandy, wondering if she should leave it for the sick man. Then she decided that it was much more likely that as soon as her back was turned Ned and Ben would finish it off and she did not want to make any explanations to her father.

'What is your name?'

She turned and realised that the man on the couch had been watching her.

'Amanda—Amanda Burke,' she said. 'I am the Vicar's daughter.'

'I should like to thank you.'

'The best way you can thank me is to get well quickly and be gone from here,' Amanda answered. 'We shall all be in a deal of trouble if you are found.'

'I realise that and I am even more grateful,' Peter Harvey said.

'Ned tells me that you have come from France,' Amanda told him. 'Is that true?'

'It is quite true. The men from Ravensrye were kind enough to bring me home,' Peter Harvey replied.

'Was it not dangerous for you being in a French port?'

'Very,' he answered. 'There were the preparations for the invasion all round me—the barges, the soldiers waiting for a fair tide and wind, Bonaparte's generals impatient for the command to sail.'

'You must have been very clever not to have got caught.'

A faint smile twisted his lips.

'I am not clever but lucky,' he said. 'Am I not lucky not to be dead? Am I not lucky to have found you?'

It was an unanswerable argument, Amanda thought. Then, as if the effort had been too much for him, she realised that even as he spoke the last words he had fallen into the sleep of utter exhaustion. She pulled the blanket a little higher up his chest.

'Whatever you do, do not let him move,' she said to Ned. 'I do not want that wound to start bleeding again.'

'Aye, Miss, Oi'll watch 'im,' Ned answered. 'Do ye think ye'd best leave th' brandy in case 'e needs a swig?'

Amanda saw the greed in his eyes and realised that her first suspicions had been correct.

'No, Ned, I do not,' she said. 'I have got to put that bottle back so that the Vicar will not know I have taken it. If you are hungry come back with me as far as the Vicarage and I will try to find you something to eat.'

'Nay, Miss, Oi'll manage,' Ned replied.

'Good night, then!'

She looked round the tiny room. Now that the flames

were leaping up the chimney it looked warm and cosy. There were only two windows and these were covered by heavy, dark curtains to keep out the cold. The panes of glass had long been smashed and only the lead frames remained.

'Be careful not to show a light,' Amanda warned. 'Shut the door quickly behind me.'

Ned crossed to the door as she spoke.

' 'Night, Miss!'

'Good night, Ned! Good night, Ben!'

She heard their voices answering her as she moved away into the darkness, taking a moment or two to accustom her eyes to the moonlight. Then she hurried back to the house, half afraid that she would find soldiers standing in the hall or waiting outside the front door.

She need not have worried. Everything was quiet. There was no sound except the distant hoot of an owl, the sudden flutter of a pigeon disturbed on its roost, and, inside, the tick of the grandfather clock in the hall.

She put back the bottle of brandy in the dining-room and crept up the stairs, once again avoiding the creaking boards, and then reached her own room. It was only then, as she put down her bag and stood staring at her reflection in the mirror, that she realised how tired she was. Could any day have been more packed with adventure and excitement?

Then, as she stood there looking at herself in the gown which had been her mother's and which had been altered so hastily to fit her, she remembered Lord Ravenscar's hold tightening on her on the terrace, felt again that sudden panic when she knew that he was about to kiss her. Those thick lips seeking hers; the lust in his eyes; his arms crushing her resistance by sheer strength.

Just for a moment she let her mind linger on what had happened, and then she put her hands up to her eyes with a little cry.

'I cannot marry him! I cannot!' she told herself. 'I will tell him so in the morning. Papa and Mama will understand. He must not . . . touch me again.'

3

Amanda was awake soon after six. Actually she had slept very little, waking fitfully or dreaming of blood and men escaping from their pursuers.

Now she dressed quickly, putting a warm shawl over her shoulders, and tiptoed down to the kitchen to fill a basket with bread, eggs and butter and a comb of honey from the hive which stood in the rose-garden. She also carried with her a fresh bandage, feeling grateful, as she took it from a pile in the linen chest, that her mother had insisted one rainy afternoon that she and Harriet should tear a linen sheet into strips ready for just such an emergency.

She let herself out into the garden and then drew a deep breath at the sheer beauty of the morning. The sun was rising in golden glory, tingeing the sky a vivid pink until it reached the sable of the night, when it became the soft purple of Parma violets. There were a few stars still twinkling overhead; but, as if they had already been forgotten, the whole garden seemed alive with the song of birds. Overnight the green buds on the trees, the plants and the shrubs had opened so that in that moment Amanda could say, 'Spring is here!'

She felt a sudden surge of happiness. Why, she did not know, because at the back of her mind lurked the darkness and the fear or Lord Ravenscar and the decision she had to make regarding him.

But just for the moment she was happy, filled with youth, joy and excitement, so that she ran towards the shrubbery on feet that hardly seemed to touch the ground. She had expected to find everyone in the Temple asleep, but when she knocked lightly on the door Peter Harvey's voice said, 'Come in,' and she entered to find him alone.

The curtains had been drawn back from the windows,

and although the fire was burning brightly it was by sunlight that she saw him clearly for the first time. He was lying on the couch and looking very pale; but he was smiling and she thought, as she went towards him, that he was the best-looking young man she had ever seen.

She reached his side. His deep-set grey eyes looked up into hers and she saw that he had shaved and tidied his cravat. He had even tried to wash away the blood from his coat and had partially succeeded, so that if she had not known the dark stains had been there she would not have noticed the traces of them.

Just for a moment she stood looking at him, her eyes held by his. And then quickly, because of something which made her instinctively shy, she asked:

'Where are the others?'

'They left as soon as it was light enough to see their way,' Peter Harvey answered. 'Ned, who said he lived only a short distance from here, was obliging enough to fetch me his razor. He will not need to come for it because that would be dangerous. I have made it possible for him to purchase another for himself.'

'You should not have given him money,' Amanda said quickly.

'Why not?' Peter Harvey enquired.

'Ned is too fond of money,' Amanda replied. 'That is why he has turned smuggler. He wants to be rich, to show off in front of his friends, to be able to treat them in the tap-room at the *Four Bells*.'

Peter Harvey put back his head and laughed.

'Have you a dossier on everyone in the village?' he asked.

Amanda flushed.

'I would not wish to sound priggish,' she said. 'But having lived here all my life and watched young men like Ned and Ben grow up, I naturally know all about them. My father has tried to make them courteous and generous to strangers and that is why I said he should not have taken any money from you.'

'He did more for me than give his razor,' Peter Harvey smiled. 'Have you forgotten that he saved my life? If he had not carried me away when I was unconscious, I should at this moment be in the hands of the Dragoons.'

'No, I had not forgotten that,' Amanda answered. 'And

that is why you must be very careful. The soldiers will still be in the village. You must stay here until they are gone. Once before they came and searched every cottage, looking for weapons and contraband, anything which enabled them to arrest those they suspected. But they could prove nothing and so they went away. I have been thinking that they will not be so easy-going this time.'

'I do not want to trespass on your hospitality,' Peter Harvey said.

'I am afraid you have no choice,' Amanda replied.

She smiled at him and once again their eyes met and it seemed to her as if something passed between them, something which made her turn her head away as if with an effort and say quickly:

'I . . . I must change the bandage on your head. I have brought one with me.'

'Let me fetch the water for you,' he suggested.

'No,' she answered. 'You are not well enough for that. What you can do is unpack your breakfast from my basket and you will find a frying pan in the corner. There are also some plates and cups which my sisters and I keep for when we picnic here.'

She picked up the bowl that she had used the night before to wash his wound and added laughingly:

'I am sure the frying pan will need dusting.'

She went out to the little stream, filled her bowl and, as she did so, saw primroses growing close down to the edge of the water. She picked a small bunch of them and carrying them in her hand went back into the Temple.

Peter Harvey, looking very white and shaky, was unpacking the things she had brought and putting them on the table. She glanced up at him as she came in and said sharply:

'Sit down at once. You know you are feeling weak and dizzy. It was foolish of me to suggest that you should get up before you had eaten. Sit down at once.'

He obeyed her with a rueful smile.

'It is so idiotic that a mere scratch from a bullet should make me feel like this.'

'You have lost a lot of blood,' Amanda said briefly.

She put the bowl of water down on the table, found the frying pan, dusted it and, putting a little butter into it to melt, set it on the fire. It only took her a few minutes to cook the eggs and put them in front of her patient. He looked at them and asked:

'Are you not going to eat too?'

She shook her head.

'I am not hungry,' she answered. 'I ate too much last night.'

Her face clouded over for a moment as she remembered where she had eaten such a large and exotic dinner; but Peter Harvey, without further argument, fell avidly upon the eggs. He was desperately hungry, she thought, and without talking further to distract him, she buttered some pieces of home-made bread and poured him a cup of milk from the jug which had reposed on top of her basket.

'I am afraid there is nothing else I could bring you,' she said when, having finished the eggs, Peter Harvey reached out of his hand towards the cup. 'Papa has the key of the cellar and Mama keeps the tea—which we only offer to important visitors— locked up.'

'I ask for nothing better than this,' Peter Harvey said. 'Everything you have brought me has seemed like food from the gods. I suppose one never appreciates what one eats until one is really desperately hungry.'

'When did you last have anything to eat?' Amanda asked.

'It must have been early yesterday morning,' he answered. 'I meant to have a meal before we left and then, as the men said their boat was slow and the tide was right, we sailed before noon. I forgot all about food, expecting —somewhat foolishly I suppose—that I should be able to get something to eat when we landed.'

'Where are you trying to get to?' Amanda asked casually.

It seemed to her that something flickered across Peter Harvey's eyes and there was a perceptible pause before he answered:

'London.'

'Your home is there?'

Again there was a pause before he replied:

'I have no home. My parents are both dead.'

'I am sorry,' Amanda said.

'So am I,' he added gravely. 'Although you do not resemble her in any way, you remind me of my mother. She, too, was gentle, sympathetic and very lovely.'

As if his words reminded her of her duty, Amanda rose.

'If you have finished,' she said, 'I must now rebandage your wound.'

He sat still while she removed the bandage, only wincing slightly when she took away the pad of linen which was soaked with dried blood. Amanda stared intently at the wound. It was ugly, raw and, because the bandage had stuck, it was now oozing a little. At the same time it was not inflamed and she knew that, as she had anticipated, the brandy had done its work.

'It is not going to look very beautiful,' she said, 'but at least it is clean. You should not have very much trouble with it.'

He winced again as she put on another pad of linen and rebandaged it deftly. When she had finished he rose to his feet and said:

'I wonder how I can thank you? Do you realise how grateful I am or how much I owe to you? I should do you a grave disservice if I let you run any risks on my behalf. I really think it would be best if I left now.'

'No, no, you cannot do that!' Amanda cried. 'It would be crazy; the soldiers would be waiting for you. Do you not understand that by now they will have searched all the village? They will have found there is not a wounded man anywhere, but they have plenty of evidence that one was injured. You were seen escaping on Ned's shoulders. They saw him and Ben—only fortunately they did not know who they were—helping you up the steps into the Castle grounds. Then you disappeared!'

She pressed her fingers to her temples as if to help herself think.

'There are only two ways in which it would be possible for an injured man to get away from this neighbourhood,' she went on. 'One is by sea—which would obviously be impossible, for the coastguards will be watching the creek and all along the coast; the other is by land and the Dragoons will have their men well posted to prevent that. With that bandage round your head you are a marked man.'

Peter Harvey smiled gently at the intensity of her tone.

'Then what do you suggest I do?' he enquired.

'Stay here until they get tired of looking for you and then go away,' she answered. 'It is as simple as that. They will wait, and when you do not appear they will have to give up the search. Lord Ravenscar has refused to allow them in the Castle park and grounds. They will therefore have a very good idea where you are. So long as he withholds his permission, there is nothing they can do about it. You must hide here. I will bring you food whenever I can; and as soon as it is safe for you to start your journey to London, I will let you know.'

'You are so small, you look like a child—a very sweet, very attractive child,' Peter Harvey said unexpectedly. 'And you are one of the most sensible people I have ever met. Are you always like this?'

'When I have to be,' Amanda replied.

'Amanda is a very pretty, unpractical name,' Peter Harvey said. 'Ned told me that is what you are called. And now there seems to me to be some magic about it—a magic perhaps that is connected with your fair hair, blue eyes and that ridiculous, tiny, upturned nose.'

Amanda said nothing, but, blushing a little, she picked up the things on the table and started to tidy them away.

'Are you angry with me?' Peter Harvey asked anxiously.

'No,' she answered. 'But I suppose I am not used to compliments.'

'They were not really compliments,' he answered. 'The English never know how to accept compliments—especially English women. No, I was just thinking aloud.'

'I suppose I ought to be flattered then,' Amanda said with a little smile. 'But actually I am worried. This is not something to be taken lightly.'

'I am not taking it lightly,' Peter Harvey contradicted in his deep voice. 'Not really. I am only overwhelmed with the knowledge of what you and Ned have done for me and wondering how I can ever repay you.'

'You can repay us best by not getting caught,' Amanda said. 'If you are there will be a lot of explaining to do which might be very uncomfortable for us both.'

'I can credit that,' he answered. 'And I will do what you tell me. Does that satisfy you?'

'For the moment at any rate,' she smiled. 'Now is there anything else that you want particularly? I am glad Ned brought you a razor because Papa might have thought it vastly suspicious if one of his had disappeared.'

'I want nothing,' Peter Harvey said. 'Unless, perhaps, when you are kind enough to come and see me you could bring me something to read. I had a book with me when I went aboard the smugglers' boat, but it must have been left behind with my overcoat.'

'I will find you another,' Amanda promised. 'Papa's library is full of books although I am afraid you would find many of them very tedious.'

'Never mind, they will help to pass the hours when you are not here,' Peter Harvey told her. He sat down suddenly on the chair by the table. 'I have got a devilish headache,' he exclaimed. 'Perhaps it is as well that I am not attempting to leave the village today. It would be awkward to be found having an attack of the vapours in the ditch.'

'You must not attempt to leave until you are really well enough,' Amanda told him.

'Ravensrye!' Peter Harvey said reflectively. 'It is a charming name. I suppose Ravenscar was originally derived from it. By the way, what do you think of his Lordship?'

There was a sudden rush of colour in Amanda's cheeks and she turned aside to put more wood on the fire.

'I have seen his Lordship—only occasionally,' she replied.

'And yet, you were dining with him last night, if Ned's version of your movements is correct.'

'Yes, my father and mother were at the Castle too.'

'Well, what do you think of him?'

'I do not think I can discuss his Lordship,' Amanda said.

'Why not? Most people are only too willing to do so,' Peter Harvey replied. 'I suppose he is one of the most disliked men in the whole of Society. And yet the Prince enjoys his company!'

Amanda sat back on her heels and looked across the tiny room at him.

'Why is Lord Ravenscar so disliked?' she asked.

Peter Harvey shrugged his shoulders.

'I cannot think that my answer to that question would be fit for your ears,' he replied. 'Let us say he is not a particularly desirable acquaintance, as, living at his gates, you have perhaps already found.'

'And yet he can be kind,' Amanda said in a low voice. 'It

was kind of him not to let the soldiers search for you last night. He knew you were there—not you, personally, but someone who was wounded—but he refused to give them leave to trespass upon his land. That was kind.'

'It was indeed,' Peter Harvey agreed. 'I wonder what he stood to gain by being kind at that moment?'

'Is that not in itself rather an unkind and unfair remark?' Amanda asked accusingly.

Peter Harvey laughed.

'*Touché!* You are right there. It was perhaps ungenerous of me. No, I must be grateful to his Lordship. When we meet, I will accede him that point at any rate in his favour.'

Amanda turned her head away from him.

'What else do you know about Lord Ravenscar?' she asked.

'So much that I would not stoop to repeating it,' Peter Harvey answered. 'He is a bad man, little Amanda. Take my word and keep away from him. From all I have heard he does not spend much time here.'

'He comes occasionally.'

'Alone?' Peter Harvey asked.

Amanda shook her head.

'Oh, no, with parties. Harriet—she is my younger sister—watches them pass. She is extremely interested in what happens at the Castle.'

'You must tell Harriet not to be curious,' Peter Harvey said. 'Whatever Lord Ravenscar does, it is certainly not repeatable to children or anyone so lovely and innocent as yourself.'

Amanda got to her feet.

'I think I must go now.'

Without rising he put out his hand and caught hers as it hung at her side.

'What is troubling you?' he asked in a low voice. 'Has anything I have said upset you? Forgive me if it has. I suppose Lord Ravenscar is a familiar topic of conversation in this village and your father must come in contact with him during his pastoral duties, but otherwise what are you likely to know about him, you and your sister?'

'I have already told you, we seldom see him,' Amanda answered quickly. 'In fact, until yesterday . . .'

She stopped, and Peter Harvey, still holding her hand, said:

'Yes, go on. What happened yesterday?'

'I . . . I had never been inside the Castle,' Amanda said.

'That is not what you were going to say,' Peter Harvey insisted. 'Was it that until yesterday Lord Ravenscar hadn't taken any interest in you?' His voice sharpened suddenly. 'That is not true, Amanda? Tell me that is not true.'

She pulled her hand free of his and picked up her warm shawl and placed it over her shoulders.

'I must go now,' she said quietly.

'Not before you have answered me. Amanda, you cannot go away after all that I have said and leave me wondering what I have done wrong.'

'You are not to blame,' she answered. 'You could not know and I suppose I would rather hear the truth.'

'What is it I could not know?' Peter Harvey asked. 'Amanda, answer me. You have got to answer me.'

Amanda drew a deep breath.

'Lord Ravenscar,' she said in a voice hardly above a whisper, 'has offered for me. That was why we were all at the Castle last night.'

'Offered for you!' Peter Harvey's voice had also sunk to a whisper. '*Nom de Dieu!* But it cannot be true! But, why? Why, when he has got himself talked about with Lady Isabel . . . ?'

He stopped suddenly.

'Never mind that. What is your answer, Amanda? Tell me what answer you are going to give him!'

Amanda threw back her head suddenly.

'I am going to say no,' she told him. 'It will mean that Papa cannot be Dean of Frackenbury. It will mean that Harriet, Caroline and Roland will be disappointed, but it cannot be helped. I cannot do it! I cannot!'

She was trembling all over and now she put one hand up to her lips as if to erase the memory of Lord Ravenscar's kiss. She knew then that, although she had tried not to think of it, her mouth had throbbed all night from the horror of his touch.

'Of course you cannot,' Peter Harvey said soothingly, and suddenly, to her surprise. He was standing close to her.

He put out his arms and quite spontaneously, without

thought, she hid her face against his shoulder.

'I cannot do it! I cannot!' she whispered.

'I know,' he answered, 'and no one must make you, no one.'

She could feel the strength of his arms around her, but somehow there was nothing personal about it. He was just someone strong, reliable and kind against whom she could lean for the moment, someone who understood the predicament in which she found herself.

'Be quite firm,' he said quietly. 'Just say to him: "I regret, my Lord, that I cannot marry you." Do not go into explanations. Do not be led into arguments. Do you understand, Amanda? If you feel you cannot do that, make your father say it for you. Tell your father there are reasons which make it a complete and absolute impossibility for you ever to marry such a man.'

'And what are they?' Amanda's voice asked, muffled against the soft cloth of his coat.

'You poor child,' Peter Harvey said, 'You should never have been subjected to this. You are too young, too innocent to know what Ravenscar is like. There are no words in which I can express myself strongly enough to condemn the viciousness of his private life, the bestiality of his interests. You have got to be firm, Amanda. You quite understand?'

She was still trembling and, still holding her close with one arm, he reached down and very gently put his other hand under her chin and raised her face towards his. He looked down into the tear-filled blue eyes, at the soft, quivering mouth and pale cheeks which a short time ago had been rosy with colour.

'Listen, Amanda,' he said quietly. 'One day you will find a man whom you love and who will love you—a decent man, and a man you can trust and of whom you will be proud, a man of your own age. Ravenscar is old and steeped in sin and degradation. If he does, indeed, wish to marry you, it can only be for two reasons. One, that he lusts after your loveliness; and the other, that it is expedient in some way for him to have a wife at this particular moment. You have got to refuse him.'

'I . . . I want to. I mean t . . . to,' Amanda stammered. 'But he is so frightening. There is something about him, something that makes me feel as if I shall never es . . . escape.'

'You will,' Peter Harvey said. 'I will see to that.'

His tone made her open her eyes in surprise.

'How?' she asked.

'I do not know at this moment,' he admitted. 'But you are not to marry him, not under any circumstance. Is that clear?'

Amanda drew a deep breath.

'I will tell him so this morning.'

'Good girl!'

Peter Harvey gave her a squeeze with his arm which might have been the action of an affectionate elder brother to a younger sister, and then she was free.

'I must go,' Amanda said, wiping the tears from her eyes. 'It is getting late and people will begin to wonder where I am.'

She turned towards the door and then suddenly Peter Harvey had dropped on one knee beside her. She looked at him wonderingly as he lifted the hem of her white muslin gown and touched his lips with it.

'Amanda,' he said, 'that is how a man, any man, should approach you. No one—least of all Ravenscar—is worthy to do more than to kiss the hem of your gown. Will you remember that?'

There was something in the tone of his voice, as well as the action which had taken her entirely by surprise, which made Amanda drop her eyes shyly.

'I will remember,' she said softly before she was gone from the Temple, running down the twisting path which led through the shrubbery and back into the Vicarage garden.

It was only as she approached the house that she realised how long she had been away. The curtains were drawn back, the windows were open, and she could see Nellie, their fat cook, moving in the kitchen. As she hurried onwards she saw, through the trees, the clock on the church tower. It was a quarter-to-nine. How could she have been so long? she asked herself, and what explanation could she make for having been up so early?

She opened the door of the house which led in from the garden and was just slipping up the back stairs hoping not to be seen when there was a cry from the landing above her.

'Amanda! Where have you been? I have been looking for you.'

Amanda looked up guiltily and was relieved to see it was only Harriet.

'What do you want?' she asked.

'Hurry! Hurry quickly!' Harriet cried.

Amanda reached the top step of the stairs to find her sister literally dancing with excitement.

'What is it, Harriet?'

'Oh, Amanda, there is so much to tell you and you are to go down at once to the drawing-room. Lord Ravenscar is there and is asking to see you.'

Amanda felt as if someone had laid a cold hand on her heart.

'Lord Ravenscar! At this hour?'

'Yes, he has been out riding and he has another gentleman with him. But, Amanda, what do you think he has told me?'

'What?' Amanda asked, hurrying to her own bedroom and throwing her shawl on the bed, then running to the mirror to tidy her hair.

'He says,' Harriet answered, her words falling over themselves in her excitement, 'that he will give a Ball for me next year when I am seventeen, and you shall take me to Carlton House and present me to the Prince of Wales. Think of that, Amanda. Carlton House and a Ball! Oh, I can hardly believe it is true. But he has promised yes, he has promised, and he says it will be the finest Ball London has ever seen. Think of it, Amanda. I might be the toast of St. James's.'

'When did he tell you all this?' Amanda asked.

'Just now, when he arrived. There was nobody else to look after him. Papa is holding an early service in the church. Had you forgotten?'

'Oh, yes, I had;' Amanda confessed.

'I thought you must have; and Mama has gone with him, so there was no one in the house but me—and, of course, Caroline and Roland, but they were getting up. I took Lord Ravenscar into the drawing-room and offered him a glass of wine, though I was not certain we had any. He luckily said no, he did not want anything, but the gentleman with him said he would have a cup of chocolate. So I told Nellie.'

She gave a little excited laugh.

'Then Lord Ravenscar started talking to me and asked me how old I was, and when I told him, that was what he said. A Ball in London at his house in Grosvenor Square! Oh, Amanda, will it not be wonderful?'

Amanda said nothing. This was bribery she told herself. She had half expected that Lord Ravenscar would use this method, and it was going to be hard to say no to Harriet and even harder to meet her reproaches later. She rose from the dressing-table.

'I will go down,' she said.

'You will not forget to thank him for saying he will give a Ball for me, will you?' Harriet asked.

'No, I will not forget,' Amanda answered.

She walked slowly yet purposefully down the stairs; it was not going to be easy, she thought, to tell Lord Ravenscar that he could not have what he wanted. And yet, as she had said to Peter Harvey, it was impossible, she could not force herself to marry him.

She opened the door of the drawing-room. Lord Ravenscar was standing with his back to the fire and beside him stood another man whose uniform Amanda recognised as that of a senior officer in the Dragoon Guards. Slowly she approached them and Lord Ravenscar stepped forward to meet her.

'Good morning, Amanda,' he said, and raised her fingers to his lips.

Before he bent his head she was conscious once again of his eyes apprizing her, taking in every detail of her appearance, making her feel as if he mentally undressed her before the touch of his warm, greedy lips made her shiver and long to snatch her hand away from him.

'You . . . are early, my Lord,' she managed to say in a voice that quivered a little.

'I was impatient to see you,' he answered, and then turning to the man standing at his side, he said: 'Besides, Colonel Dovercourt was on my doorstep almost as soon as it was light.'

'The matter was urgent, my Lord,' Colonel Dovercourt said.

'That I understand,' Lord Ravenscar replied. 'But let me present you. Colonel Dovercourt, Miss Amanda Burke, the lady who I hope will do me the great honour of becoming my wife.'

Colonel Dovercourt bowed, but not before Amanda had seen the incredulity and disgust in his eyes.

'My congratulations, my Lord,' he murmured.

'No, no, you must not congratulate me yet,' Lord Ravenscar said. 'That would be premature, would it not, Amanda? I am in the position, Colonel, of being a humble suitor waiting impatiently for the word which will turn me from an apprehensive, anxious man into a supremely happy one.'

Amanda drew in her breath and her lips parted, but before she could say anything Lord Ravenscar continued:

'But I must not take up your time with my intimate affairs. We must explain to Miss Burke why we are here.'

'Is that really necessary, my Lord?' Colonel Dovercourt asked.

'But, of course,' Lord Ravenscar replied.

With a courteous gesture which somehow made him seem very elegant and worldly beside the more stolid Colonel, he indicated to Amanda that she should be seated. Obediently, although she would rather have stood, she did as he said, sitting upright in the winged armchair rather like a child at school.

'And now let me explain, Amanda,' Lord Ravenscar said. 'The position is this. Colonel Dovercourt has come to me with an urgent and almost peremptory request that his Dragoons should be allowed to search the Castle grounds and park. I told him that it was no longer in my power to say yea or nay, for the simple reason that I have promised you—or, rather, I was quite certain that it was your wish—that his men should not trespass further in pursuit of their prey. Am I right?'

Amanda felt the blood drain from her face.

'Y . . . yes, my Lord. You . . . you did say last night that . . . that you would not allow the soldiers to . . . trespass on your land.'

'That is what I said and what I meant,' Lord Ravenscar

replied. 'At the same time, it seemed discourteous to refuse Colonel Dovercourt's request, and also rather unnecessary —unless, of course, we have something to hide. And we have nothing, have we, Amanda?'

His eyes were searching her face and she knew that he must have seen the fear there, the sudden gesture which made her instinctively bite her lower lip, the trembling of her hands so that she was forced to lock her fingers together in an effort to conceal her agitation.

'But what I have told the gallant Colonel,' Lord Ravenscar went on, 'is that if it should offend you in any way that the soldiers should go tramping over the flowers, searching amongst the shrubberies and the woods just in the nesting season, disturbing the primroses and the violets as their heads come peeping between the leaves, then I shall, of course, keep to my original promise to you that the sanctity of my grounds shall be preserved. As my future wife you have but to command, and I, Amanda, to obey.'

'As my future wife . . .' Amanda heard the words as if they were the door of a trap closing behind her. She knew now that she could never escape. He had caught her, just as she had known instinctively from the very beginning that he would do. She was his prisoner, his captive.

Just for a moment she imagined herself saying that she could not marry him and that he must do as he pleased about letting the soldiers search the park and gardens. And then she saw Peter Harvey's grey eyes looking up into hers, felt his arm round her, saw him kneeling at her feet and raising the hem of her gown to his lips.

Just for one second she shut her eyes. Then, with a sense of utter despair she said clearly:

'I am afraid, my Lord, that as your . . . fu . . . future wife I must hold you to your promise of last night, that the soldiers shall not, as you say, desecrate the gardens and the p . . . park.'

She saw the sudden expression of triumph on Lord Ravenscar's face and wondered how soon one could cease to feel anything, even disgust and fear.

4

Lord Ravenscar spoke first.

'Well, Colonel!' he said. 'That seems to be your answer.'

Colonel Dovercourt did not look at him. Instead, watching Amanda, he said quietly:

'I hope you will excuse me, Ma'am, if I beg you not to make any hasty decision in this matter. I must, of course, respect his Lordship's instructions as regards any trespass on his grounds. At the same time, I am in duty bound to carry this matter further.'

'Further!' Lord Ravenscar interjected. 'What the devil do you mean by that?'

'I mean, my Lord,' the Colonel replied, 'that I have reason to believe that the man we seek is no smuggler but someone of a far more important character—someone whom it is my duty as a loyal and faithful servant of His Majesty to seek out.'

'You speak in riddles,' Lord Ravenscar said testily. 'Miss Burke has given you her answer. Does that not suffice you?'

'I wish it might,' Colonel Dovercourt said. 'In which case it would be quite simple for me to withdraw my troops and leave your Lordship's gardens and park to harbour whatever yokel had been pleased to indulge his sense of adventure by smuggling a keg of brandy or a roll of lace across the English Channel.'

'We have not admitted that any such person is taking refuge on my preserves,' Lord Ravenscar remarked irritably.

The Colonel bowed.

'No, my Lord, and I stand corrected. But from the reports of my own men, and from what we have found in the boat, there is no doubt at all that the local smugglers of Ravensrye had a passenger with them last night.'

'How can they be sure?' Lord Ravenscar enquired

loftily. 'It was dark. You admit yourself that your men fired too soon. The smugglers escaped and you would be a wise man, Colonel, if you forget the whole episode. It does not bring much credit to your soldiers or your own organisation.'

The Colonel flushed a little at the arrogant tone in which Lord Ravenscar addressed him, but he stood his ground and replied courteously:

'Everything you say, my Lord, has its foundation in truth. But what you do not seem to know is that this passenger, of whom I am speaking, left two things behind in the boat. One an overcoat which is of a fine quality and cut such as could not possibly have been worn or purchased by one of the local men; and, secondly, in its pocket was a book.'

'A book!' Lord Ravenscar said incredulously. 'For a trip at night across the Channel! 'Tis ridiculous!'

'It is in my possession,' Colonel Dovercourt said, 'and the reason I am deeply concerned with it, my Lord, is that the book is written in French.'

For a moment there was silence, broken only by the tiny gasp that Amanda gave as the full import of what the Colonel was saying sank into her mind.

A man making a stealthy entrance into England carrying a book written in French in his pocket! A man coming from the shores of the enemy! So that was why the Colonel was so insistent that he must search the garden and grounds. A French spy! Someone sent, perhaps, by Bonaparte himself!

She clasped her fingers even tighter together; she raised her eyes to Lord Ravenscar piteously, as if she believed that in some miraculous way he could reassure her.

'A spy!' Lord Ravenscar said ruminatively, as if to himself. He gave Amanda a sidelong glance. 'That puts a very different complexion on the whole affair.'

It was not true. Of course it was not true, Amanda thought. How could she convince them? How could she tell them that Peter Harvey was as English as they were without revealing that she knew of his presence?

'I think, Colonel,' Lord Ravenscar said softly, 'that I should like to speak in private with my future wife. We shall not keep you long, if you will be kind enough to wait in the hall.'

He crossed the sitting-room as he spoke and opened a door which led into the hall. Colonel Dovercourt bowed to Amanda.

'I beg you, Ma'am, in your consideration on this matter, to remember that we are on this island fighting for our very existence. It is reported, as you well know, that Bonaparte has built hundreds of barges with which to invade our land.'

'I do not forget that, Sir,' Amanda said in a low voice.

The Colonel bowed again and went from the sitting-room. Lord Ravenscar shut the door behind him.

'Amanda!' he expostulated. 'What mischief is being hatched in your little head?'

Amanda rose to her feet.

'My Lord, the man they have wounded is no spy,' she said. 'He is English, just as you and I are. He had been washed overboard and has been hiding along the French coast with some fishermen until chance gave him the opportunity to return here.'

'And his name?' Lord Ravenscar asked.

There was something in the way he asked the question which made Amanda feel that she must be cautious for Peter Harvey's sake. After all, he had trusted her with his life and his liberty. She should not betray his confidence or even share it until he gave her permission to do so.

'I do not know,' she answered. 'He . . . he has not been well enough to endure much questioning.'

Even as she lied she wondered what her father would say to her. And yet she believed that such lies, given in defence of someone helpless and in her charge, did not count as any terrible sin.

'Where is he?' Lord Ravenscar asked.

She had anticipated this question and answered lightly, forcing a smile to her lips.

'That is my secret, my Lord. It is not that I would not wish to confide in you, but I could not do so without my fugitive's permission. Besides, even these walls may have ears.'

Lord Ravenscar's eyes narrowed for a moment and she knew he was displeased. Then he laughed.

'Have it your own way, child, if it amuses you. You have promised to marry me, so we have other and more important things to concern us at this moment. The good Colonel is likely to be a nuisance. I think the best thing I can do is to tell him that you are, at the moment, adamant; but that if he will call on me tomorrow I shall, by then, have persuaded you either to hand over this supposed spy to me or to have told me where he can find him.'

'Oh, no, you cannot do that!' Amanda cried piteously.

'Wait,' Lord Ravenscar replied. 'Do not be so impetuous. What I suggest is that tonight we will get your protégé away. Is he well enough to ride?'

'I . . . I think so,' Amanda said.

'Good. I will have a horse saddled and ready for him at any point in the grounds you may wish to name. The soldiers will be waiting until tomorrow and they will not be on the look-out. He can therefore escape while they are still unsuspecting.'

'Oh, how kind of you! How very kind!' Amanda exclaimed.

In her relief she held out her hands towards him. Lord Ravenscar took them in his and holding them said, 'I want a greater reward than that, my dear,' and his eyes rested greedily upon her lips.

Just for a moment Amanda hesitated, feeling almost sick that he must touch her. Then pride and his sense of gratitude made her force herself to lift her mouth towards his. He swept her into his arms.

She shut her eyes, striving not to shrink or to fight herself free of him. She felt the lecherous hunger of his mouth on hers, felt him hold her so tightly as if he would squeeze the very breath from her body. And then, even as the horror of it swept over her, she felt his hand fumbling with her muslin fichu and recoiled from him with a sudden hasty movement which set her free.

'I . . . I must go, my Lord. There is so much to do,' she said. 'But, nevertheless, I thank you.'

'You are eluding me,' Lord Ravenscar said thickly. 'You are like a bird that escapes even as I try to cage it. But it'll not be for long. We shall be married and then you will be mine, Amanda. Do you hear me? Mine!'

'Yes . . . yes . . . my Lord,' Amanda said moving towards

the door, and even as she did so she realised that Lord Ravenscar was following her, saw his hands outstretched towards her and knew, from the look in his eyes, that he had no intention of letting her go.

'Please, my Lord . . .' she said, but it was too late. He was at her side.

'There is no hurry,' he murmured, and she hated the thickness in his voice and the fire she could see smouldering behind his eyes.

In a sudden panic she tried to run, but his arms were round her. Then, at that moment, the door opened and her father came into the room.

'Oh, Papa!'

She gave a little sob of utter relief and turned towards him.

'What is it, Amanda?' the Vicar asked, and she knew by his tone that he was displeased.

He did not wait for her to answer but said to Lord Ravenscar:

'There is a Colonel Dovercourt in the hall, my Lord, who informs me that my daughter is betrothed. I was extremely surprised to learn such information from a stranger.'

'It happens to be true, my dear Vicar,' Lord Ravenscar said: Amanda heard the insolent note in his voice as if he resented that even her father should question him on the matter.

The Vicar ignored him.

'Is it true, Amanda?' he said. 'If so, I consider it somewhat impetuous on your part that you should have informed this gentleman, whom I have never seen before, without first acquainting your mother and me of your intention.'

'I am sorry, Papa,' Amanda said. 'It was . . .'

She stopped and hesitated. How could she explain that Lord Ravenscar had forced her hand? How could she tell even her father that unless she had promised to marry him, as he fully intended she should, he would have sent the soldiers on to the track of a wounded man, like foxhounds running to earth an exhausted fox.

'Pl . . . please, Papa, may I go?' she asked.

'Yes, indeed,' the Vicar said. 'You may leave it to his

Lordship to explain what has occurred.'

Thankfully Amanda turned towards the door, and yet, as she reached it, she was forced to look back.

'You will keep your promise, my Lord, as regards the horse?' she questioned.

'It shall be exactly as I have told you,' Lord Ravenscar replied, and Amanda ran across the hall.

'A horse!' she heard her father ejaculate, and wondered what explanation Lord Ravenscar would give to that.

She hurried upstairs but did not go to seek her mother. Instead she ran to her own room and, shutting the door behind her, ran to the wash-hand-stand and started to wash her face with cold water. She wanted to scrub away the touch of Lord Ravenscar's mouth, and yet it seemed that her lips would always bear the imprint of his.

She knew with a kind of terror that now there was no looking back, that she was, as he had said, his, and all too soon he would claim the fulfilment of the promise she had given him.

'What else could I do?' Amanda thought wildly. The overcoat; the French book. How could Peter Harvey have been so crazed as to have left them behind? And then, even as she thought of them, she remembered something else—the words he had been muttering when he had been unconscious when she had first found him in the Temple, wounded.

She had thought nothing of it at the time, but now she knew why they had seemed so strange. Words broken, disjointed the mutterings of a man who was concussed and delirious, a man who was speaking in French!

With a sudden terror she put her hands to her temples and remembered something else. '*Nom de Dieu!*' That was the exclamation he had made when she had told him that Lord Ravenscar wished to marry her. Was there anything else? Please God there was nothing else that might incriminate him.

The conversation they had had together repeated itself clearly in her mind and she could hear him saying: 'The English never know how to accept a compliment, especially English women.' Was that the sort of thing an Englishman would say? Or would it more likely be the remark of a Frenchman?

She felt as if her suspicions must tear her in half. Supposing he was not what he seemed? Supposing he was really a spy of Napoleon Bonaparte? Could she, as an Englishwoman, let him escape? Was she not, as a patriot and a subject of the King, in honour bound to hand him over to the soldiers?

But he could not be a spy. It was this thought which made her suddenly feel as if a heavy weight had been lifted from her shoulders. Of course not, and if he was innocent he could clear himself.

Why, then, was he hiding? Was it because he must not give away the others? From what Colonel Dovercourt had said he was quite prepared to take a very lenient view with regard to the smuggling. If Peter Harvey should go forward and say who he was, well then, the charge of smuggling could be withdrawn or forgotten. He could establish himself as a British subject.

At least, Amanda thought, she could suggest this to him, and as quickly as possible. If he was to get away that night then he would have to make his preparations. And, anyway, in his present weak state he must rest as much as possible.

She went from her room and stood at the top of the stairs. Colonel Dovercourt was no longer in the hall, so he must be in the sitting-room with her father and Lord Ravenscar. Quickly she picked up her shawl and put it over her shoulders, then she slipped down the back stairs and out through the garden door.

When she reached the shrubbery, she waited for some moments to see that she was not being followed. She had the feeling that she should not, at this moment, trust anyone. The Colonel, knowing that she knew where the fugitive was hiding, might easily have her watched by some of his men.

But nothing stirred in the garden. There were only the daffodils, blowing a little in the breeze, the sunshine making the first yellow azaleas come into bloom, and the wood-pigeons cooing in the shrubbery as if they invited her to enter.

She turned and ran along the path which led to the Temple. She opened the door and found, as she had expected, that Peter Harvey was lying on the couch half asleep. He woke up at her precipitous entrance.

'Amanda!' he exclaimed. 'I didn't expect to see you so soon. Is anything wrong?'

'I do not know if it is wrong or right, as far as you are concerned,' she answered.

'What has happened?' he asked briefly, watching her face.

'When I got home,' she began breathlessly, 'I found Lord Ravenscar was there with Colonel Dovercourt of the Dragoons.'

'Looking for me?' Peter Harvey asked.

'Asking for permission to search for you,' Amanda answered. 'They had found your overcoat an . . . and the book you were reading.'

He got up from the couch and walked towards the fire.

'How could I have been such a fool?' he asked. 'I ought to have chucked it in the sea. But I was in the middle of the tale and it rather amused me, so I slipped it into the pocket of my coat.'

'You know what they think?' Amanda said.

'That I am a spy,' Peter Harvey replied. 'It is obvious, is it not?'

'Yes,' Amanda agreed unhappily. 'It is obvious.'

He turned from the fire to where she was standing in the centre of the little room, both hands pressed against her breast, her eyes dark and troubled.

'And you? What do you think?' he asked.

Her eyes met his and for a long moment she looked at him, seeking something in his face and in his expression that would tell her the truth, that would reassure her fears.

'Tell me, Amanda,' he said very softly, 'what do you think?'

'I know,' she said hardly above a whisper, 'that you would not work for our enemies. I do not know why, but I . . . I trust you.'

He gave a cry of sheer joy, his voice seemed to echo and re-echo around the Temple.

'That is what I wanted you to say!' he cried jubilantly. 'Oh, Amanda! Amanda! If you had failed me, then I think I should have walked out and given myself up.'

She felt the blood rising in her cheeks.

'I do believe in you, I do,' she said. 'But, please, explain why you had a book in French, why you were talking in French when you were unconscious, and why, when I told you Lord Ravenscar had asked for me to marry him, you said, "*Nom de Dieu!*"'

'Did I do all that?' he asked. 'I should not make a very good spy, would I, if indeed I were one? Poor little Amanda! No wonder I have worried and frightened you. I swear to you I am not working for Bonaparte; but, nevertheless, I speak French—well and fluently. I should not have been able to live so comfortably or so freely the other side of the Channel if I had been able to speak only English.'

'No, of course not,' Amanda said in utter relief. 'It was stupid of me even to have wondered about it. But now I have news for you.'

'What is it?' he asked.

'Because they think you are a spy, Lord Ravenscar says that tomorrow he must give the Colonel permission to search the park and grounds.'

'I am safe for today?' Peter asked quickly.

Amanda nodded.

'His Lordship has promised,' she told him. 'And he suggested something else as well. Tonight he will have a horse ready at any place we like to name, so that you can escape, and when they do search they will not find you.'

She expected Peter to be pleased, but the expression on his face seemed to darken as he said:

'That is extremely accomodating of his Lordship. And why should he take this interest in me?'

'He . . . he has done it for my sake,' Amanda said. 'He knows that I am hiding you although he does not know where or what your name is.'

'And so just out of kindness and goodness of heart he is prepared to assist me to evade His Majesty's soldiers who are quite convinced that I am a French spy?'

'Yes, yes, that is what he said,' Amanda replied.

'And what did you promise him in return?'

The question sounded almost like a pistol shot. Amanda started and now her fingers crept up to her mouth as if she would still the trembling of her lips. She turned her head away; but now, with one stride, Peter was at her side and taking her by the shoulders turned her round to face him.

'What did you promise him?' he asked. 'Answer me.'

She would still have avoided looking at him, but he took her chin in his fingers and turned her face up to his, so that she had no alternative but to look at him.

'Tell me,' he insisted sternly. She trembled and the tears gathered in her eyes as she whispered:

'I . . . I promised to . . . marry him.'

'For my sake? To save me? Oh, Amanda, how could you have done such a thing?'

He released her and walked towards the door.

'I am going to give myself up.'

'Do you think that would solve anything?' she asked, running to stand in front of him, her back to the door. 'Listen to me, Peter. He will never let me go. I gave him my promise because he said that as his future wife I could forbid the soldiers to search the gardens and the grounds. He will not release me if you give yourself up voluntarily. I do not think he would release me under any circumstances—not now.'

Her voice broke on the words and she covered her face with her hands. Then she felt Peter's arms around her and started to sob against his shoulder.

'Amanda! I beg of you!' he said. 'Do not cry. Amanda—stop, you are breaking my heart.'

She raised her head at that and through her tears saw him looking down at her with a tenderness in his expression such as she had never imagined she would see on any man's face.

And then quite suddenly, in the passage of a second, she knew—knew that she loved him and knew, in that inexpressibly glorious moment, that he loved her too.

5

The whole room seemed to swim dizzily around Amanda. She was conscious of only one thing—Peter's eyes looking down into hers, his arms holding her, a feeling of wild delight like a sudden flame rising in her heart.

Slowly, very slowly, and with a wonderful tenderness, his lips found hers. Just for a moment their mouths touched; the petal of a flower against the petal of a flower. And then her arms were around his neck and he was straining her to him.

'Amanda! Amanda!' he cried. 'What have you done to me? What has happened to us? Oh, my sweet, my little love, I knew it, I think, from the very first moment I felt your hand against my forehead.'

His mouth sought hers once more and it seemed to her as if the whole world was swept away from them and they stood alone above the clouds in the glory of the sunshine, which had something divine about it.

'I love you,' he said. 'I love you, Amanda! Tell me this is not a dream. Tell me it is really happening.'

'I love you, too, Peter,' she answered. 'From the very first moment, I think.'

'Oh, my darling! Heart of my heart! The woman I have been looking for all my life!'

His voice shook with emotion and now, once again, he was kissing her, wildly, passionately, on her lips, on her eyes, on her cheeks and on her white throat where a little pulse was throbbing madly.

'I love you!' he said again and again, his mouth holding hers until she quivered with an ecstasy which was like wine in her veins.

Her breath was coming quickly, her eyes were like stars.

'I love you,' he said again and thought how inadequate the words were to express the glory which, radiating from them both, seemed to fill the room and reach outside towards the sunlit sky.

'Oh, Peter. . . . Peter. . . .'

A log falling in the fireplace made them remember the danger which beset them. Instinctively they drew apart, but Amanda still clung to one of Peter's hands.

'What are we going to do?' she asked in a whisper.

He did not answer and after a moment she went on:

'Why cannot you see the Colonel and inform him of what has happened? Tell him how you have been hiding in France and this was the only way that you could return to England. You need not in any way implicate the men who brought you over. The Colonel is a gentleman and I think would understand that you could not give him their names.'

'That, of course, is the obvious way,' Peter said. 'But I cannot do it—and I cannot tell you why.'

She looked at him enquiringly and, still holding her by the hand, he made her sit down in the chair by the fireplace. then he knelt beside her on one knee.

'Look at me, Amanda,' he said. 'I am kneeling here beside you because I want you to put your hands in mine and look into my eyes and tell me that you will trust me. It is not going to be easy for you—in fact it is going to be very hard, but you must believe in me and I must beg you to give me your trust, simply because there is nothing else I can do.'

'You cannot tell the Colonel the truth?' she asked.

He shook his head.

'No, and I have to steal away from here in secret. You will not understand, and because I cannot make you any explanations I can only pray that our love is big enough for you to accept this.'

'It is! It is!' Amanda cried. 'I love you—I trust you.'

He took her little hand and, opening it, kissed the palm, slowly and passionately. And then, as she trembled beneath his touch and put out her other hand to touch his dark hair, he said:

'I never believed in love at first sight. I always thought it was something rather ridiculous which happened to poets. But, Amanda, I think I have loved you, not only from my first sight of you, but ever since I was born. Perhaps through all eternity we have been waiting for each other.'

'What shall I do if you go away?' Amanda asked in a troubled voice.

'I do not know,' he answered. 'But one thing you must promise me. Whatever happens, however long I may be gone, you will not marry Ravenscar.'

'Supposing he tries to make me?' Amanda asked.

'You must play for time,' Peter said. 'Do you understand? If you cannot refuse to marry him, then you must stave him off, make excuses to put the wedding as far ahead as possible.'

Amanda shivered.

'I have a feeling that he will want it to be soon.'

'He shall never marry you.' Peter said fiercely, 'Do you understand, Amanda? He shall never marry you—not while I am alive to prevent it. But just for the moment I cannot challenge him, I cannot come out into the open. Oh, my poor darling, if only I could tell you what is hidden in my heart it would be so much easier.'

With a pride which was somehow infinitely pathetic, Amanda drew herself up.

'I will not ask it of you,' she said. 'I know you would tell me if you could. As it is, I will just wait until you can tell me.'

It was the voice of a woman who spoke, but it was followed by the cry of a child.

'Oh, Peter, do not let it be long. I am frightened.'

He put his arms round her and put his lips against her forehead. 'Trust me,' he said. 'Trust me, Amanda, and it shall not be one second longer than I can help.'

He got to his feet.

'When I think of that swine trying to touch you,' he said hoarsely, 'I could go and kill him now. Promise me never to be alone with him.'

The words trembled on Amanda's lips to tell him that she had already been alone with Lord Ravenscar, twice, and that each time he had forced his kisses upon her. And then she knew that if she did tell Peter this, he might, indeed, do something desperate.

It was perhaps in that moment that Amanda grew from a child into a woman. 'Do not worry about me,' she said. 'I will wait. But, please come back quickly.'

He kissed her, but she had the idea that his thoughts were

already preoccupied with something else.

'Where do you suggest that his horse waits for me?' he asked.

'Almost anywhere in the park is safe,' Amanda answered. 'And with a horse you can go across country. I think we have a map here somewhere. It is only an old one that my brother used for his studies, but I can show you the direction to take in which you will come out beyond the Dover road far away from here.'

She rummaged amongst the miscellaneous collection of books which were arranged on a small shelf in the corner of the Temple.

'Roland used to work here last summer,' she explained, 'when Caroline and Harriet were making so much noise in the Nursery that he could not get his lessons ready for Papa who was teaching him. Ah, here is the map. I was sure it was here somewhere.'

She spread it out on the table. Peter looked at it.

'You see how you can go,' Amanda said, tracing a route with her finger.

'And the horse?' he said.

'There is a little dell to the north of the Vicarage,' Amanda answered. 'It dips down steeply from the wood and it would be quite impossible for anyone crossing the park to see if a horse or anyone was hiding there. That appears to be a good place.'

'And is there any way that we can approach the dell and overlook it without being seen?' Peter asked.

'You think someone might follow the horse?' Amanda questioned, remembering how she was afraid of being followed. 'Yes, that will be easy. If we keep to the high ground, we can approach the dell through the wood. From among the trees we shall be able to see and yet not be seen.'

'That is what I meant,' Peter said. 'Tell Lord Ravenscar to have the horse in the dell at nine-thirty of the clock tonight. It will be on the edge of darkness and I can journey a little way before it is too dark.'

'I will tell him,' Amanda answered.

'How I hate to ask you to do this for me,' Peter said, and she knew by the rawness in his voice that he was suffering.

'I was willing to do it before I knew that you loved me,' she answered. 'And now . . .'

'Now it only makes it all the harder,' he said. 'I have found you, Amanda. I love you and yet I have got to leave you, leave you in the clutches of that beast.'

He hesitated a moment and then he said:

'It would not be possible even now for you to draw back, to refuse to marry him?'

'Not unless we are prepared to let the soldiers come here now, at this moment,' Amanda answered. 'They would find you, Peter. They might even shoot you down before you had a chance to make any explanations.'

'I suppose that is the risk we should not take,' Peter frowned.

'You must take no risks except those that are absolutely necessary,' Amanda pleaded.

'I have everything to live for,' Peter answered simply, his eyes on her face.

'I must go back now,' she said. 'I think, in a way, it was indiscreet of me to come as quickly as I did. But I had to see you, I had to tell you what was happening.'

He opened his arms. 'I love you, Amanda!'

She went to him like a bird homing to its nest. For a moment they clung together. She could feel his heart beating against hers.

'Go,' he said at last. 'And do not come back until it is dark, for fear that it should be dangerous.'

'I will come as soon as I can,' she answered, 'and I will bring you food. And, Peter, what about money?'

'Fortunately I have plenty of gold in my purse,' he said. 'Try not to worry, Amanda. Everything will come right in the end.'

She had a feeling that he was only saying this to cheer her up. Because she did not want to add to his difficulties, she pressed her cheek against his for one moment and then, turning from the shelter of his arms, went to the door.

'You promise me you will rest?' she asked.

'I promise,' he answered. His eyes followed her until she was lost from sight amongst the bushes, and then he dropped his head in his hands in an attitude of utter despair and despondency.

Amanda hurried back to the Vicarage. To her relief she saw that the horses had gone and knew that Lord Ravenscar and the Colonel had ridden away. She went into the sitting-room to find her father and mother talking together in low voices and from the anxious expressions on their faces knew they were discussing her.

She had a feeling that her father was angry and yet, for the first time in her life, she was not afraid. The knowledge of Peter's love was a treasure in her heart like the crock of gold at the foot of the rainbow. She might not be able to rely on his help; he might not be able to stand by her at the moment; and yet somehow she knew that eventually they would be together.

All through the day she felt as if she walked in a dream. The rebuke from her father, the anxious consideration from her mother, the jubilation of Harriet over her engagement, and even the flowers which arrived in great profusion from the Castle, were things which could not perturb or touch her. They were all apart from herself.

She bade the groom who brought the flowers wait, and writing a note to Lord Ravenscar which she marked *Private* she said:

My Lord,

Please have the Horse of which we spoke waiting in Oak Dell at nine-thirty o'clock. Anyone in your Stables will know where that is, but Please make sure that They speak of it to No one.

Amanda.

It was only after she had written to Lord Ravenscar that she found, amongst the flowers he had sent her, a note written in his hand. She opened it slowly and read:

To Persephone, that she may soon be in the arms that ache to hold her.

The words seemed to spring out of the page and she felt as if Lord Ravenscar was there and once again his lips were seeking hers. But for the moment even this had no power to hurt her. Because of her secret love for Peter she seemed to walk on air.

'I have never seen you look so happy,' her mother remarked as she went up to change her gown before dinner. 'Lord Ravenscar told your father and me this morning that he wishes to announce your marriage as soon as possible.'

The words seemed to awaken Amanda for a moment from her reverie.

'Surely there is no hurry, Mama,' she said.

'Lord Ravenscar is very anxious that you should be in London for the Season this year. He says it is difficult for him to get away very often as the Prince demands his company so frequently at Carlton House.'

'I have a great desire for a winter wedding,' Amanda said in a low voice.

'Then you will have to talk to Lord Ravenscar,' Mrs. Burke replied.

'Yes, yes, I will speak to him,' Amanda answered, escaping to her own bedroom.

Lord Ravenscar would have to wait, she thought. At the moment she could think of only one thing—of Peter and of getting him away. If he did not go tonight, she was quite certain that the soldiers would be looking for him at dawn. Colonel Dovercourt would not be a person to delay hunting down the fugitive once he had permission.

Dinner seemed to drag as she had never known a meal drag before. The chatter of Harriet and the solemnity of her father's voice seemed to come to her from a great distance.

Immediately the dessert was finished, Amanda said gently: 'I have a headache, Mama. May I retire to bed?'

'I will come and rub your forehead with lavender water,' Harriet said eagerly, and Amanda knew she was longing to talk over the plans for her marriage and all the benefits which it would bring to the family.

'No, no,' she said quickly. 'I want to be alone.'

'I wonder Lord Ravenscar did not invite us to dine at the Castle tonight,' Harriet said.

'It is rather strange,' Mrs. Burke agreed. 'Of course, we were there last night, but that was different. Amanda was not then engaged to his Lordship.'

'I expect we shall see him tomorrow,' Amanda answered. At the same time she wondered anxiously what was afoot. Was the Colonel dining at the Castle tonight? Did Lord Ravenscar's preoccupation mean an added danger to Peter?

Her anxiety made her determined to hurry to Peter whatever the rest of the family might think. She told everyone she did not want to be disturbed and slipped out of her room, locking the door and putting the key in her pocket.

If they knocked and she did not answer, perhaps they would think she was really asleep.

She had collected some food in a basket earlier in the day when the cook was engaged in making butter in the dairy. There was some cold chicken which had been left over from luncheon, several slices of ham, and even a bottle of wine she had managed to take from the cellar because her father had left the key on his desk.

She hurried through the bushes to find that Peter had pulled the curtains over the windows in the Temple and had lit the candle.

'I was afraid you would never come,' he said, taking her arms and relieving her of the heavy basket all in one gesture.

'Oh, Peter, are you doing the right thing in running away?' Amanda asked. 'I have been worrying about it all the afternoon.'

'And so have I,' he answered. 'It shows, my darling, that our minds think alike. But I have got to go. There is nothing else I can do.'

'You are going to London?' she asked.

'I am going to London,' he answered.

She would have asked him more, but he stopped her mouth with kisses.

'We have got to be sensible,' Amanda said what seemed to her a long time later. 'It is quite late. I could not get away before. They would talk to me.'

He drew a watch from his vest pocket.

'It is twenty minutes to nine,' he said.

She forced him to eat some of the food and drink a little of the wine.

'You must carry the rest with you,' she said; but he refused and they left the basket on the table and stood locked together in one long, last kiss before they left the Temple.

Amanda led the way, moving through the shadows of the trees into the park and then entering a little copse.

'Oak Dell is on the other side,' she told Peter in a whisper. Then she stopped. 'Are all these precautions really necessary?' she asked.

'I think they are,' he said gravely. 'Show me in which direction to go and I will go first. Be careful how you walk;

we do not want anyone to hear twigs breaking or leaves rustling. If anyone has followed the horse, they are likly to be hidden anywhere amongst these trees.'

They moved very quietly, keeping to the shadow of the trees. Peter did not speak to Amanda again and she kept behind him. Every so often he stopped and appeared to listen.

A few minutes later they reached the edge of the wood and could see Oak Dell ahead of them. The horse was there under a tree with a stable boy at its head. Amanda was just about to point it out to Peter when she felt his hand clasp hers and the fingers of his other hand touch her lips. She knew then that she must be silent and they stood very still under the branches of an ancient tree.

It was then, with her eyes already accustomed to the darkness, that Amanda saw ahead of them the outline of two heads. Just for a moment she thought she must be mistaken, and then she realised that two soldiers were lying full length at the edge of the wood. She could see their muskets, which were pointing downwards to where the horse was standing.

Amanda drew in her breath. She felt as if she had been turned to stone. For several minutes they stood there, not moving, only watching the soldiers' heads, until Amanda began to wonder when Peter was going to make a move.

One of the soldiers stifled a sneeze.

' 'Ere, look out,' the other man said in a whisper, his voice being carried to Amanda's ears quite clearly. 'Ye don't want to warn 'im, do ye?'

' 'E couldn't 'ear us, not up 'ere,' his companion answered. 'The Colonel said as 'ow 'e'd be coming from the direction of th' Vicarage.'

'Does the Colonel know where 'e is, then?'

'No, but 'is Lordship told 'im I suppose. 'E was there when we got our instructions. Don't seem right, some'ow, that we should fire without giving 'im any warning.'

'Orders be orders,' the other man said laconically.

Peter grasped Amanda by the hand. Very quietly, yet moving as swiftly as they dared, they began to retrace their steps in the direction from which they had come.

6

They stopped in the shadow of an oak tree some way outside the wood. Amanda was trembling, not so much with fear as with rage.

'How dare he?' she exclaimed. 'How dare he? After he had given me his solemn word?'

Peter shook his head.

'Be fair,' he said. 'Lord Ravenscar promised you that he would not allow the soldiers to search the gardens and grounds. They are not searching, they are just waiting with the certainty that they have a sitting target in front of them.'

Amanda put her hands to her face.

'To shoot you down in cold blood,' she said. 'To shoot any man for that matter. He is a fiend. Everything that anyone has ever said about him is true.'

Peter did not answer. After a moment she added in a voice that was no longer angry, but frightened and broken:

'And . . . I . . . I am betrothed to him. What am I to do?'

'You must play for time,' Peter answered. 'You have given your word and to break it would only bring retribution upon your family. Trust me, Amanda. I will find a way, I swear it to you. But I must have more time.'

'How long?' she asked.

He shook his head.

'I cannot answer that question,' he said. 'I cannot tell you anything. I can only beg you, as I have done before, to trust me.'

She stared up at him and the first rays of moonlight coming through the branches of the trees touched her face with silver. She was very beautiful in that moment. She heard him draw a quick breath before he said:

'I must go now.'

'But where? Where can you go, Peter? They will be looking for you as soon as it is dawn.'

'But not until dawn,' he answered. 'That gives me six hours at least.'

'You cannot get far in that time, not without a horse,' Amanda said.

'Then I must get one,' he replied almost gaily.

He put out his hand and touched her lips with his fingers, checking questions she was longing to ask.

'There is no time to talk,' he said. 'Besides, it is dangerous. At any moment someone might come across the park and see us. I want you to go home.'

'And leave you here, without knowing what is going to happen to you? How can I?' Amanda asked.

'Nevertheless, it is what you must do,' he replied. 'I have told you to trust me. That is all I can say, except . . .'

He looked down at her, the expression on his face serious, yet tender.

'Take care of yourself,' he said in a low, deeply moved voice. 'Never be alone with him if you can help it, and play for time. I shall be thinking of you, Amanda, every moment of the day and night, and loving you, my darling, with every breath I draw.'

'But how shall I know if you are safe?' she asked.

'I think,' he replied, 'that our love has wings. When we are thinking of each other, however far we may be apart, my heart will fly to your heart and somehow we shall know, each of us, that the other still cares.'

'I shall never love anyone else,' Amanda said.

On the ends of her eyelashes there were tears which glistened in the moonlight like tiny stars. He looked down at her and then he dropped down on one knee, as he had knelt to her once before.

'I worship you, Amanda,' he said, almost as if he made a vow.

Still he did not touch her. She waited, every nerve in her body yearning for the feel of his arms and his lips on hers. But when he rose to his feet, his face was grim.

'Go back to the house now,' he said, 'while I can watch you. Walk there as quickly as you can and don't look back. Promise me, Amanda, you will not look back until you reach the Temple.'

'I . . . I promise,' she said, because he expected it of her.

'When you get there,' he said, 'tidy up everything so that the soldiers, when they search it, will not have the slightest idea that anyone has rested there. Take away the food, make sure the ashes in the fireplace are not warm, and then go home and go to bed. In the morning you know nothing; remember that, Amanda, nothing.'

'I will remember,' she repeated through her tears, like a child repeating a lesson.

'Oh, my love . . .' he said, his voice breaking. 'Go swiftly or I shall not be able to let you go and they will find me here when dawn comes, still clasping you in my arms.'

She knew then that his iron control was breaking. He wanted her as she wanted him. Because she loved him and because she knew that what he asked of her was for both their sakes, she turned and went without another word.

She longed, as she had never longed for anything in the whole of her life, to turn back and look at him; to see him once again, so proud, so handsome, standing under the spreading branches of the oak tree. But she had given her word, and she kept to it. When she reached the Temple she tried to look back through the thickness of the surrounding shrubs, only to find it was impossible.

He must have known that, she thought. For a moment a sense of desolation made her long to throw herself down on the couch on which he had lain and give way to her storm of weeping. But because in obeying his instructions she felt she was in some way helping him, she carried out all he had commanded her.

She tidied the room and damped out the fire. Finally she picked up her basket of food from the table and went from the Temple, closing the door behind her. As she did so, she had a sudden terror that she was saying 'Good-bye' for ever to her secret happiness, to the love which seemed to beat in her heart like a caged bird.

'Trust me.' She could hear his deep voice saying the words.

Resolutely she turned from the little Temple and slipped back to the house like a ghost moving amongst the dark shadows of the garden. Only when she reached her own room was she able to give way to the tears of desolation and loss which seemed almost to choke her with their intensity.

She had thought she would not sleep, but her weeping had exhausted her. She fell into a deep, dreamless slumber from which she was only awakened once because she thought she heard horses' hoofs galloping down the drive. She sat upright and listened, but there was no sound and she thought she must have been mistaken and after a little while she slept again.

She awoke as the door was burst open and Harriet came hurrying into the room.

'Wake up, Amanda!' she called. 'Wake up! What has got into you that you should be so tardy this morning?'

'What is the matter?' Amanda asked. 'What time is it?'

''Tis nearly eleven o'clock,' Harriet answered. 'Mama said I was to let you sleep, but now Lord Ravenscar is here and wishes to see you immediately.'

'Eleven o'clock!' Amanda repeated.

How could she have slept so soundly, she wondered, when Peter was in danger and anything might have happened to him?

Harriet was pulling back the curtains.

'It is a lovely day,' she said, 'and I have brought you a glass of milk. Mama did not think you would want anything more.'

'No, indeed, this is sufficient,' Amanda answered. 'Thank you, Harriet.'

She sat up against her pillows to sip from the glass and Harriet jumped on to the bed and sat there, clasping her knees in a manner for which she had often been reproved.

'Such excitements, Amanda! Everyone says the fugitive slipped away last night on one of his Lordship's best horses.'

'The fugitive!'

Amanda put down the glass of milk with an unsteady hand.

'Yes. Harry, the verger, is full of it. He says that a man burst into the stable-yard last night and cried out that his Lordship was being attacked down at Oak Dell. The stable hands all rushed to his assistance, and when they had gone the man must have saddled one of Lord Ravenscar's best greys and ridden off on it.'

Harriet was breathless with excitement.

'Nobody saw him go,' she continued, 'but the stable was

empty and, of course, his Lordship was not in Oak Dell. He was at dinner in the Castle.'

'Did . . . did anyone see the man who gave the alarm?' Amanda asked.

'I asked Harry that,' Harriet replied. 'But he said nobody seems to have got a clear picture of him. Some say he was very tall, others that he was short and fat. Some say he was a gentlemen and others say he was a gipsy. I wonder what he was really like?' Harriet gave Amanda a glance from under her eyelashes.

'I do not expect that we shall ever know now that he has got away,' Amanda said deliberately.

Harriet sprang off the bed.

'Well, that is all the news up to date,' she exclaimed. 'Except that Lord Ravenscar is closeted downstairs with Mama and Papa, and they said you were to come down as quickly as possible. Oh, Amanda, what thrilling things are happening round here!'

Amanda wished she could feel as excited as Harriet. Instead, as she walked down the stairs a little while later, she felt her heart heavy with apprehension. What could Lord Ravenscar be talking about to her father and mother?

She entered the sitting-room to find them grouped around the fireplace. She fancied that her father looked unusually grave. She dropped Lord Ravenscar a deep curtsy without looking at him, raised her face dutifully for her father's morning kiss and bent to kiss her mother.

'You are keeping late hours this morning for a country lass,' Lord Ravenscar said. 'Did you also keep late hours last night?'

It was an innocent enough question spoken in a jocular tone, but Amanda knew only too well what he meant.

'My mother will tell you, my Lord, that I retired early,' Amanda answered. 'So much happened yesterday that I am afraid I must have been over-fatigued.'

'That is why I left you to sleep, my love,' Mrs. Burke said.

'Yet I rather suspect that you owe me a horse and a new saddle,' Lord Ravenscar said.

He spoke as if to her alone, but Amanda's chin went up and she faced him bravely.

'I am afraid I cannot fathom your Lordship's meaning,' she said.

His lips curled a little and she knew he was amused at her defiance.

'He will not get far,' he said ominously. 'You can be sure of that.'

'I am afraid I do not exactly follow what this conversation is about,' the Vicar interposed. 'Are you referring, my Lord, to that fellow the soldiers were looking for? I heard some vague rumour that he had escaped.'

'He has not escaped,' Lord Ravenscar answered. 'Shall we say he has merely postponed his capture?'

'But what has Amanda got to do with it?' Mrs. Burke enquired.

There was a moment's silence before Lord Ravenscar said:

'I think, Ma'am, we are wasting our time even discussing this tiresome wretch who, from all accounts, is in the employment of our enemy across the water. Shall we turn to more pleasant matters? The plans that we were discussing.'

'Yes, of course,' Mrs. Burke agreed.

'What plans?' Amanda asked suspiciously.

'I thought you would be interested,' Lord Ravenscar replied. 'I was talking with your father and mother about your marriage.'

'There is no hurry,' Amanda parried. 'We have not known each other very long, my Lord.'

'And yet there is no reason why we should delay our nuptials,' Lord Ravenscar said. 'As I have been saying to your father and mother, a marriage during the Season when the Prince is in London could be attended by all the *beau monde*.'

'No, no,' Amanda said quickly. 'This summer is impossible, my Lord. I could not be ready in time. There is my . . . my trousseau, for one thing.'

'That is something else which I have been discussing with your father and mother,' Lord Ravenscar replied.

'We told his Lordship that we were very anxious to do the very best for you, but . . .' Mrs. Burke said hastily.

'What is the suggestion?' Amanda interrupted.

'Something with which I hope you will agree,' Lord

Ravenscar replied for Mrs. Burke. 'As I explained to your parents, in your position as my wife, you must be dressed in the very height of fashion. You will be competing with all the beauties of St. James's and with the élite of Society who frequent Carlton House.'

'If you believe that I will allow you to pay for my clothes,' Amanda said, 'then, my Lord, you are very much mistaken.'

She spoke hastily, her pride making her protest sound almost rude. Lord Ravenscar raised his hand in almost a theatrical gesture of horror.

'My dear Amanda, as if I should conceive such an indiscretion!' He exclaimed. 'Indeed, it would be most ill-bred of me to make such a suggestion. But, as I have explained to your father and mother, my sister, Charlotte—the recently widowed Countess of Standon—has suggested that she should give you your trousseau as a wedding present.'

He paused, then continued:

'I could not help feeling it was a very practical suggestion and, as I pointed out to your parents, what would be the point of straining their resources to the uttermost limit all to no avail, for it is impossible to buy anything in this part of the world that you could possibly wear in London?'

His heavy-lidded eyes were glinting with amusement and Amanda knew that he was enjoying the predicament in which her hasty words had thrust her. To say that she refused such a generous offer from his Lordship's sister would be quite unnecessarily rude. At the same time, she was convinced in her heart that Lord Ravenscar would, in fact, be paying for any clothes that might be bought by Lady Standon.

Wildly she thought that his generosity was like a golden chain which, encircling her, made her more and more effectively his prisoner. 'It is extremely generous of Lady Standon,' she said cautiously. 'But I cannot conceive why she should make me so magnificent a present when I have not yet had the honour of her acquaintance.'

'That is something which is soon to be remedied,' Lord Ravenscar said with the air of a man who draws out a trump card. 'My sister is here at the Castle. She arrived last night and I have been suggesting to your parents that we should all leave this afternoon for London.'

'For London!' Amanda ejaculated. 'But why should we do that?'

'To get your trousseau, of course,' Lord Ravenscar replied. 'There is not a great deal of time if we are to be married, as I have suggested, at the beginning of June.'

'It is too soon, much too soon!' Amanda cried.

'My dear,' the Vicar interposed. 'I feel that while we should not be hasty in this matter, Lord Ravenscar has put forward some very sensible suggestions. If the Prince, as his Lordship intimates, wishes to be present at the wedding, it would be unaccommodating, to say the least of it, to ask His Royal Highness to return from Brighthelmstone where he will be staying during the latter part of June.' He could not help a little note of satisfaction creeping into his voice. After all, it was not every day that the daughter of a poor and obscure country vicar had the Prince of Wales at her wedding.

'What is more,' he went on, 'as a personal friend and an important member of the Prince's entourage, Lord Ravenscar cannot be away from London for long periods. He would find it hard to come down here frequently to see you, as naturally he would wish to do.'

'But . . . but June is less than two months ahead,' Amanda protested.

'We must, of course, consult the Prince,' Lord Ravenscar replied smoothly. 'He may wish the ceremony to take place even sooner.'

'No, no, let us make it June then!' Amanda cried.

She knew that he was driving her into a corner, getting what he wanted in a subtle manner which made her realise, even while she hated him, that he was a clever and a dangerous opponent. Already her parents were convinced of his good sense. He was making her appear childish and rude, and now there was this suggestion of leaving for London.

'Your parents have agreed,' Lord Ravenscar was saying, 'that under my sister's chaperonage you should stay for a short time at my house in Grosvenor Square. It is not an ideal arrangement, of course; but under the circumstances I do not think people will gossip unduly, and I shall make all haste to rent a house for my sister so that you shall not be under my roof while she purchases your trousseau and introduces you to Society.'

'But, Mama, cannot you come too?' Amanda asked in the lost voice of a child.

She ran to her mother as she spoke and knelt by her side. Mrs. Burke put her hand up and smoothed Amanda's hair back from her forehead.

'I wish I could, my dearest,' she said. 'But you know Papa would never agree to my leaving him. And what about Harriet and Caroline? What would happen to them? Not to speak of Roland, who is still a baby although he thinks he is a man now that he wears long trousers. No, my love, I am afraid I cannot accompany you to London, much as I should wish to do so.'

There was a wistful note in Mrs. Burke's voice and Amanda said quickly:

'But could you not go instead of me, Mama? I will look after Papa and you could choose the clothes with Lady Standon. You know my measure so well.'

Before Mrs. Burke could answer, Lord Ravenscar said:

'Are you afraid, Amanda? It was not my estimation of your character the other night when you defied the Dragoons at the gates of my garden. I thought then that you were a girl of spirit.'

With a sense of despair Amanda got to her feet.

'I hope I shall not disappoint you, my Lord,' she said with a meaning behind her words.

'That, I am sure, you will never do,' he said with mock courtesy. 'You will, I am convinced, often surprise me, Amanda, but you will not disappoint me.'

He looked at her small, troubled face and would have said more if the Vicar had not stepped forward to take Amanda's hand in his.

'I understand, my dear child,' he said, 'that this is a big step for you to take. It means going out into the world; it means leaving your mother and me behind. But you must remember that you have a man who loves you at your side, a man to whom in a very short space of time you will be married.'

'Yes, I know,' Amanda said in a very small voice.

'It is settled then,' Lord Ravenscar said. 'My sister will call upon you this afternoon and my travelling coach shall convey you both to Ravenscar House. I shall not accompany you on the journey, but will follow later in my curricle, which is a much faster mode of transport.'

Without waiting for Amanda's reply he bowed to Mrs. Burke and then taking Amanda's unwilling hand lifted it to his lips.

'We shall meet in London,' he said.

The Vicar accompanied him to the door and as soon as they were out of earshot Amanda turned towards her mother.

'Mama, I am astonished!' she cried. 'How can you let me go to London with a perfect stranger? To stay in his Lordship's own house with Lady Standon, of whom, until this moment, we have never heard.'

'But of course I have heard of Charlotte Standon,' Mrs. Burke contradicted. 'I remember her as a girl when we first came here. She was a sweet person and we missed her sadly when she got married. She never seemed to come to the Castle much after that, but I believe her husband lived somewhere in Dorset or Wiltshire—I cannot remember which.'

'Why should she take an interest in me? Giving me all my trousseau!'

'Oh, Amanda, what has come over you?' Mrs. Burke exclaimed. 'It is so kind of Lady Standon. And, besides, as Lord Ravenscar said so sensibly, what would be the point of Papa and me spending money which we could ill afford on buying clothes that he would never permit you to wear? It is undoubtedly a little unconventional, but then we live in unconventional times. There is a war on and one should not be needlessly extravagant just for the sake of old-fashioned social conventions and traditions.'

'Oh, Mama, cannot you see he has put all those ideas into your head?' Amanda asked. 'You would never have thought of them yourself. He is so wily, he manages to make wrong things seem right and right things seem wrong.'

She stopped suddenly. Mrs. Burke had risen from her chair, a very worried look on her face.

'Amanda, why are you talking like this?' she asked. 'Can it be that you really do not want to marry Lord Ravenscar? Because if you do not, Papa and I will quite understand. You must refuse his offer if you do not love him and do not think you will be happy with him. After all, dearest, we have always brought you up to realise that money and position are not of the least import when it comes to marriage, neither Papa nor I would wish you to marry anyone whom you do not love.'

Amanda was silent. She wondered what her mother would say if she told the truth.

'All the same,' Mrs. Burke went on, 'it would be wonderful to think that you were happily married and in a position where you would not have to skimp and save. It is hard trying to bring you all up on such a very small stipend as your father earns,' she sighed. 'It would have been different if I had had money of my own. Although my father was the Squire of Hanley Swan, as you have often heard me say, I had three brothers so there was nothing left for my sister and myself. I have often wished that you could have even half the things that I enjoyed as a child.'

Impulsively Amanda turned and put her arms around her mother and laid her cheek against hers.

'I know how difficult it has been, Mama,' she said. 'And you have been so kind and generous to us all. I know that you and Papa have gone without lots of things that you wanted so that we could have extra treats and pretty clothes.'

Mrs. Burke smiled:

'That is why, my love, it seems so marvellous that everything is going to be different now that Lord Ravenscar has offered your father this living at Frackenbury, and he has promised that next year Roland shall go to Eton, where he himself was educated. Think of that, Amanda, Eton! And we had thought we should not have been able to afford a public school of any sort for him.'

'He is buying me! He is buying me!' Amanda wanted to tell her mother, and knew that the words could not pass her lips.

Roland at Eton! Caroline at a fashionable school! Harriet to have a Ball in London! Her father Dean of Frackenbury! Could the impulses of her heart really weigh against such things? And even if they did, how could she tell her mother that she did not love Lord Ravenscar, but had given her solemn promise that she would become his wife in order to save an unknown stranger from being lawfully captured by His Majesty's Dragoons. It was all impossible. She was trapped and she knew it.

'I will go upstairs and get ready, Mama,' she said in her quietest and most amenable voice.

'I will come and help you,' Mrs. Burke said. 'I wonder what Harriet is doing? She must run and fetch old Harry to bring the trunks down from the attic. We have very little time.'

There was, indeed, so little time that Mrs. Burke was still putting the last things into Amanda's round-topped leather trunk when the carriage from the Castle drew up at the front door.

'It is here, Mama!' Harriet shouted. She ran to the window to add excitedly: 'Four horses and an outrider. Amanda will be travelling in style! And the carriage has a coat of arms painted on the door!'

'Hurry, Amanda, you have not got your bonnet on yet,' Mrs. Burke said in a flustered tone. 'And where is the sash which goes with your blue gown?'

'The footman is opening the door of the carriage,' Harriet reported from the window. 'There is a lady getting out. Oh, she is all in black! I hoped she would be wearing something pretty and gay.'

'Lady Standon has not been widowed very long,' Mrs. Burke answered. 'Let me see, it cannot be more than nine months, if that.'

'She looks a bit dull,' Harriet said doubtfully. 'I cannot see her any longer. She is under the porch.'

'I must go downstairs,' Mrs. Burke said, rising from her knees. 'Harriet, get old Harry to fasten the trunk and carry it downstairs. Are you ready, Amanda?'

'Yes, Mama,' she murmured.

Amanda barely glanced at herself in the mirror as she set a plain little chipstraw bonnet on her fair hair and pulled on the dull grey cloak of cheap cloth that had been her winter wrap for nearly three years.

'If there had been time, we might have retrimmed that bonnet,' Mrs. Burke exclaimed. 'Oh, well, there is nothing we can do now. I hope Lady Standon will not change her mind when she sees you.'

'There is no hope of that,' Amanda wanted to say, but her mother had gone hurrying down the front stairs to greet the guest, who had already been shown into the sitting-room.

Amanda turned to Harriet.

'Look after Mama and Papa, Harriet,' she said. 'You know how good and unworldly they are. Somebody has got to look after them.'

'I will do my best,' Harriet answered, suddenly serious.

'And . . . oh, Harriet, do not forget me,' Amanda begged. 'I am so unhappy to be going away.'

'Amanda! Amanda! I shall miss you every moment,' Harriet cried, flinging her arms round her sister. 'But think of the glorious time you are going to have in London. Balls, Receptions, Assemblies! Oh, it is all so exciting! Write and tell me about everything, every person you meet, everyone with whom you speak. And do not forget to tell me, too, what the Prince really looks like.'

'I will write you pages every day,' Amanda promised.

She hugged Harriet, then said:

'I must go downstairs now or Mama will be annoyed. Fetch old Harry as she asked.'

'I will not be a moment doing that,' Harriet answered. 'I want to see Lady Standon. I hope she is going to buy you more exciting clothes than she is wearing herself.'

Amanda could not help hoping the same thing when she was presented to Lady Standon in the sitting-room. She had expected, from her mother's words, someone young; but it seemed to her that it was an old woman who stood there—a woman with a grey, set face and rather tight lips, whose dark crêpe widow's weeds gave her an austere and somewhat frightening appearance.

'This is my eldest daughter, Amanda!' Mrs. Burke said by way of introduction, and Amanda sank down in a low curtsy.

Lady Standon seemed surprised.

'You are so young,' she said. 'I had expected someone older.'

'I shall be eighteen in three months' time,' Amanda answered.

'My brother will be forty next October,' Lady Standon said, a sudden edge on her voice.

'I had forgotten there was such a gap in their ages,' Mrs. Burke said conversationally, as if to cover up an embarrassing moment.

'There was a brother and sister between us,' Lady Standon answered. 'My brother was killed in the Army, and my sister, as I expect you may remember, Mrs. Burke, died soon after you came to the Vicarage.'

'Yes, I remember it well,' Mrs. Burke said. 'It was a sad tragedy when she was so young and attractive.'

'Sometimes I thought she was lucky!' Lady Standon said.

There seemed to be nothing anyone could say to this strange statement and there was an uncomfortable pause until Lady Standon said with what was obviously an effort:

'I think we should be leaving. My brother will be annoyed if we do not arrive in London precisely at the time that he is expecting us to do so.'

'If you will excuse me, I will go and see if the trunk has been brought downstairs,' Mrs. Burke said, hurrying from the room.

'I must thank you, Ma'am,' Amanda remarked to Lady Standon, 'for your very generous wedding present. I understand that you are giving me my trousseau. I should, indeed, be most grateful.'

Lady Standon opened her lips as if to say something, then obviously changed her mind and substituted:

'I hope we shall find something that will suit you.'

Her tone was uncompromising and Amanda was relieved that Harriet came hurrying into the room, her cheeks crimson, her curls dancing on either side of her face.

'Everything is ready, Amanda,' she cried. 'And another outrider has appeared. Fancy, you are travelling to London with two outriders. I had never dreamt of anything so smart.'

'Harriet,' Amanda reproved her, and turning to Lady Standon said: 'May I introduce my younger sister, Ma'am? She is rather over-excited at my departure.'

Harriet curtsied.

'I am sorry, Ma'am,' she said apologetically, 'but nobody has ever journeyed to London from this household before. And next year it is going to be me.'

'Indeed! I hope you find it very enjoyable,' Lady Standon said stiffly, and moving away from the two sisters walked slowly from the sitting-room into the hall.

Harriet's eyes met Amanda's, and then she giggled.

'You are not going to have much fun with her,' she whispered.

'Hush!' Amanda answered, and then she was hugging Harriet to her and holding her arms out to Caroline and Roland, who came running down the stairs from the schoolroom.

'Good-bye, Amanda! Don't forget us. Write us lots and lots of letters.'

Their shrill voices mingled with the deeper tones of her father and mother as, finally, with her handkerchief in her hand, she waved and waved as the coach turned from the drive into the road. A few seconds later they were out of sight.

Amanda sank back against the cushioned seat and pulled the fur rug, which had slipped a little, over her knees. Lady Standon was sitting in the far corner staring straight ahead of her, her face white and set.

Amanda surreptitiously wiped away her tears and, after a moment because the silence seemed uncomfortable, said:

'It is horrid saying good-bye to people whom you love.'

'That is what I thought when I drove down this same road fifteen years ago,' Lady Standon said.

'Were you, too, going to London?' Amanda asked.

'I was going to be married,' Lady Standon replied.

'And . . . and you were not happy?'

It seemed an impertinence to ask the question and yet Amanda could not prevent it. It seemed to leap from her lips.

'Happy!' Lady Standon ejaculated, her black veil rustling as she spoke. 'I had no idea what unhappiness meant in those days. I had no idea what torture, misery and degradation it could be to marry a man whom one did not love.'

She spoke with utter bitterness; and then, turning towards Amanda, she said:

'You little fool! Why are you marrying my brother? Is it for his money?'

7

Amanda was thankful when early the following afternoon they drove into London. She leant forward in the coach, looking out at the crowded streets with their glittering bow-windowed shops and smartly dressed crowds.

To her everything was fascinating, for she seldom visited even the market towns near Ravensrye; and this seething, traffic-filled metropolis made her feel as if she were a spectator at the playhouse.

There were wagons jostling coaches drawn by four horses, fast cabriolets, and phaetons driven by dashing young bloods with their tall beaver hats set at an angle. There were street criers crying their wares and men roasting chestnuts on glowing braziers. It was all so unlike anything she had seen before and she exclaimed excitedly at each new sight, forgetting the uncomfortable embarrassment which existed between herself and Lady Standon.

After her first outburst as they left the Castle Lady Standon had lapsed into a gloomy, disdainful silence, while Amanda, who could not explain why she was marrying Lord Ravenscar, could only sit with crimson cheeks, feeling that her visit to London was ill-omened from the start.

They had stayed the night at a posting house and immediately after a somewhat indifferent meal, served in the private sitting-room, Lady Standon had retired to bed. While they were dining Amanda had looked at her curiously. It was difficult to believe that this white-faced woman who seemed old and tired of life could ever have been the gay, attractive girl whom her mother had known when first they came to Ravensrye. What had happened to change her? Amanda had asked herself; and then was afraid to guess the answer.

Now she forgot everything except the thrill and interest of what she was seeing.

'Oh, look at that monkey with the organ-grinder!' she cried.

The animal was wearing a little red cap and holding out a cup to the passers-by.

'Look at that curricle! Did you ever see anything so smart? And the gentleman holding the reins is wearing an orchid as big as a saucer.'

Lady Standon made no answer and Amanda did not expect one. It really did not matter what her companion said. She was already planning in her mind the letter she would write to Harriet describing everything.

Now the horses were leaving the streets where there were shops and driving through a more residential quarter where the houses were high and imposing, and Amanda had glimpses of powdered flunkeys opening big mahogany doors or rolling strips of carpet over the pavement so that the ladies could alight from their coaches without dirtying their slippers.

It was quite a surprise when the horses drew up and she saw they had stopped outside a large mansion. Footmen wearing the claret-and-gold livery of Lord Ravenscar came hurrying through two large doors which, when open, revealed what seemed to Amanda as enormous marble hall with stone pillars and impressive statuary.

A Major-domo bowed before Lady Standon.

'Good afternoon, your Ladyship! I hope you and Miss Burke have had a pleasant journey. We received his Lordship's instructions and everything is prepared for you.'

'Thank you,' Lady Standon said in a cold, disinterested voice.

Amanda smiled at the man.

'We seem to have got here very quickly,' she said. 'But, then, the horses were magnificent.'

'His Lordship is always very particular about his horse-flesh,' the Major-domo replied.

He led the way into a Salon where a fire was burning brightly in the grate. It was a high, impressive room hung with what even Amanda's inexperienced eye recognised as being magnificent portraits.

'Will your Ladyship partake of a glass of Madeira?' the Major-domo enquired. 'Or tea and chocolate will be prepared instantly should you desire it.'

'I should like tea, if you please,' Lady Standon said. 'But first of all I wish to be taken to my bedchamber and I am sure Miss Burke will desire to do likewise.'

'The housekeeper is here, your Ladyship,' the Major-domo replied with a bow.

Amanda turned to see an elderly woman, wearing a black gown and over it a black satin apron, standing in the doorway. From her belt hung a huge bunch of keys. She dropped a respectful curtsy.

'If your Ladyship will follow me,' she said.

For the first time Lady Standon seemed to unbend.

'It is Mrs. Hewitt, is it not?' she said.

'It is, indeed, your Ladyship.'

'I am so glad to see you,' Lady Standon said. 'You have not changed.'

'Your Ladyship is most gracious,' the housekeeper said.

They started to ascend the stairs. To Amanda's surprise, now that the ice was broken Lady Standon went on talking.

'The house has been decorated,' she said. 'I should not have recognised it.'

'His Lordship has just spent a great deal of money doing it up,' the housekeeper replied. 'Lady Is . . .' She stopped suddenly.

Amanda guessed what name she had been about to say and wondered what the mystery was about Lady Isabel. It was the second time she had heard her name mentioned.

Lady Standon was shown into a large room at the top of the stairs, while Amanda had a slightly smaller one next to her. Alone, because Mrs. Hewitt had gone with Lady Standon, Amanda looked around her chamber and wondered at the luxury of it.

The gay brocaded bed, set in an alcove with a coronal of gold cupids, was beautiful in itself. So was the furniture, the pictures and the fine Aubusson carpet which covered the floor.

'How rich Lord Ravenscar must be!' she thought, and just for a moment wondered if such luxury could ever, in any way, bring happiness to those it indulged. And even as she thought of it, the ache in her heart, which had been there all through the journey, throbbed with a sudden intensity.

Where was Peter? What was he doing? What had happened to him? She had lain awake last night in the inn. wondering where he would be and trying, as he had suggested, to send her love winging towards him. If only she could have told him that she was coming to London, there might have been the chance of a meeting. And now, when it was too late, she told herself how stupid they had been to part without arranging any sort of rendezvous or even a go-between to whom they could send their letters.

'Peter! Peter!' she had cried in the darkness, and had wanted him so much that she felt he must know how she yearned for him.

There was a knock at the door; two footmen carried her trunks into the room and a maid, wearing a white mob-cap, appeared to unpack her things. Amanda washed her hands and tidied her hair. She was wearing a simple little muslin gown which was rather creased from the journey, but there was nothing she could do about it and so she was ready to go downstairs. But she hesitated, wondering if she should wait for Lady Standon, and then thought that perhaps she had already descended.

Slowly, rather overawed with her surroundings, Amanda walked down the staircase. A footman sprang forward to open the door into the Salon and she saw that a table had been laid by the fireplace. There was a heavily embossed tray on which was set a silver teapot, a lighted kettle, tea-caddy, cream jug and sugar basin. There was every type of delicacy to tempt the appetite—scones, biscuits, cakes, wafer-thin slices of bread-and butter and at least three different sorts of jam in cut-glass jars, each with its own special silver spoon.

'You must be hungry after such a long journey, Miss,' a voice behind her said and made her jump. It was the Major-domo and Amanda realised that he was an elderly man.

'Have you, too, been here a long time?' she asked.

'Not as long as Mrs. Hewitt,' the Major-domo replied. 'I think it will be only twenty-three years this next Christmas since I first came to his Lordship.'

'You must like being here,' Amanda smiled.

It seemed the obvious conclusion to draw and yet she would have been very obtuse if she had not seen a shadow pass over the Major-domo's face.

'His Lordship keeps us very busy,' he said quietly.

Amanda would have asked another question, but at that moment Lady Standon came into the room.

'I must apologise for having kept you waiting, Amanda,' she said stiffly, and moved with a rustle of her black skirts to seat herself at the tea-table. Amanda followed her and the Major-domo withdrew, closing the door behind him.

As Lady Standon seemed busy with the cups, Amanda seated herself on a low chair near the table and waited, feeling rather like a child in the presence of the teacher.

'May I pour you a cup of tea?' Lady Standon asked.

'Thank you,' Amanda replied.

'Please help yourself to something to eat,' Lady Standon went on.

Amanda did as she was told, and having taken a tiny hot scone filled with melting butter felt as if even a mouthful of it would choke her. The journey had been exciting, but now that they had arrived she felt uncertain and depressed. Could she bear many days of this atmosphere of oppression? she wondered.

She glanced at Lady Standon. Now that she had removed her widow's bonnet, Amanda could see that her hair had many strands of white in it. It was arranged unbecomingly—strained back from her forehead with what seemed to be a quite unwarranted severity.

'What are you staring at?' Lady Standon asked sharply.

Amanda started.

'I . . . I am sorry,' she stammered. 'I did not mean to be rude.'

Her eyes met those of Lady Standon and suddenly the older woman put down her cup with a little bang.

'I am sorry,' she said. 'I should not have spoken to you like that or said what I did yesterday. You must forgive me. I am overwrought.'

'I can understand that,' Amanda said softly, looking at the black crêpe round the collar of her dress and on her sleeves.

'Can you?' Lady Standon asked with a mirthless smile. 'I do not think you can and I cannot explain. But I promise you I will try not to be disagreeable. I will try to do what is required of me and buy you a trousseau befitting to the future Lady Ravenscar.'

There was so much bitterness in her voice that Amanda felt desperately embarrassed. She was not sure how to answer such a remark and was wondering whether she dare question Lady Standon when, at that moment, the door was thrown open and Lord Ravenscar came into the room.

Vaguely, as they had been sitting at the tea-table, Amanda had heard sounds in the hall outside. But somehow she had not expected him so soon and the mere sight of him made her heart leap with a sudden fear.

She rose quickly to her feet and as she did so was aware that Lady Standon had risen too.

'So, you are here exactly at the time I predicted!' Lord Ravenscar said.

He walked across the room, still wearing his travelling coat with its many-tiered cape, and the Major-domo hurried after him to take his hat and gloves. Amanda curtsied and he took her hand and raised it to his lips.

'You had a good journey, I trust?' he said, and his eyes bored down into hers so that it took all her will-power to answer quietly and with what she hoped was dignity.

'A very comfortable journey, I thank you.'

'And what do you think of my house?' he asked, still holding her hand although she tried rather ineffectively to pull it away from his.

'I . . . I have not had time to see it yet. It is very magnificent.'

'It pleases you. I am glad of that.'

Amanda's eyes dropped before his and to her relief he released her hand so that he could take off his travelling coat.

'Your Lordship will have a glass of wine?' the Major-domo enquired.

'Bring me brandy,' Lord Ravenscar commanded; and before the Major-domo had left the room, he turned to his sister.

'Have you not had time to get out of those monstrous garments yet?' he asked. 'I told you I would not have you sitting about looking like a bird of ill omen. Good God, Charlotte! Many women would be glad to be in your shoes.'

'As I told you, I have nothing else to wear.' Lady Standon replied.

'Then get something, and quickly. It gives me the creeps to see you sitting there suffering. If I have much more of it, you will go back from where you came.'

'Nothing you can say or do can hurt me any more than I have been hurt already,' Lady Standon said in a low voice full of suffering.

'Stop moaning,' Lord Ravenscar said roughly. 'The Lord knows I loathe respectable women, with their whining and their tears, their reproaches and their accusations. If you want to be miserable, be miserable; but for the love of the devil do not let us have to suffer with you.'

Lady Standon rose to her feet.

'If I could only find one way to make you suffer, Hugo,' she said, 'I should be glad of it.'

There was so much hatred in her tone that Amanda stared at her in amazement.

Lord Ravenscar threw back his head and laughed.

'At last,' he exclaimed, 'you are showing some feeling. It is better, at any rate, than your mealy-mouthed acceptance of the cross that you have to bear.'

'You are intolerable, Hugo. You always have been and you always will be.'

There were tears in Lady Standon's eyes now, but Lord Ravenscar still laughed at her.

'I suppose you are evoking past ghosts,' he taunted. 'Do you remember standing in this very room and defying me? Let me see, it must have been sixteen years ago. You told me then that you hoped I would rot in hell for what I had done to you. But I have not—I am still here! You are the one who looks as if you are rotting.'

'Say what you like,' Lady Standon said in a low voice. 'Nothing you can say can really touch me.'

She swept across the room, her skirts billowing behind her. The sound of her brother's laughter, rude and mocking, followed her as she reached the hall and started up the wide staircase.

Amanda had been spellbound at this exchange and now she moved to follow Lady Standon.

'Wait!' Lord Ravenscar called.

'I must go to her,' Amanda said. 'How . . . how . . . could

you speak to her like that? How could you speak to . . . to anyone in such a way?'

It was the expression on her white face which impressed Lord Ravenscar more than her faltering words.

'Have I upset you?' he asked. 'I am sorry. You must excuse me, Amanda, but Charlotte infuriates me—she always has. But needs must when the devil drives and there was no one else I could get to come at a moment's notice to chaperon you—no one, that is, whom your parents would have accepted. She is an old crow, but respectable!'

'You should not speak to her like that,' Amanda said. 'She is your sister and she is unhappy.'

'She has made herself unhappy,' Lord Ravenscar replied. 'But do not let us talk of her; it bores me. I would rather talk about you.'

He made a movement towards her, but Amanda was too quick for him. She ran to the door.

'I am sorry, my Lord, but I must go to Lady Standon,' she said a little breathlessly as she reached it. And then, before he could prevent her, she had reached the safety of the hall and begun to run up the stairs.

She had a vague idea of comforting Lady Standon; but when she reached the landing outside her bedroom, she hesitated before knocking on the door. She was quite certain, for one thing, that Lady Standon would look on her championship as an impertinence. She had already made it very clear what she thought of her brother's intended bride.

How could Lord Ravenscar be so rude? Amanda wondered, and while she hesitated she heard voices inside the room and guessed that Mrs. Hewitt was with Lady Standon. Amanda went to her own bedroom.

Her unpacking had been finished and the big trunk taken away. Now was her opportunity, she thought, to start a letter to her parents and perhaps one to Harriet. She wondered how much she dared tell them of what was happening here. She could certainly never put into words the rudeness of Lord Ravenscar or the insolence of his tone.

'Oh, Peter, Peter!' her heart called. 'When are you coming to save me from this? When will you take me away?'

In a kind of terror she remembered that she had given

her word of honour to marry Lord Ravenscar. How was Peter to extricate her from that tangle? At home they would already be packing preparatory to moving to Frackenbury.

'I must not think about it. I must trust him to save me,' Amanda whispered, and ran to the writing-desk, hoping to distract her mind from the questions which hovered there, evil and frightening, like vultures awaiting their prey.

There was a freshly cut quill. There was ink in an exquisite little Sèvres inkpot—but no writing-paper. Amanda opened drawers in the beautiful little inlaid secretaire, but to no avail. She wondered if she should ring the bell, and then shrank from fetching a servant upstairs for so trivial a request. She had already felt that she would never be able to give orders to the servants with their superior airs and disdainful expressions.

She remembered noticing as she had come up the stairs that there was a large Salon on the other side of the landing to their bedchambers. She had guessed it was the main reception room and thought now that it would be easy for her to cross the landing. There was certain to be a writing-desk somewhere in the room and she would be able to take a few sheets on which to write her letter.

She opened the door. There was no one about and she crossed the landing. Large, gilt-painted doors opened into the Salon and when she entered it she stood for a moment both amazed and entranced by what she saw.

The walls were covered in rose-pink brocade which matched the curtains. There were huge, glittering, crystal chandeliers and sconces filled with tapers to light great gilt mirrors which made the room seem even bigger than it was. The furniture was gilded with nymphs and cupids rioting with golden dolphins, and everywhere there were great bowls of hot-house flowers which gave the room an overpowering fragrance. It was both lovely and awe-inspiring.

Forgetting for a moment what she was seeking, Amanda walked over the Persian rugs, looking around her with wide eyes. The Salon ran the whole length of the house. At the far end was a large bow window with a door opening on to a balcony that overlooked the formal gardens in which played a fountain.

The pale afternoon sunshine was glinting on the water and it seemed to Amanda that she could see a rainbow as it rose and fell. She was kneeling on the brocade window-seat watching it like a child when she heard someone come into the Salon behind her.

'I will tell his Lordship that you are here,' she heard the Major-domo say, and swiftly, hardly thinking what she did, she hid herself behind the long, brocade curtain.

The window was so wide and the curtain so voluminous that she was completely obscured from anyone in the room. Besides, whoever might be there was quite a way from where Amanda was hiding.

There was a moment's complete silence and then Amanda, realising that she was being foolish, decided that she would come out and make her apologies.

'I must say I was watching the fountain,' she told herself. 'I must introduce myself.'

It required quite a lot of courage, and while she was forcing herself to make the effort it was too late. She heard the door open again and heard Lord Ravenscar's voice say:

'Wassell! I was not expecting you.'

'I did not know you were back until someone told me but five minutes ago that he had seen you in Piccadilly,' a man's voice replied.

'I have just arrived from the country,' Lord Ravenscar said. 'I should have sent for you to come or have looked for you at White's.'

'The Prince has been asking for you.'

'I thought he would have been,' Lord Ravenscar replied. 'Well, I am going to Carlton House right away.'

'I will go with you,' the man said. 'But, by the way, Ravenscar, I think your man must have taken leave of his senses. He told me that your sister was here and—I could hardly credit my ears—he added that she was accompanied by Miss Burke, to whom you were betrothed. Can this be true or am I dreaming?'

Amanda heard Lord Ravenscar's laugh.

'You see, I cannot keep a secret for more than five minutes,' he said. 'Yes, it is true, Wassell. You shall be the first to congratulate me.'

'But, good Lord, Ravenscar! Is this the moment for such junketing?'

'This moment more than any other, my dear man,' Lord Ravenscar said. 'Apart from anything else, think how it will allay suspicion, or indeed, interest, in any other activity.'

'I had not thought of that. But I had imagined that had you intended to marry anyone it would have been Lady Isabel,' the other man replied.

There was a little pause.

'No,' Lord Ravenscar said firmly. 'I do not intend to marry Isabel, whatever she may feel about it.'

'But she has more or less announced that you were to do so. You let her choose the decorations for this house. It was accepted by everyone, I think, as a foregone conclusion.'

'Isabel is both extravagant and curious, Wassell.'

'Curious?'

The question came sharply.

'Yes, curious. It would be unwise to underrate the intelligence of one's wife.'

'In which case I can only commend you on your foresight.'

'I thought you would do so,' Lord Ravenscar said suavely.

'And this new lady? Who is she?'

'She is the daughter of my local vicar at Ravensrye.'

'A vicar's daughter. My God, Ravenscar! That is doing it a bit brown. No vicar's daughter would accept you.'

'I assure you that she has done so.'

'But is such sacrifice really necessary?'

Lord Ravenscar chuckled.

'It is not particularly a sacrifice. She is extremely desirable and will make me, when I have trained her and improved her, the type of wife that I prefer. I am getting older, Wassell. It is about time I had a son and heir.'

'To inherit, of course.'

'As you say, to inherit. It is important, do you not agree, if everything goes according to plan? Very important.'

'Can you look ahead as far as that?'

'I think so. But in the meantime, what news for our feathered friend?'

'Good news. News which will delight you, Ravenscar. I heard from our informant in the Admiralty that three ships . . .'

The voice broke off suddenly as if a hand had been put on his arm, or perhaps a finger to his lips.

'What is it?' the man called Wassell asked apprehensively.

'I do not know,' Lord Ravenscar replied. 'I thought I heard a sound—or was it just my imagination? Anyway, do not talk here. This room is too big. I always feel that anything we might say could be overheard. Come into my bedroom. I have got to change before I go to the Prince; but be careful what you say in front of my valet. He served with the Gordon Highlanders and never forgets to let me know it.'

'I will come with you,' was the reply. 'But, Ravenscar, I want to see the parson's daughter.'

'There is plenty of time for that,' Lord Ravenscar replied. 'And do not go trying to seduce her away from me. I should hate to have to call you out.'

This was a joke which made them both laugh and Amanda could hear their laughter echoing down the passage long after they had left the room.

She stood there shaking until she felt as if her legs could not hold her, and then she sat down on the window-seat. She was not angry at the way Lord Ravenscar had spoken of her. She was only disgusted and shocked. She had not believed that such men existed. Though she had shrunk from him because personally he revolted her, she had believed, in her innocence, that he loved her. Why else would he have wanted to marry her? But now she knew that what she had thought to be love could only be described by a very much uglier word.

She felt almost faint at the horror and the degradation to which she was subjecting herself. And then her mind slipped away from the insults to herself and began to question what were the secrets Lord Ravenscar and Mr. Wassell were exchanging. What had they meant by what they had said? And why should they be ashamed to speak in front of someone who had served in the Gordon Highlanders?

It was all a mystery that Amanda could not fathom, and for the moment she found it difficult to dwell on anything but Lord Ravenscar's references to herself—the parson's daughter; the woman who was to bear him a child because it was time he had one; the woman who was not to be curious.

Curious about what? The question had asked itself and she had no idea of the answer. She felt only with a kind of intensified impatience that there were too many secrets for her to cope with. First Peter and now Lord Ravenscar.

She had a sudden intuition that this was important; and yet, because she could not understand, it was like quicksilver slipping away through her fingers so that she could not catch it and could not understand it.

She felt suddenly very helpless and utterly alone—alone in this big room, in this vast mansion; alone amidst so much luxury and so much wealth; alone when all she longed for were the arms of the man she loved around her, to feel safe because her head was on his shoulder.

She shut her eyes, imagining it, imagining that he was there. She could almost feel him holding her, hear his deep voice telling her that he loved her.

'I love you! Oh, Peter, I love you!' she tried to tell him, and then felt the curtain which hid her being roughly dragged back and opened her eyes to find herself staring straight into the dark and angry face of Lord Ravenscar!

8

'So you were spying on me!'

Lord Ravenscar's words combined with the expression of anger on his face rendered Amanda speechless for the moment.

'I . . . I do not know that . . .' she began, only to be interrupted by Lord Ravenscar's voice, furious and accusing, saying:

'Who told you to spy on me? Was it that fugitive you helped to escape?'

As she did not answer, feeling by now almost paralysed with fear and astonishment, he took her by the shoulders and shook her.

'Answer me,' he said. 'I will get an answer from you if I have to kill you to do so.'

She felt her head rock backwards and forwards on her shoulders, and then, with a sudden movement, she was free as he almost flung her from him, saying:

'No, it cannot be. This fellow was of no consequence and he would have been captured by now.'

With her hair disarranged about her forehead, her eyes wide with apprehension and her breath coming quickly, Amanda said:

'I . . . I was not . . . spying, my Lord, I swear it. It was just . . . just that I was here in the room when your . . . your guest was announced. Feeling shy I . . . hid behind the curtain. It was stupid and discourteous of me, I admit, but there was no . . . other reason, it was only shyness which prevented me from . . . making my presence known later when you . . . were there. It was wrong and extremely remiss of me . . . and I must offer you my deepest apologies.'

As she spoke, she knew Lord Ravenscar was watching her with narrowed eyes. Then his face cleared.

'I believe you,' he said. 'It was only that I have an ingrained dislike of being spied upon.'

'I . . . I can understand that,' Amanda said. 'And, please, my Lord, believe me when I say I am ashamed of my stupidity. It was, indeed, very foolish of me.'

'It was,' he said, a faint smile curling the corners of his lips. 'But I have forgiven you. Come, we must be friends again. But first you must pay forfeit for your foolishness.'

'Forfeit, my Lord?' Amanda enquired.

'Yes, you must give me your apology with your lips, and I shall feel cheated if they are not so sincere as your words.'

Amanda stiffened. Instinctively her hands went towards her breast as if to soothe the sudden frightened leap of her heart.

'I . . . I think, my Lord, that Lady Standon requires me,' she said.

'Then my sister must wait,' Lord Ravenscar replied. 'Come, Amanda, you are too honest not to pay your debts.'

With a feeling of dismay she realised that he was waiting, standing in the light from the window with an amused expression on his face, his thick lips parted as they waited for her approach.

Slowly, with leaden feet, she drew nearer, longing to run away and yet prevented by some pride which told her that in this, at any rate, he had right on his side. Nearer and nearer, and now she was close to him so that he could see the troubled rise and fall of her breasts, the fear in her eyes and the quick intake of her breath between lips which had seemed suddenly to grow pale.

'Do you hate my kisses so much?' he asked.

'My Lord, I . . . I wish to kiss no one,' Amanda said with a little convulsive movement of her hands.

Even as she spoke she knew it was a lie. She had a sudden longing for Peter, for the sanctuary of his arms, for the comfort of his cheek against hers.

'It is perhaps that which attracts me so much about you,' Lord Ravenscar was saying. 'Most women seek my embraces—indeed, they are insatiable in their desire for them. But you will learn; yes, Amanda, I promise you that you will learn—to want me to kiss you. And then, only then, is there any possibility of my becoming bored with you.'

He gave a little laugh.

'Until that moment comes, you are utterly desirable. A wild animal to be trained by the hunter who was clever enough to trap her.'

He put his arms round her. Amanda closed her eyes. It was coming, this moment she dreaded, this moment from which she shrank with her whole being—the feeling of his lips, hungry, hot and possessive. It was, she thought, a degradation worse than anything she had encountered or even dreamed of in her whole life.

And then, as she shrank from his touch, even as she waited for it as a man might wait for the stroke which would mean destruction, they were interrupted. The door opened and a flunkey's voice announced:

'Lady Isabel Mannering, my Lord!'

Lord Ravenscar gave an exclamation and Amanda was free. She turned to see entering the Salon a most beautiful and striking woman.

Lady Isabel was at the height of her loveliness. She was tall and had raven-black hair, about which the bucks of St. James's had written a dozen poems, a heart-shaped face with sculptured features. She was wearing a gown daringly transparent and seductively low-cut, and there were diamonds glittering round her white throat and on the fingers which held a fur-lined wrap around her shoulders.

She swept into the room rather like a tidal-wave entering a harbour; and then, facing Lord Ravenscar, she said abruptly:

'What is going on here? Why did you not inform me of your return?'

Lord Ravenscar went forward to take her hand and raise it to his lips.

'My dear Isabel,' he said. 'I am enchanted to see you. I have but this moment arrived and I did not expect such an honour as having you here to welcome me.'

'Fustian!' she said sharply. 'You did not expect me because you took good care not to tell me of your arrival. Fortunately I saw your coach driving round into the stables a short while ago and guessed you were back. Who is this?'

She pointed a finger at Amanda, who dropped an embarrassed curtsy.

'I think, Isabel.' Lord Ravenscar said shrewdly, 'that you have already heard that Miss Burke has done me the honour of promising me her hand in marriage.'

'It is true then!' Lady Isabel exclaimed. 'And do you imagine, Hugo, for one second, that you can do this?'

'As far as I can see, there is no one who will prevent me,' he said.

'You overestimate your own power,' she answered. 'I shall prevent you.'

'Delightful though you are, Isabel,' he replied, 'fond though I shall always be of you, I reserve the right to marry where and whom I choose.'

Her lips curled icily.

'And so you have chosen this puny country chit,' she said. 'For what reason? What hold has she got over you? Good Lord, Hugo! There would be no reason for you to offer marriage to someone in that position.'

With a heightened colour Amanda turned towards the door, only to be stopped by Lady Isabel who stepped in front of her.

'Where are you going?' she asked.

'I think, Ma'am, it is unnecessary for me to stay here and listen to such insults,' Amanda said in a voice that quivered a little, however proud she tried to make it.

'I should like you to hear them,' Lady Isabel said. 'I should like you to know once and for all that Lord Ravenscar and I had an understanding which in all honour he cannot ignore. All London expects us to announce our engagement this Season. All London knows that I have chosen the decorations for this house, that we have been constantly in each other's pockets for over six months. The Prince himself only last week asked me when the wedding was to take place.'

'As a man I still have the right to propose to whom I please' Lord Ravenscar said.

'Proposal!' Lady Isabel said with scorn. 'Do you imagine that a proposal would come well from your lips, Hugo? You take what you want. For some reason I cannot for the moment fathom, you want this wench. It cannot be merely lust. If it were, there would be no reason for marriage. What is it? Tell me. Let me hear why your inclinations are at this moment honourable.'

She was white with rage and Amanda watched her with both dismay and fascination. Never had she seen anybody so beautiful. Never had she seen a woman so angry.

'You cannot hurt me,' Lord Ravenscar sneered.

'I can and I will,' Lady Isabel stormed. 'You shall pay for this, Hugo; and in the end you will come cringing back to me with your tail between your legs, like a dog that has been whipped.'

She turned to look at Amanda and continued:

'And as for this pale-faced milksop, I will make her the laughing stock of St. James's. To begin with, it is not likely that she will be accepted by anyone who matters seeing that she is staying here under your roof.'

'I think on this count you have forgotten me,' a voice said from the doorway.

They all turned with surprise as Lady Standon came into the room, her sober black gown contrasting strangely with the colourful elegance of Lady Isabel.

'Who is this?' Lady Isabel demanded.

'May I present my sister, Charlotte, Countess of Standon?' Lord Ravenscar replied. 'I assure you, Isabel, that the proprieties are well observed. Amanda is under her chaperonage.'

'You think of everything, do you not, Hugo?' she asked, her eyes smouldering. 'Well, I will leave you to the black crow and the little white pullet. I presume you are going to add to your aviary of rare birds!'

She turned away from him, looked Lady Standon up and down in a very insolent manner, and then, fixing her eyes on Amanda, she said commandingly:

'Go back to the country, wench, to where you belong.'

There was so much venom and dislike in her voice that Amanda recoiled instinctively, stepping back as Lady Isabel swept past her through the open door and down the staircase.

To Amanda's surprise Lord Ravenscar seemed almost shaken by the interview. He took out his handkerchief, mopped his forehead, and then, with a sudden burst of irritability, said to his sister:

'Keep Amanda with you. If she had not been in here, this would not have occurred.'

He walked away and Amanda, with a sense of utter relief, turned to Lady Standon.

'Thank you,' she said. 'I could not fathom what would happen next.'

'So that is the notorious Lady Isabel,' Lady Standon said reflectively.

'She is very beautiful,' Amanda remarked.

'And very vicious,' Lady Standon added. 'I wonder my brother dares to defy her.'

Amanda had wondered the same thing, and she wondered again the next day when, as they were shopping in Bond Street, they saw Lady Isabel stepping from an open carriage, looking exquisitely beautiful and escorted by three attentive young bucks.

Amanda saw her and drew back into the shop which she and Lady Standon were just leaving.

'Lady Isabel,' she whispered.

Lady Standon looked through the window and also turned back, making a pretence of looking once again at a gown which they had already refused to buy.

'She has gone,' Amanda whispered a moment or so later.

'No, I do not think I will take it after all,' Lady Standon said to the shopkeeper. 'Please send the other garments as soon as possible.'

'They shall be there within an hour, your Ladyship,' she was promised.

Lady Standon and Amanda stepped into the coach that was waiting.

'There is no reason why we should be afraid of her,' Lady Standon said.

'I know,' Amanda answered. 'But I am.'

Even as she said it she thought of how many people she was afraid of already—Lady Isabel, Lord Ravenscar and even Lady Standon, except that at this moment she seemed more approachable.

The previous night Amanda had lain in bed thinking over the events of the day and trying to make some pattern out of the jig-saw puzzles and problems, fears and anxieties. It seemed to her that so much of it made no sense. She only knew that she had been vastly relieved when the Major-domo had brought a message that Lord Ravenscar was dining at Carlton House.

Lady Standon had immediately said that she was fatigued and would have a light meal brought to her bedroom and Amanda had elected to have the same. She had found as soon as she had eaten that she, too, was tired. But though she had gone to bed, she had not been able to sleep. She had found herself going over and over the scene with Lady Isabel; Lord Ravenscar's strange action in shaking her when he had thought she was spying on him; his conversation with Mr. Wassell, and, most of all, her anxiety and fears for Peter.

Where was he? she wondered. Had he escaped? Or had the soldiers captured him? How could she find out? How could she learn what had happened after he had taken Lord Ravenscar's horse and ridden away from the stables?

As they had driven through the streets to go shopping, Amanda found herself looking out of the window of the coach at the passers-by. What would she do, she wondered, if she suddenly saw Peter walking amongst the bloods in Bond Street or tooling a phaeton down Piccadilly?

Oh, Peter! Peter! She felt as if the ache in her heart had been there all her life—that ache which persisted whatever else was happening, because always at the back of her mind there was the thought of him.

As she and Lady Standon chose the gowns for her trousseau, she found she could think of only one thing—what would Peter think if he could see her in them? There were gauzes and satins, muslins sprigged with tiny flowers embroidered by fairy hands, silks and velvets, ribbons which seemed to portray every colour of the rainbow; shoes and gloves; bonnets and shawls; fans and reticules.

Long before they had acquired even half the things that Lady Standon said were necessary, Amanda's mind had ceased to register. It was too much, too fantastic, to be able to spend money like this, when never before in her life had she bought more than one gown at a time, and that of the very cheapest kind of material.

'Surely it is too expensive?' she whispered once to Lady

Standon as they hesitated over a gown of silver gauze embroidered with tiny pearls.

Lady Standon did not answer her.

'I will take it.' she said to the shopkeeper who, curtsying delightedly, produced more gowns for their approval, each more elegant and more expensive than the last.

Finally they drove back to Grosvenor Square to find that many of their purchases had already arrived and were being unpacked by one of the maids. Lady Standon swept into her bedchamber and after a moment's hesitation Amanda followed her. To her surprise Lady Standon was standing in front of the looking glass staring at her own reflection. She must have seen Amanda move behind her and she turned sharply and said:

'What do you want?'

'I just wanted to say, thank you,' Amanda said. 'I am so grateful for your generosity, although I feel that you have spent much more than is necessary.'

'There is no need to thank me,' Lady Standon replied.

'But there is,' Amanda said. 'I do not want you to think I am not grateful, I am. It is only that I wish . . .' She stopped suddenly.

'Go on,' Lady Standon prompted. 'What do you wish?'

'N . . . nothing,' Amanda stammered, conscious that she had been on the verge of being indiscreet. 'No, nothing.'

'I think,' Lady Standon said, 'that you were about to say that you wished you were looking forward to wearing them. Is that not the truth?'

Amanda averted her eyes.

'I shall of course be entranced to wear such beautiful garments,' she said in a flat voice.

'But not so that they shall delight my brother,' Lady Standon insisted.

'I did not say that,' Amanda exclaimed.

'No, but I did,' Lady Standon answered. 'Do you suppose I have not seen your face when you have been with him? Do you suppose that you hide your feelings towards him? Amanda, do not be foolish. Run away before it is too late. Do what Lady Isabel suggested and go back to the country. You will be happier there; much, much happier than you would ever be here.'

Lady Standon spoke with real feeling in her voice, her

eyes kind and sympathetic for the first time since Amanda had known her. Amanda turned her head.

'I cannot,' she whispered. 'And I cannot explain either. I have got to go through with it. It is too late to do anything else.'

Lady Standon sat down in front of the mirror.

'Look at me,' she said. 'Look at me in this mirror. What do you see?'

Amanda did not answer and she went on:

'I will tell you what you see—a woman aged beyond her years, a woman drained of all feeling. No, that is not true—a woman drained of youth, of joy, of happiness, of love; but a woman who can still feel miserable and degraded. I hoped I was numb. I hoped I was immune to everything. But I can still feel. Today has brought it all back; things I had hoped were dead and forgotten.'

Her voice broke on the words and the tears which had gathered in her eyes ran down her pale cheeks. Amanda never could remain unmoved by suffering, and now she went forward impulsively to kneel at Lady Standon's feet, to put her hands on hers.

'I felt you must be unhappy,' she said. 'Oh, please, can I not help you?'

'We neither of us can help the other,' Lady Standon said. 'But look at me and think what you are doing before you become like me. Once I was young and the world was full of excitement and beauty. And now there is only darkness, loneliness and ugliness.'

'But why? Why?' Amanda asked.

Lady Standon looked down at her.

'Because I obeyed my brother's commands. Because I was forced to marry a man I did not love. No, that is not telling the truth—a man I hated; whom I loathed and despised. If only I could relate to you the degradation of those years with him, you would understand.'

'But why did you have to marry him?' Amanda asked.

'Because my brother insisted and because he sent away the man I loved, the only man I shall ever love.'

'Sent him away?' Amanda asked. 'What has happened to him now?'

'I do not know,' Lady Standon answered. 'Every day I used to wonder despairingly what had happened to him. I used to lie awake at night thinking of him, imagining that he might be dead or wounded in some foreign land. But what was the use? I was married at my brother's command to the Earl of Standon. A brilliant match, was it not, for a girl of seventeen to a man of great wealth and great possessions? A man so evil and sunk in shame that it is strange that my hair did not turn white in the night, as I thought it must.'

She gave a little sobbing sigh.

'I used to pray to die,' she went on. 'But my prayers went unanswered and I went on living—living to become as I am now, something withered and dried up, a woman who has no further use for life.'

'But you must not talk like that, you must not!' Amanda cried. 'You are still young. You have many years to look forward to.'

'What sort of years?' Lady Standon asked. 'Living with a querulous and disagreeable old mother-in-law who is nearly eighty. Trying to repair some of the broken lives and unhappiness of those on our estates, and conscious all the time that my name, simply because it was his, stinks in the nostrils of all decent people. Do you suppose I have any friends? Of course not. The people I should have liked to know would not deign to come to the house, and those whom he entertained so royally would not give me a thought now that he is dead, even if I wanted them to do so.'

She wiped away her tears and added bitterly:

'Once I longed to have children. But now I am glad that the title and the family will die out and perhaps one day people will be able to forget.'

'Oh, I am sorry for you, desperately sorry for you,' Amanda said in her soft voice. 'I only wish I could help you.'

'No one can help me,' Lady Standon replied. 'But do you not understand? Do you not realise why I am telling you this? My husband and my brother were great friends.'

The eyes of the two women met, and Amanda rose unsteadily to her feet.

'Thank you for telling me,' she said dully. 'But there is nothing I can do . . . nothing.'

All the same she felt a sudden chill pass over her and her

hands were trembling as she added quickly:

'Will you not tell me more about the man you loved? How did Lord Ravenscar contrive to send him away?'

'Captain Graham Munro was in the Royal Fusiliers,' Lady Standon said in a flat tone. 'And Hugo had influence. He had Graham's battalion sent overseas. Hugo would not even let us say good-bye to each other. He saw him, told him that I was going to marry the Earl of Standon, and confiscated all our letters—mine to Graham and his to me.'

She put her hands up to her eyes.

'It was only later that I learned of this from my maid. I cannot tell you what agonies I went through; waiting, waiting for a letter which never came. When I discovered the truth it was too late; by then I was married and there was nothing I could do about it.'

'You never tried to find out where he was?'

'How could I?' Lady Standon replied. 'And, besides, I was ashamed that he should know of the life I was forced to lead.'

'Why should your brother have been so ruthless? Did he not care for you?' Amanda asked.

'Hugo has never cared for anyone but himself. His friend wanted me. I can see Lord Standon's eyes now, the day he first saw me. It was at the Castle and I had come downstairs to greet Hugo's friends who had arrived from London. I should have been warned. I should have run away, retired to my bedchamber, said I was ill. But perhaps even then it was too late.'

Lady Standon covered her face with her hands.

'And now, you are free,' Amanda cried.

'I think Graham is dead,' Lady Standon said, her voice suddenly sharp. 'And if he is not, can you conceive that I would want him to see me like this? Besides, he may be married, he may have a family of his own. I could not bear to learn of it. No, some things must remain for ever in the past.'

She got up from the dressing-table as the housekeeper came in to say that a number of boxes had arrived from a shop in Bond Street.

'There are some for you, m'Lady, and some for Miss Burke,' she said.

'And there are still more to come,' Lady Standon answered in a tired voice. 'Bring them in, Mrs. Hewitt. His Lordship does not wish me to wear mourning any longer.'

'Well, that is a good thing, Miss Charlotte . . . I . . . I mean, m'Lady,' Mrs. Hewitt approved. 'Mourning is always depressing, not only for those who wear it but for those who have to look at it.'

'You see, Amanda, we have to be gay,' Lady Standon said with a bitter twist of her lips.

Amanda went to her own room. The gowns were laid out on the bed and she looked at them with awe, wondering what Harriet would think of such magnificence. Yet, at the very thought of her sister, she felt homesick for the quiet Vicarage; for her mother and father reading together in the sitting-room, for the children chattering upstairs in the schoolroom.

Quite suddenly she felt lost, as if she was wandering in a maze to which she could never find the way out. She went to the window, which looked out on to the gardens of Grosvenor Square. There were tulips blowing in the wind, the shrubs were in bud and the faint scent of lilac came to her on the breeze.

'I want to go home!'

She said the words aloud and yet she knew they were not entirely true. It was Peter she wanted. A man she had met only a few times in her life and yet who was already so much a part of it that she could not imagine her life without him. It was ridiculous and absurd, and yet love was something which could not be denied, could not be set on one side.

'It is time to dress, Miss,' a respectful voice said behind her. 'There is a dinner party here tonight, and afterwards you and her Ladyship are to go to Carlton House. You will see the Prince, Miss, and meet all the famous people in London. You must look fine for that.'

'I suppose so,' Amanda said with a sigh which came from the very depths of her being.

She was remembering how she had run through the garden to the Temple; how Peter had waited there for her. How willingly she would change the grandeur of tonight for the simplicity of yesterday!

Yet when she was dressed she could not help feeling surprised and thrilled at her appearance. She had chosen, from all the lovely gowns which they had bought, one of white satin embroidered with tiny sprigs of forget-me-nots. There was a wreath of forget-me-nots for her fair hair and white satin slippers with little diamanté buckles for her feet.

The gown fitted her to perfection and while accentuating her youth it gave her an air of elegance and distinction which she had never had before.

Shyly she went from her own room to Lady Standon's, to find an almost similar transformation had taken place. The heavy black robes were gone and in their place Lady Standon wore a gown of soft dove-grey with ribbons of pale mauve and a stole lined with the same colour to drape elegantly over her arms.

But what was so surprising was that in discarding her crêpe Lady Standon had discarded many of her years. She looked younger. For the moment she even looked happier and a little more animated.

'You look lovely!' Amanda exclaimed.

'It is certainly a pretty gown,' Lady Standon agreed without much enthusiasm. 'And yours, my dear, is charming. You cannot fail to hold your own, whoever we meet at Carlton House.'

Both women knew that the reference was to Lady Isabel, but they did not speak her name, and as a flunkey announced that Lord Ravenscar was waiting they crossed the landing to the Salon where already a number of guests had arrived.

Tapers were sparkling in the chandeliers. The room was fragrant with the scent of hot-house flowers. Amanda had a sudden vision of women wearing jewels and men in knee-breeches. She could not, for the moment, see an individual face. She only knew that everything seemed to glitter and sparkle and that it was all rather grand and frightening and that she was very much alone.

And then Lord Ravenscar was beside her, his eyes flickering over her, apprizing everything—her new gown, the whiteness of her skin, the arrangement of her hair, the way her dark eyelashes fell before his gaze and touched the delicacy of her soft cheeks. She felt his lips burn against her hand.

'You are madly desirable.'

His voice spoke against her ear and almost without meaning to she moved sharply away from him.

'Still afraid of me?'

The words were hateful because she knew that he was mocking her. She did not answer and after a moment he said:

'Before I present you to my friends, who are, of course, most anxious to meet you, I have news for you.'

'News?'

She felt herself stiffen as she asked the question. Her fingers were still in his and he felt them tremble.

'Yes, news,' he answered, his eyes watching her as a cat will watch a mouse before it strikes it down.

He waited for the quick intake of her breath before he said:

'You will be interested, I know, to learn that the fugitive who escaped from His Majesty's Dragoons has been apprehended.'

'They . . . caught him?' Amanda asked.

She thought for one moment that the lights must have gone out. The whole room seemed dark.

'Yes, they caught him,' Lord Ravenscar said, and still his eyes watched her. 'But, unfortunately, they were able to discover very little about him. You see, in resisting arrest he was killed!'

9

Amanda sat blindly through the dinner that followed. She stared with unseeing eyes at the great, gold ornaments which loaded the polished table, at the orchids which were festooned around the candelabra holding a dozen tapers. She ate, though she did not taste, the exotic dishes which were served by powdered footmen, one behind each chair, and drank the wines, which were poured into monogrammed crystal goblets.

She had no idea who sat on her right or her left. She must have smiled and made a pretence of joining in their conversation for the gentlemen seemed quite pleased with her. She had a vague idea that they were paying her compliments.

All she could see was a figure lying on the ground, shot, perhaps in the back, and a riderless horse galloping away.

'Peter! Peter!' she cried to him in an agony of desolation, and knew that now her love, as it went winging from her heart, would have no place to rest.

Only one thing caught her attention while she was still under Lord Ravenscar's roof. It was that in the Salon where they gathered before dinner there was, at one end, an aviary built between the long French windows and the little paved and statued garden which lay outside. It was filled with wonderful birds of all descriptions, from mere morsels of turquoise and crimson to their larger brethren with long tails and beautiful crested heads.

They only intensified her sense of loss. She could see the smile on Peter's lips, hear his low, grave voice speaking to her, feel his dark eyes looking down into hers as he spoke of their love winging to each other's hearts. It seemed almost intolerable that he should be dead while these exquisite creatures flitted from perch to perch.

'What are you thinking, Lady-fair?' someone asked her flirtatiously.

'I was thinking of death,' she replied blankly, and moved away, leaving him staring after her in astonishment.

She had the vague impression that, when they went towards the coaches waiting outside, many of the gentlemen carried too much wine, that the ladies' voices were shrill and the patches of vivid colour on their cheeks were not entirely due to artifice.

But she did not really care how they looked or what they did. She only knew that her own private world was blank and empty, a desert where no flower bloomed and no bird sang.

The coaches drew up outside the great Corinthian portico and Ionic pillars of Carlton House. A large crowd had gathered to watch the Prince's guests disembark in their finery.

Dazed and unhappy, Amanda moved like a puppet. She did not even say to herself, 'I am here, in Carlton House!' She did not even wonder what Harriet would have had to say at the great hall with pillars of porphyry and sweeping staircase, or at the reception room hung with Chinese yellow silk and furnished with Chinese furniture.

'I must ask the Prince's permission to present you,' Lord Ravenscar said in her ear, and even that could not bring a flicker of interest to her eyes or a quickening of her pulse.

She could see the Prince at the far end of the room and had a momentary disappointment. She had expected him to be handsome and dashing, the Prince Charming they had always whispered about as having innumerable love affairs, as being so crazily in love with Mrs. Fitzherbert that he had even proposed marriage to her.

But now he was forty-three and looked fifty-three! For despite his pearl-powdered cheeks and juvenile curls, his too-solid flesh weighed heavily upon him. It was obvious by his stiff movements that he wore a corset, but even that could not disguise his paunch.

Vaguely, as if in a dream. Amanda saw Lord Ravenscar, much more sober than his compatriots, bustle to the Prince's side and seizing his opportunity whisper in his ear. The Prince nodded and looked around, as if pleased at the idea of some new diversion, and Lord Ravenscar came back to her.

'His Royal Highness will receive you,' he said. 'Be careful to curtsy low and speak up when he addresses you. He hates women who mumble.'

At any other time Amanda would have been overcome with nerves and shyness. But now it did not seem to matter to her whether she spoke to the Prince of Wales or to a crossing sweeper. She only knew that her whole future stretched ahead, dark and empty.

Lord Ravenscar drew her forward.

'May I, Sir, present Miss Amanda Burke, who has honoured me by the promise of her hand in marriage.'

Dutifully Amanda sank to the ground in a low curtsy.

'A child! A child, Ravenscar!' she heard the Prince exclaim. 'But, at the same time, a nymph! I had not expected such simple tastes from you.'

'Your Highness has obviously misjudged me,' Lord Ravenscar replied with a hint of laughter in his voice.

'You are up to something,' the Prince said with glee. 'I know it and you have got to confide in me what it may be. Come on, no secrets from your old friend.'

'The secret is a very simple one,' Lord Ravenscar answered. 'I have experienced an affliction which has often befallen Your Royal Highness. I have been smitten by the arrow of Cupid himself.'

The Prince wobbled all over with laughter.

'Egad, that is a joke!' he exclaimed. 'You, of all people, Ravenscar. But I do not blame you. I do not blame you at all. She is enchanting, quite enchanting.'

He patted Amanda on the shoulder and turned away to speak to someone else who was trying to attract his attention.

Amanda saw that Lord Ravenscar was well satisfied. All around her there were envious and curious glances. She could not mistake the jealousy on some of the women's faces or the suspicion in their eyes. There was also something peculiar, something that would not bear investigating.

And then for the first time she felt a sudden wave of shyness sweep over her. She dropped her eyes before the crowd of strange, unrecognisable faces, but not before she had seen one that was familiar. A beautiful face with dark eyes glowering at her across the glitter of jewels, the flutter of feathers and the sparkle of decorations.

She thought in that moment that never before in her life had she really believed that one woman could look at another with such an expression of hatred as to make her blood run cold. But there was such enmity, such cruel vindictiveness, in Lady Isabel's eyes, that instinctively Amanda shrank towards Lady Standon as if in need of protection.

To her surprise she found Lady Standon surrounded by a number of old friends.

'Where have you been?'

'Why have we not seen you?'

'What are you doing in London?'

For once her Ladyship's air of unhappiness and indifference seemed to have lifted a little and there was almost a sparkle in her eyes as she realised that after all these years she had not been forgotten.

But before Amanda could claim Lady Standon's attention Lord Ravenscar was at her side again.

'I want you to meet my friends,' he said, and presented her to a stream of people, rather, she thought, in the manner of a farmer exhibiting a prize heifer.

Only one person was of interest to her, and he was a sparse young man with a very large nose, who was wearing a sombre coat of grey without trimmings or decorations, a strange contrast amongst the glittering, colourful, brilliant throng.

'Who is that?' she asked Lord Ravenscar. 'I did not hear his name.'

'Sir Arthur Wellesley,' was the reply. 'A soldier, and someone who is not of the slightest interest.'

Amanda had not missed the look of scorn, indeed almost of disgust, with which Sir Arthur Wellesley had responded to Lord Ravenscar's greeting. He would almost certainly not have spoken to him at all had he not been in conversation with a very overdressed and overpainted lady who had held out her hand to Lord Ravenscar with a cry of exaggerated pleasure.

Lord Ravenscar stopped to speak with someone else and impulsively Amanda crossed the room to where Sir Arthur stood staring into the crowd.

'Sir, I need your help,' she said a little nervously.

'At your service, Ma'am,' he said in an uncompromising manner which would have daunted even a stouter heart than Amanda's.

He waited for her to speak, frowning a little, and she thought how very unapproachable he was. And yet, at the same time, there was an air of integrity about him which contrasted to his advantage with most of the men around.

'I am Amanda Burke,' she said, 'and I have just been presented to you by Lord Ravenscar.'

She felt she must introduce herself again, for she had the feeling that he had not noticed her previously. He inclined his head, but he still said nothing.

'I have a great desire, Sir,' she went on, 'to know if an officer by the name of Graham Munro is still alive.'

'Graham Munro!' Sir Arthur replied.

'Yes, that, indeed, is all I know about him, save that he was in the Royal Fusiliers in . . . Well, I am not quite certain of the year, but over fifteen years ago.'

'He was then a cornet?' Sir Arthur asked.

'I am afraid I do not know,' Amanda answered. 'He was sent abroad and then no more was heard of him. If you could make enquiries . . .'

'Yes, of course,' Sir Arthur replied. 'I will do my best. If I learn of his whereabouts, you shall be informed.'

He spoke to her as if she were a trooper under his command, and, curtsying, Amanda moved away from him.

'It might have been a ridiculous request to make, she thought, and yet the tragedy in Lady Standon's eyes, the unhappiness in her voice when she had spoken of the man she had once loved, had awakened in her the deepest sympathy.

Perhaps there was just one chance, Amanda thought, that the lovers, parted so tragically, might be reunited. For her there was no such chance.

Talking to Sir Arthur Wellesley she seemed to have lost her escorts. She looked around her but she could see neither Lady Standon nor Lord Ravenscar. Curious for the first time since she had entered the house, she moved with the crowd into other rooms, looking at the brocades and velvets, satins and plush, which covered the walls and furniture; at the *objets d'art* in glass cabinets; the fabulous porcelain and the extremely fine pictures.

She found herself in what she guessed must be the

dining-room. It was walled with silver and supported by columns of red-and-yellow granite. All around her people chattered and talked and paid her no attention, until she felt she might be a ghost moving amongst them and wished, indeed, that she were.

She could not help hoping that she would not see Lady Isabel again. The hatred in her eyes had seemed to sear its way almost like a weapon across the space that separated them in the reception room, and quite unaccountably she felt herself shiver.

'Excuse me, Ma'am,' a respectful voice said at her elbow.

She turned to see one of the footmen in the royal livery standing beside her.

'You are Miss Burke, Ma'am?'

'That is my name,' Amanda replied.

'I have a message for you,' the flunkey said. 'My Lady Standon has been taken ill. She asks that you will join her immediately. There is a carriage waiting for you at the front door.'

'Oh, indeed, I must go to her,' Amanda exclaimed.

'If you will permit me to show you the way,' the footman answered.

'Yes, please,' Amanda said, having no idea how she could find the front door.

The footman went ahead and she followed. Almost immediately she found herself in the hall. Another flunkey brought her cloak. She pulled it over her shoulders and hurried down the steps on which dozens of linkmen stood and at the bottom of which a coach was waiting, its door open.

Amanda jumped in, the door was shut behind her and a footman sprang on to the box. She felt the coachman whip up the horses; and then, as they moved away, she had a glimpse of the light pouring out of the windows, of the guests moving almost like coloured ants up and down the grand staircase.

Amanda sank back against the cushioned seat of the coach. Poor Lady Standon, she thought. It had been too much for her, coming to London in such a hurry, shopping all day, attending this reception and, perhaps, feeling upset and distressed by meeting old friends and reliving past memories.

'I will be kind to her,' Amanda resolved. 'I will try to make her forget what she has been through.'

She could hear again the horror and the humiliation in Lady Standon's voice, and with a little throb of fear she could hear her saying:

'He was my brother's great friend!'

In the darkness of the coach, Amanda put her hands over her eyes. Now that Peter was dead, she had to face what lay ahead. It had been easy to believe—because she had wanted to believe it—that Peter would save her; that she would not have to fulfil her promise; that somehow she could escape from this marriage which both frightened and nauseated her.

Now she knew there was no escape. She was in honour bound to marry Lord Ravenscar, and her sacrifice, as far as Peter was concerned, had been all in vain. And yet, even without Peter, she was honest enough with herself to admit that it would have been hard to refuse his Lordship's offer. She had heard the sudden joy in her mother's voice when she learned that her father had been offered the Deanery at Frackenbury. She had seen the excitement on Harriet's face, and she had known only too well what their improved circumstances could mean to Caroline and Roland.

Would she ever have been strong enough to put her own selfish feelings before their well-being? And yet at the mere thought of Lord Ravenscar she felt her flesh creep.

'I cannot do it! I cannot!' she told herself in the darkness but knew that she was only repeating words and that she was being carried along relentlessly, as by a tide against which even the strongest swimmer could not prevail.

There were no tears in her eyes, but she felt as if her whole body wept tears of blood because the man she loved could no longer help her. He was dead, gone from her, gone where she could never see him or hear him again until she, too, lost her life.

'Trust me.' It seemed to her that he said the words beside her, and she could have cried out aloud because it was all so hopeless and such a waste of happiness.

She tried to feel his lips on hers in that glorious, wonderful kiss in which the world had stood still and they had been alone, man and woman in an Eden of their own.

She tried to recapture that moment when he had knelt at her feet and lifted the hem of her white muslin gown to his lips.

She knew then that the memory of him would haunt her so long as she lived. There would never be another man who could mean to her what Peter had meant. 'We were made for each other,' she thought. 'I must have known at once, in that very first moment when I looked at him, that he was a part of me and I of him. And he knew it when I bent over him as he lay on the couch in the Temple, and he opened his eyes and looked up into mine. I think it was in that moment that our souls were joined.'

She felt the tears well up in her eyes. Sternly she fought them back. It was Lady Standon she had to think of at this moment, she thought, and not of herself. That would come later, in the darkness of the night—in the darkness of many, many long nights—when she would remember Peter and all that he had said and done.

She bent forward to look out of the window. The coach was travelling fast but was taking an unconscionable long time, she thought, to get from Carlton House Terrace to Grosvenor Square. They were driving down a road filled with shops and now they turned up what seemed to be a narrow, rather disreputable-looking street; but it was difficult to be certain in the darkness.

Suddenly the horses came to a standstill. Amanda peered out. They had stopped at a house, but it was certainly not Lord Ravenscar's. It was low and not at all imposing, but the windows were bright with lights and there was the sound of music, gay, jingling music.

The coach door was opened by a man in livery, but he had not the appearance, Amanda thought somewhat vaguely, of a gentleman's servant.

'I think there is some mistake,' she said. 'I am looking for Lady Standon and I expected she would be at Lord Ravenscar's house.'

'You are Miss Burke?' the man asked.

'Yes, that is my name.'

'You are expected,' he said. 'Get out.'

There was something familiar and almost insolent about his manner, but Amanda could only obey him, thinking that it was a strange place for Lady Standon to have been brought to, but perhaps it was the house of a friend and she preferred to come here rather than return to Grosvenor Square.

The entrance hall was brightly painted, with strange pictures on the walls, and she had a sudden glimpse as a door opened of a large room crowded with people; and she thought—although, of course, she must have been mistaken—that there were card-tables and people seated round them.

The footman turned aside to show her up a flight of stairs. A man and a woman were coming down them. He was obviously a dandy, dressed in the latest fashion, with his cravat somewhat crumpled and his face flushed as if with drink. But the woman was extraordinary, with a painted face and dressed with an indecency which made Amanda avert her eyes quickly.

'Who is that?' she heard the man ask as they passed on the stairs.

'Oh, another novice for the Abbess, I suppose,' the woman answered, and their laughter followed Amanda up to the next floor.

What was Lady Standon doing in such an extraordinary place? she thought, but she did not wish to question the insolent footman and so could only keep her surprise to herself as they moved along a passage.

A door burst open suddenly and a woman appeared. She was middle-aged, or perhaps older; but her hair was dyed with henna and her eyelashes were mascara'd to stick out from her tired, deeply lined eyes like fir trees in the snow. She had a full red mouth, her evening gown was cut shamelessly low, and there was, Amanda thought, an air of coarse vulgarity about her.

'Here she is, Ma,' the footman said jocularly.

The middle-aged woman turned on him.

'Don't you "Ma" me, you young jackanapes. Get downstairs and be more respectful, or you'll find yourself out on your neck tomorrow morning—and without a reference.'

'Where would a reference from here get me?' he asked with a grin.

She made a threatening gesture at him, half in fun, half seriously, and he ran away laughing, leaving Amanda staring after him in utter perplexity.

With an effort she forced herself to make a small curtsy.

'I beg your pardon, Ma'am,' she said, 'but I was informed that my chaperon, the Countess of Standon, was here. Can there be some mistake?'

'No, dearie, there's no mistake,' the woman answered, looking her up and down in what Amanda felt was a most common way. 'Come upstairs with me.'

She walked ahead, disclosing that her gown was practically transparent and had been done up so hastily at the back that several of the hooks were in the wrong eyes.

'Why should Lady Standon come here?' Amanda asked.

She received no answer to her question and, feeling it would be impolite to stress the unsuitability of such a place for a lady of quality, she could merely follow the middle-aged woman up another flight of stairs, while bursts of raucous laughter seemed to come from every room they passed.

On the top floor the woman produced a large key from a reticule she carried on her arm, and inserted it in a door half way down the passage. Amanda followed her into the room. There was no sign of Lady Standon, but a girl was lolling in an armchair. She was wearing a soiled dressing-gown ornamented with torn frills and from the expression on her pale face Amanda thought that she must be ill.

'Hello, Rosie,' the woman said.

'What do you want, Ma?' the girl asked. 'I'm feeling like hell. It's no use bringing anyone up here.'

'It's all right, Rosie,' the woman answered. 'I told you you could have the night off. But I've nowhere to put her.' She jerked her thumb towards Amanda.

'I am sorry,' Amanda said firmly, 'but I do not understand what is happening. I was told that Lady Standon was here—the Countess of Standon, Lord Ravenscar's sister—and I wish to see her at once.'

'Here, Rosie, you tell her what to expect,' the woman said. 'I haven't got time for all these frips and fraps. It's full already downstairs and there'll be a lot more coming along later from Carlton House.'

'What is happening?' Amanda asked angrily. 'Where is Lady Standon?'

The woman shrugged her shoulders and looked at the girl.

'You see,' she said, 'when we get 'em raw I always say we need time. But her Ladyship was insistent that it should be tonight, so tonight it had to be. Don't pull your punches, Rosie. We haven't time for nursery games these days.'

While Amanda stared at her, the woman pushed her to one side and, before she realised what was happening, had gone out of the room, slamming the door to behind her. Amanda heard the key turn in the lock.

In a sudden panic she ran to the door and rattled at the handle.

'What are you doing? Why are you leaving me here?' she called. 'Let me out. Help!'

She pulled and hammered on the door. Even while she did so, she knew it was hopeless.

'It's no use,' the girl called Rosie said from the armchair. 'It's easier if you don't make a fuss. They always win in the end.'

'What is all this about?' Amanda asked.

She was really frightened by now, but she realised that there was nothing to fear from the pale, rather miserable-looking girl seated in the chair. She drew nearer to her.

'Please explain to me what is happening,' she said. 'I was told at Carlton House that Lady Standon was here.'

'You were at Carlton House?' the girl interrupted. 'She's flying a bit high this time! I should have thought it might have got her into trouble.'

'Who?' Amanda asked.

'Ma, of course.'

'What has she got to do with it?' Amanda enquired. 'Is Lady Standon here? Is she ill?'

'No, of course she isn't,' Rosie answered. 'That was just a trap, see, to get you here.'

'A trap!' Amanda repeated. 'But why? What for?'

Rosie looked at her as if she felt she must be pretending not to understand. And when she saw the innocence in Amanda's face she gave a little sigh.

'You might be me four years ago,' she said. 'I was just like you, but they told me they had a wonderful post for me; personal maid to a lady of title, that's what it was supposed to be. I was ever so excited about it until I got here. It didn't take me long to realise I wasn't going to see no ladies—but plenty of gentlemen.'

'I . . . I still do not understand,' Amanda said. 'Could you explain to me exactly what this place is?'

Rosie told her and after one startled, horrified gasp, Amanda said nothing. She just sat, growing paler and paler, until Rosie put out a hand and guided her into a chair beside her own.

'It's all right,' she said soothingly. 'You'll get used to it after a bit. It's a bit awful at first. I remember crying like anything when I was alone—which wasn't often. But you get used to it.'

'But . . . but I . . . I will not . . . I mean . . . I cannot . . .' Amanda managed to say at last, the words coming between her lips hardly above a whisper. 'But, who could . . . have done this . . . this thing to me . . . ? She—that woman —said, "her Ladyship . . ." Who did she mean . . . by that?'

'I don't rightly know,' Rosie answered. 'There aren't many ladies that come here, you can be sure of that. But there is one Ma talks about sometimes—one of those grand bits o' muslin who were born in the right place, but try to do us wretched girls out of our jobs. Now, what was her name? Let me think. Lady Irene? No, Lady Isabel something or other.'

'Lady Isabel!' Amanda gasped the name. She could see the hatred in those beautiful eyes, the hard, bitter line of that pouting, red mouth.

'Yes, that's it—Lady Isabel,' Rosie said. 'I remember now. That's the name.'

Bit by bit the jigsaw began to fall into place, Amanda thought. Lady Isabel's anger that she should have engaged Lord Ravenscar's affections; her threats when she had come into the Salon at Grosvenor Square; the fury in her eyes at Carlton House.

'But she cannot do this to me!' Amanda gasped. 'She cannot! I must speak to somebody. They must let me go.'

'Now, look here, duckie,' Rosie said. 'You haven't got a chance. No one ever gets out of here. If you're once in, they keep you.'

'But surely, surely, I can escape?' Amanda asked wildly.

'They will stop you and all you will get is a good whipping.'

Amanda felt herself shudder.

'They would not dare.'

Rosie laughed.

'You tell that to Ma when she comes round with her riding whip. Oh she does it very cleverly—not too many marks to spoil your looks and your value—but it hurts and goes on hurting.'

Amanda covered her face with her hands, and after a moment Rosie went on:

'And she's got other ways, worse than the whip, to make you see sense. She gives you something to drink. I don't know what it is, but after you've taken it there's no question of you being able to refuse to do what she wants you to do. Your brain doesn't seem to work. You just do anything you're told. So you'd better give in from the beginning and make the best of it.'

'I cannot b . . . believe this is h . . . happening to me,' Amanda managed to stammer.

She thought of her mother and father, of the little grey church next to the Vicarage where they had worshipped every Sunday. She thought of how one day she had dreamed that she would meet a man whom she would love and marry. That they would be joined together by their love and because of it every kiss and touch would seem a thing of beauty and of wonder.

With the sudden cry of an animal that has been caught in a trap, Amanda sprang to her feet. She ran across the room and pounded on the wooden door with her fists.

'Let me out! Let me out!' she screamed, and knew even as she cried out that no one would hear her.

How long she stood there bruising the soft flesh of her hands, Amanda did not know. But suddenly the utter hopelessness of her position swept over her and she turned and staggered back to the chair, sinking into it, exhausted and almost on the point of fainting.

'Poor little thing!' Rosie exclaimed. 'You've got it bad, haven't you? But take my advice. Don't argue with that she-devil. If you defy her she half kills you, and you have to give in in the end.'

'There must be something I can do,' Amanda managed to whisper.

'There's drink,' Rosie said. 'Drink whatever you can get a gentleman to pay for. It helps, it does really, and it's worth a headache the next morning.'

Amanda drew a deep breath. With an almost superhuman effort she tried to get control of herself, to stop the shaking of her hands and the sudden chattering of her teeth.

'Thank you,' she managed to say to Rosie. 'You mean to be kind and I am grateful. But I have got to get out of here somehow.'

'I've told you, you haven't got a chance,' Rosie retorted. 'All you'll be doing is buying trouble for yourself. One girl made a bolt for it, but Ma tripped her at the top of the stairs and she broke her leg. She was sent to another house in north London with a different type of client altogether. She died after two years there. No, if you have to be in this sort of life you can't do much better than to be in Madame Barclay's house.'

'Is that her name?' Amanda asked.

'It's supposed to be,' Rosie said, 'but it might be anything, and nobody worries so long as she produces the goods.'

The implication of the words made Amanda give a little groan. And then, suddenly, she heard the key turn in the lock, and she stiffened with an expression of horror on her face.

As she had expected, Ma came into the room. To Amanda's surprise she seemed to be in a very good temper.

'Well, dearie, has Rosie told you how happy you're going to be here?' she asked, in what was almost a wheedling tone.

'You know I have no intention of staying,' Amanda answered.

Even as she spoke she felt Rosie give her a nudge with her arm.

'Don't annoy her,' she whispered out of the side of her mouth.

'Now, you mustn't talk like that,' Ma said. 'You'll be grateful to me one day, when you realise what I have done for you and a lot of girls like you. Now, just listen to reason. There's a gentleman here who wishes to see you. He asked for you very special, he did, and is prepared to pay a pretty penny for the privilege! Are you coming to see him like a good girl, or shall I give you a drink to make you feel better?'

Amanda's heart gave a sudden leap. A gentleman who had asked specially for her! Could this possibly be someone who had seen her leave Carlton House? Could it, indeed, be Lord Ravenscar? She knew at this moment that even he would be welcome. Anything, anyone, would be better than the horror of what she had learned from Rosie. Whoever it might be, she decided quickly, she would have a chance of telling him the truth, of begging him to help her.

'Well, are you coming?' Ma asked impertinently.

'Yes, I am coming,' Amanda said.

'Now, there's a good, sensible girl,' Ma smiled. 'We don't often get anyone who settles down so quickly, do we, Rosie?'

'No, we don't,' Rosie answered.

She nudged Amanda again.

'Be careful,' she whispered. 'She takes it out on you if they're not satisfied.'

Amanda walked resolutely towards the door.

'I am ready,' she said, with a courage that she was far from feeling.

'You look a bit pale,' Ma said critically, 'but perhaps you're best as you are, without rouge. Some men like them ladylike, and this one seems to think you're just what he's been waiting for!'

She gave Amanda a leer and then, going from the room, led the way downstairs. They stopped on the first floor which was better decorated and, therefore, Amanda guessed, was probably more expensive. Ma put her hand towards the door and then stopped.

'You behave yourself,' she said in a warning tone. 'If you don't, I'll make you wish that you'd never been born. Do you understand?'

She thrust her face into Amanda's. Her breath, heavy with wine, and the smell of her cheap scent, was nauseating. Without waiting for Amanda's answer she opened the door.

'Here you are, Monsieur,' she said. 'If she's not to your liking I've plenty of others who will be.'

She gave Amanda a push into the middle of the room. In the softly diffused, pink light it was difficult for a moment to focus her eyes. Then Amanda saw that the room was partially filled by a draped and canopied bed. There was a table in the centre of the room, on which were two bottles of wine and some glasses, and standing beyond the table with his back to the door was a man.

For a moment as she looked at him she felt her heart contract with fear. It was not Lord Ravenscar. He was too tall. Then he turned round. Her lips parted, but no sound came from them.

It was Peter who stood there!

10

For a moment Amanda could not move and it seemed as if her heart stopped beating. Then, as she would have cried out in the utter joy of seeing him, Peter raised his fingers to his lips.

Swiftly he moved across the room and taking off his cloak slung it over the lintel of the door so that it hung like a curtain, preventing anyone who might have peeped through the keyhole, or any other spy-hole, from seeing anything.

Then he turned and held out his arms. She ran to him and hid her face against his shoulder. There was nothing she could say. She was conscious only that her whole being was vibrating with the relief and wonder of knowing that he was not dead but here, here in this place, where she had expected something so terrible, so unspeakable, to be waiting for her.

He did not kiss her, he only held her very close. And when at last she raised her face it was to find him looking down at her with an expression so gentle, so tender and, at the same time, so adoring, that for the first time since she had entered the room she felt the tears prick her eyes.

'He . . . told me you were . . . dead,' she managed to say at last—the first words that she was able to force through her lips.

'It was a lie, as you see,' Peter said quietly.

'Oh, take me away! Take me away from here!' Amanda begged, and now the terror that had encompassed her ever since she had come to this horrible house swept over her in a flood-tide so that all at once she was trembling in an uncontrollable panic.

'Let us go now, at once,' she pleaded. 'I cannot breathe here, it is evil.'

'My poor little love, if only it was as easy as that,' Peter said sadly.

'Easy?' Amanda questioned.

'They would not let us,' he said quietly.

Amanda remembered the arrogant flunkey who had led her upstairs. She remembered, too, having seen half-a-dozen like him in the doorway and in the hall when she had entered.

'But they cannot hold me,' she said in a whisper.

'Since you are here, it would be hard to prove that they had no right to do so,' Peter answered. 'And while they were arguing, finding people to come forward to identify you, it would be too late.'

She understood what he meant and the blood crept up her cheeks in a sudden crimson flood. And then, panic-stricken, her little hands were reaching up to him, beseeching him.

'But I cannot stay here, I cannot. Oh, Peter! Peter!'

It was a cry of sheer terror; a cry of an animal in a trap.

'No, you shall not stay,' he answered. 'I will take you away. But we have got to be clever about it. If we are caught, I shall be found tomorrow morning in the river with my neck broken and you will be a prisoner here for life.'

'How can we do it?' Amanda asked.

He pulled her a little closer to him for a moment, as if he would protect her with his own body; and then resolutely he set her free to stand looking down at her, his eyes watching every movement of her face.

'There is only one chance,' he said gently. 'And it means you will have to trust me.'

'What is it?' Amanda asked quickly.

'Go and look out of the window,' he commanded.

She did as he told her, pulling aside the tawdry curtains of cheap pink satin to reveal dirty, unpolished panes of glass through which it was hard at first to see. Then, as her eyes grew accustomed to the gloom outside, she saw that the window overlooked a narrow alley at the side of the house. It was deserted, and opposite there was only the blank wall of a warehouse or shop, which was obviously closed for the night.

They were on the first floor but to Amanda it looked a very long drop to the ground. At the same time, she knew that if this was her only chance of escape she would take it, even if it meant jumping into a burning fiery furnace, or a cauldron of boiling oil.

She looked round to find that Peter was stripping the bed. He was knotting the sheets and blankets together and when they did not seem long enough he added the silk counterpane to his hastily improvised rope, and then the curtains from the window. He worked without talking; and now, realising the urgency, Amanda was silent too, just watching him, her whole being tense for fear that there should come a sudden knock at the door.

At last Peter seemed to think the rope was long enough. He tested the knots and then tied one end round the leg of the heavy bedstead, pulling against it with all his strength to see that it would not give. Then he looked at Amanda.

'I am going to take you in my arms, my darling,' he said. 'Shut your eyes and pray that good fortune is with us.'

'I will do exactly what you tell me,' Amanda replied.

She was very pale, but she was not trembling. Nothing, she thought, could ever be really frightening if she was with Peter.

He opened the window and dropped the rope out of it. Then he picked her up in his arms and carried her to the window-sill, holding her very tightly, almost as if he said good-bye to her in case anything should happen.

'Link your hands behind my neck,' he commanded, 'and shut your eyes. Do not look down. Try not to move. Whatever happens, my darling, I love you!'

'I love you too,' Amanda answered. 'Oh, thank God you came in time!'

'Amen!' Peter said briefly; and then, with his hands on the rope and holding her as close as he could with the inside of his arms, he swung them both out of the window.

Amanda shut her eyes as he had told her. She felt the sudden strain on her hands behind his neck; felt him, too, take the full impact of their joint weight, and knew, as they moved slowly, slowly down the rope, that it was a race against time. If anyone saw them now they were lost. A cry from the window would bring the flunkeys at the front door hurrying round the side of the house.

They were still swinging high above the ground and she knew that her weight, light though it was, impeded Peter's progress and made it, inevitably, extremely slow. Down!

Down! Amanda was beginning to feel as if her own fingers would crack behind Peter's neck. Then suddenly she felt his feet touch the ground.

There was no time for her to feel relief or anything else. Taking her by the hand he turned and ran as swiftly as he could down the alley, away from the house, into a murky darkness which seemed almost impenetrable.

The cobbled stones were rough against Amanda's feet in her new, thin, satin slippers. She smelt the stench and dirt of the place; the dampness of the air seemed to catch her throat.

She tried to keep pace with Peter. Her wreath of blue flowers fell from her hair, but she did not check her speed. And then, suddenly, after twisting several times, the alleyway came to an end and they were out in a broad street with prosperous, well-to-do shops and pavements.

Peter paused for a moment, looking about him. There were few people in sight—a night-watchman asleep in his box, his brazier growing cold for lack of fuel; a coach drawn by four horses was turning down a side road. And then coming towards them Amanda saw another coach drawn by only one horse and proceeding at a slow, almost snail-like pace.

'A hackney carriage!' she heard Peter say beneath his breath. 'The gods, indeed, are with us.'

He waved and the man drew up his tired horse.

'Oi be a-going 'ome, Sir,' he said.

'If you will take us to Grosvenor Square, I will give you a guinea,' Peter answered.

Amanda saw the man's eyes glint in the light of his candle lanterns.

'Jump in, Sir,' he suggested. 'Oi'll give the old mare an extra bag of oats for keeping 'er up so late.'

Peter opened the door and helped Amanda in. When he sat himself beside her and closed the door she felt as if they had entered a little world of their own.

'Oh, Peter, you have saved me!' she said in a tremulous voice.

She felt relief seep over her so strongly that it was an inertia almost like an attack of the vapours. She put her head against his shoulder and his arm went round her.

'How did you find me?' she asked in a strangled voice.

'I saw you,' he said. 'It was quite by chance. Oh, my God! When I think what might have happened if I had not been there!'

'When did you see me?'

'Coming out of Carlton House,' he replied. 'I was in the crowd watching the guests enter and leave. For a moment I thought I must be mistaken; but then I knew it was you and looking so lovely, Amanda, that I ached to step forward and claim you as my own.'

'If only you had,' she breathed.

'I saw that a coach was waiting,' Peter went on. 'It had been standing there for nearly a quarter-of-an-hour and I knew that it was empty. Therefore, when you stepped into it alone, unaccompanied, I felt that something must be wrong.'

'So you followed me,' she prompted.

'Yes, I followed you,' he answered. 'And when I saw where it was taking you I thought I must have taken leave of my senses.'

'They told me that Lady Standon was ill and wanted me,' Amanda explained.

'I knew you had been trapped; but I could not imagine how or why anyone should want to do such a thing to you.'

'It was Lady Isabel Mannering, I think. She hates me.'

'Yes, of course!' Peter exclaimed. 'But I did not think that even she would sink to such depths of iniquity as to send you, an innocent girl, to a living hell.'

'She hates me,' Amanda repeated. 'Why should she hate me so bitterly? There are other men in the world besides Lord Ravenscar.'

'Not for Lady Isabel,' Peter answered grimly. 'She is notorious, Amanda. Her reputation stinks to all decent and respectable people. If Ravenscar will not marry her, then there is no one else fool enough to offer her the shelter of his name.'

'Does she love him?' Amanda asked.

'Love?' Peter questioned. 'I do not think love is a word that Isabel Mannering has ever known. No, she does not love Ravenscar, but she needs his money. In a few weeks, perhaps sooner, her father will be taken to the debtors' prison and their house will be sold up, unless she can find someone to go surety for him.'

'So that is why she hates me,' Amanda said in a wondering voice.

'When have you met her?' Peter asked.

'She came to the house last night when we first arrived,' Amanda answered. 'She walked into the Salon and found Lord Ravenscar attempting to embrace me.'

She felt Peter stiffen beside her and his arm about her tighten.

'I was trying to evade him,' she said quickly, 'when Lady Isabel interrupted us. I was glad of her presence, but I could not understand her rudeness.'

'What did she say to you?' Peter enquired.

'Oh, she was very scornful about my coming from the country; and then, when Lady Standon championed me, she told Lord Ravenscar we were a crow and a pullet to add to his collection.'

'What did she mean by that?'

'I think she was referring to the aviary of birds that he had downstairs,' Amanda replied. 'When I looked at them tonight, I kept thinking of how you told me that our hearts would wing towards each other.'

'Mine could not do that,' he answered tenderly, 'because it is yours already.'

'Oh, Peter, when I heard that you were dead, I wanted to die with you,' Amanda whispered. 'Lord Ravenscar told me just as we were going downstairs to dinner and I wanted to scream out, to cry, but I suppose pride would not let me. I could not let him, or anyone else, know that my whole life had ended. I had been so certain that I would see you again.'

'I told you to trust me,' he said quietly.

'I did, I did,' Amanda protested. 'It was just that everyone seemed so certain that you would be captured. All the soldiers were after you and you were wounded! How is your wound?'

'Nearly healed, as you can see,' he answered. 'It will not add to my beauty, but then you, my darling, have enough for both of us.'

'And you got to London safely?'

'I got to London and found friends,' Peter smiled.

'And you were afraid to let me know you were safe?' Amanda said reproachfully.

'I had no way of communicating with you,' he replied. 'I have none now. Amanda, we have got to be very careful. One foolish step and everything may be lost.'

'I will bear anything so long as I know that you are somewhere in the world and that I shall see you again,' Amanda said simply.

'You will do that,' he answered. 'But, once again, my darling, I have got to ask you to trust me. I can tell you nothing. I shall not be able to see you. Amanda! Amanda! For God's sake take care of yourself.'

'I will try,' she said. 'But I did not know such horrible things existed in the whole world as the place to which I was taken tonight. Peter! Those poor girls! They are kept there as prisoners!'

'Forget them,' he said. 'Do not think about them. You cannot help; you can do nothing about it. Just forget that you have ever been there. And, Amanda, for your own sake you are to tell no one—do you understand?—no one, what has happened tonight.'

'And how shall I explain that I came home alone?' she asked.

'That is easy,' he answered. 'You got lost in the crowd at Carlton House. You could not find Lady Standon or Lord Ravenscar. Thinking that perhaps they had gone home without you, you asked a footman to find you a hackney carriage. Now, be sure of your story. Do not speak of anything else.'

'And if I see Lady Isabel again?'

'Behave as if nothing had happened. Do not be alone with her. Do not be alone with anyone if you can help it; and, of course, never leave the house alone. If you get a message asking you to go anywhere to meet anybody, take a maid or a footman with you. Do you understand? This is important, Amanda, for it is obvious that Lady Isabel will stop at nothing to be rid of you.'

'I will remember,' Amanda said humbly.

There was silence for a moment and glancing out of the window Amanda saw, with a sense of dismay, that they were moving through quiet, residential streets lined with important-looking houses.

'Peter,' she said impulsively.

'What is it?' he asked.

'Do you still love me as much as you did?'

'You know I do,' he answered.

'Then . . . then why . . . ?' her voice faltered. 'Why have you not . . . kissed me?'

There was silence for a moment and then he answered in a voice hoarse and a little broken.

'Oh, Amanda, you child, you baby! Do you not understand?'

'What should I understand?' she asked, wide-eyed.

'That I dare not,' he replied. 'I love you, Amanda, so overwhelmingly, that if your lips touched mine I should not be answerable for the consequences. I should carry you away regardless of what might happen in the future. I should marry you this very night and make you mine, and that I must not do.'

'Why not?' Amanda breathed.

'Because I have nothing to offer you,' he replied. 'Nothing but embitterment and a life of concealment. Only the best is good enough for you, Amanda. Only the best is what I plan to lay at your feet. Trust me! Believe me! Do not for a moment doubt my love, because I promise you it is stronger than both of us.'

She heard the sudden passion in his voice and now he put his hand under her chin and turned her face up to his. She could see his face very faintly in the light from the lantern shining through the glass window in front of them. She could see his eyes looking down into hers and thought she saw a sudden fire.

She felt a quiver go through her. She felt herself tremble beneath his hands and knew that she was melting towards him. She felt as if her whole body yearned and ached for him and wanted to be part of him. She heard him draw in his breath sharply and then his hand dropped and he turned his head away from her.

'Do not tempt me, Amanda,' he said harshly. 'There are some things which a man cannot think about and remain sane. You are so utterly desirable, child and woman in one body, and I love them both.'

He put out his hand and rapped on the glass window. The carriage drew to a standstill.

'I am going to leave you here, Amanda,' he said. 'We must not arrive together.'

'Oh, do not go! Do not leave me!' she pleaded. 'Peter, let me go with you. I will do anything; I do not mind what happens.'

Her hands went out towards him, her fingers holding on to the lapels of his coat. Very gently he disengaged them.

'Have you forgotten your parents?' he asked. 'Have you forgotten what this means to them, Amanda?'

'Yes, I have,' she said defiantly. 'I know now that none of the things that I thought were important matter beside you. Money, position, clothes, jewels—they are not even worth a thought beside the fact that I love you.'

'Amanda, you are making it unbearable for me,' Peter said, and his voice sounded as if it was strangled.

'You do not want me,' she said.

She saw a sudden twist of his lips.

'One day I will make you apologise for that,' he said. 'Just as one day I will kiss you until you cry for mercy. Until that day comes—and pray God it will come soon—take care of yourself, my little beloved.'

He took both her hands and raised them to his lips. Instead of kissing the back of them he turned them over. She felt his lips kissing the palms with a reverence and, at the same time, a hungry passion which made her thrill until her whole body trembled with a sudden ecstasy.

And then he had left her, the coach door had slammed and she heard him pay the coachman and his voice giving directions to Lord Ravenscar's house. The tired horse was whipped up again. She had a glimpse of Peter standing almost to attention as she passed; and then, as she pressed her face against the window to see more of him, the darkness had swallowed him up.

For one moment she contemplated flinging open the door and running after him. It was agony to let him go; and yet, because he wished it, she knew that she must do as he had told her and go back to the terrors and fears of Lord Ravenscar's house.

It was only just the other side of the square and yet it seemed to her, in that short passage of time between Peter leaving her and her arrival, that she grew immeasurably older. She began to see that life was not so simple as she had always thought it to be, but complex, strange, frightening and, at the same time, when one least expected it, magically wonderful.

She shut her eyes and remembered the note in Peter's voice when he told her he loved her. She lifted her hands to her lips and kissed the palms where his mouth had lingered.

A sleepy footman opened the door as the coach drew up outside. Amanda, looking out, saw his surprise that she was in a hackney carriage; but his training stood him in good stead and with an impassive face he rolled down the strip of carpet across the pavement and hurried to open the door of the coach.

Amanda stepped on to the pavement.

'Please give the coachman five shillings,' she said, 'for I have no money with me.'

'Very good, Miss,' the footman said.

She hoped the driver would have the sense not to say he had been paid already; and then she walked into the house and was just about to go upstairs when the door of the library was flung open. Lord Ravenscar stood there, and behind him, looking agitated, was Lady Standon.

'Where have you been?' Lord Ravenscar roared.

Amanda walked past him and going up to Lady Standon made a little curtsy.

'I must apologise for being so stupid, Ma'am,' she said in her soft voice, 'but I'm afraid I got lost at Carlton House.'

'There, Hugo, what did I tell you?' Lady Standon said sharply to her brother. 'I told you I was sure that Amanda had not gone home without us.'

'How did you get here?' Lord Ravenscar enquired.

'A flunkey found me a hackney carriage,' Amanda answered. 'It was foolish of me to lose you both; but I was looking at the pictures and the beautiful *objets d'art* and I seemed to get swept away in the crowds.'

'Somebody told me you had left with a man,' Lord Ravenscar said, his eyes narrowing.

Twenty-four hours earlier Amanda would have asked innocently enough who had told him that and wondered why anyone should have invented such a lie. Now, with the new-found wisdom she had acquired in just a few hours, she understood. That was to have been Lady Isabel's explanation of her disappearance—that she had run away with someone else.

'No, indeed, my Lord,' she said with a little laugh. 'No one offered to take me home. I came by myself and I am afraid that as I had no money with me your Lordship will have to pay the fare.'

She saw him relax and the suspicion die out of his face.

'There you are, Hugo,' Lady Standon said again. 'You were always one for getting in a pucker about nothing.'

She turned to Amanda.

'I am sorry, dear, that we should have been so inconsiderate as to leave you behind; but if Hugo had not been so insistent that you had already left I would have searched for you further.'

'There is no harm done,' Amanda smiled, 'and it is not surprising that we lost each other in such a crowd. I never imagined that anyone would give such a big party or have so many people in one house all at the same time.'

'I thought Isabel intended to play some trick on me,' she heard Lord Ravenscar mutter as he walked across the room and poured himself a glass of wine from a decanter standing on a side table.

'I dislike that woman,' Lady Standon said. 'And the less you see of her, Hugo, I should have thought the better.'

'I agree with you for once, Charlotte,' Lord Ravenscar said, drinking down his wine as if he were thirsty. 'At the same time, some women are like leeches, 'tis devilish hard to cast them off.'

'It is not a subject I care to discuss,' Lady Standon said coldly. 'Come, Amanda, it is time for bed.'

She turned towards the door, then stopped.

'What has happened to your wreath?' she asked. 'It was a pretty thing and I thought how well it became you.'

The question took Amanda by surprise. She felt the blood rush to her cheeks. Just for one wild, irresponsible second she thought of telling the truth, of saying it was lying in the mud in some dirty alley, above which floated in the wind the sheets, blankets and curtains from a bawdy house. And then she caught a sharp look in Lord Ravenscar's eyes again and realised that his suspicions, engendered by Lady Isabel, were not entirely allayed.

'My wreath?' she repeated vaguely. 'Oh, dear! How foolish of me. I must have left it in the hackney carriage. I took it off because it made my head ache. I set it down beside me and now he must have driven away.'

'It does not matter,' Lady Standon said. 'It was an expensive trifle, but we can purchase another.'

Without saying good night to her brother she swept through the door. Amanda stopped and dropped a small curtsy.

'Good night, my Lord.'

Lord Ravenscar set down his glass.

'Wait, Amanda! I want to talk to you,' he said, holding out his hand.

'No, indeed, my Lord,' Amanda replied hastily. 'My Lady is expecting me to join her.'

He moved towards her; but she had gone, running across the hall and up the stairs behind Lady Standon who, as if she guessed that danger lay in waiting, had already reached the bend of the stairs.

They were at their bedroom doors before Lady Standon said anything. Then, as Amanda waited for her good night, she said in a low voice:

'For Heaven's sake be careful, child. If anything should happen to you he will kill me, as he has threatened to do.'

Amanda's eyes widened in astonishment.

'It is true,' Lady Standon said, looking into her face. 'He is besotted with you, do you not realise that? And he has other reasons too—reasons which I cannot relate.'

'Please tell me,' Amanda begged.

'No, for I am not sure of them,' Lady Standon replied. 'But . . .'

There was a sudden interruption from below. Lord Ravenscar's voice came echoing up the stairs.

'Charlotte! Amanda!' he shouted. 'Come here! Come here at once! I have something to say to you.'

The two women looked at each other. For the first time, it seemed to Amanda, there was a glint of mischief in Lady Standon's face and she looked young, almost like a girl again.

'It is too late,' she whispered. 'We are already asleep!'

With an incredible swiftness they both moved together. Two bedroom doors opened. Two bedroom doors shut.

Two keys were turned firmly with a determined click in the locks.

'Amanda! Charlotte!' Lord Ravenscar shouted again.

But he got no answer. There was only the silence of the sleeping house.

In her bedroom, with her door firmly locked, Amanda flung herself down on the bed and gave herself over to thinking about Peter. After a long time she undressed, slowly and dreamily, to creep between the cool white sheets and go on thinking about him.

When finally sleep overtook her, her lips were still parted as if she spoke his name. And she awoke in the morning with a sudden sense of gladness.

'He is alive!' She wanted to shout the news from the housetops and for a moment, because of the intensity of her joy, she did not remember that they were parted or that she could not get in touch with him.

In retrospect, what had happened last night seemed a strange, almost unbelievable nightmare. Could she really have been taken to such a ghastly place? Had she perhaps imagined the awful people she had met there, the frightful things that had been said to her?

It all seemed a bad dream. All that mattered was that she had found Peter again. He was not dead, but alive. She wanted to dance and to sing. She even found new pleasure in putting on one of the beautiful gowns that Lady Standon had bought for her and she wondered if Peter would see her as he moved along the street or stood at the back of some jostling crowd.

Why had he been outside Carlton House last night? she wondered. He was gentleman enough, she knew that, to have been inside. And yet, for some mysterious reason that he would not tell her, he had been watching the Prince's guests alight from their coaches.

What was the mystery that surrounded him? And then, suddenly, like a little arrow striking her when she least expected it, she remembered something.

'Here she is, *Monsieur,*' Madam had said as she had shooed her into that ominous *cabinet d'amour* and shut the door behind her.

'*Monsieur! Monsieur!*' The word seemed to echo and re-echo in Amanda's mind. Once again the full flood of suspicion overtook her—the French book in the boat; the muttered words of a man in his delirium; the sentences he had spoken about English women and their compliments.

And now '*Monsieur*'. Why had that woman called him that? Surely 'Sir' would have been a more obvious choice.

Suddenly the sunshine seemed to go behind a cloud. Was this Peter's secret? Was this, indeed, why he was hiding? A Frenchman sent to London from France! She could not believe it of him. Besides, there were many Frenchmen in London and they were not in the least ashamed of their nationality. Men who had escaped from the Revolution, who had settled here amongst the English and had not returned to see upstarts and commoners usurp the places they had once occupied.

But if he was not a spy why could he not come forward and say who he was? Why could he not tell her, at any rate? He knew she would not betray him. And then as she questioned who and what he might be, she knew that, in all truth, it did not matter. If he were a spy of Napoleon, then she would still love him and follow him, if necessary, to prison or before a firing squad.

Love knew no boundaries, either of country or nationality. It was something which created a world of its own, a world in which there were only two people—a man and a woman.

It was with a sense of serenity that Amanda greeted Lady Standon; and, having breakfasted together, they set off on their shopping expedition. It was not so bewildering for Amanda as it had been the day before. Now she found that she could make a definite opinion on this gown or that, where before they had both been but a blur of luxury and expense. Now she could choose a bonnet and be quite positive which one she preferred and which set off her fair hair to its best advantage.

She could not help being slightly appalled at the extravagance with which Lady Standon ordered things and she guessed that for all their pretence Lord Ravenscar was footing the bill and his sister was determined to make him pay handsomely.

At last they were tired and turned their faces homewards.

'The white gauze we bought this morning is the prettiest gown I have ever seen,' Amanda remarked conversationally.

'It is pretty enough for a wedding gown,' Lady Standon replied.

Amanda felt a little tremor go through her. She had forgotten at the moment that these gowns were all supposed to be for the delectation of Lord Ravenscar. When she had been looking at them this morning, she had thought of Peter and what she would look like in his eyes when she appeared in them.

'It is a long time ahead,' she said quickly. 'I feel that the fashion may have changed before I get married.'

'My brother is talking of June,' Lady Standon said.

There was always that reserve in her voice, Amanda noticed, when she spoke of her brother's marriage.

'I would rather wait,' Amanda answered. 'But, indeed, anything may happen before June.'

'Such as?' Lady Standon prompted.

Amanda did not reply. She had imagined for one moment that she had seen a tall, broad-shouldered figure moving amongst the crowd. It was only in her imagination, she knew that; and yet every second, every minute, she kept expecting that she might see Peter.

How she loved him! How her heart beat only for him, she thought. She realised that she was being rude.

'I apologise, Ma'am,' she said quickly. 'I was thinking of something else. Did you ask me a question?'

'It is of no consequence,' Lady Standon said, her voice suddenly dreary and empty of all emotion.

They drove in silence back to the house.

'I will go upstairs and take off my shawl and bonnet,' Lady Standon said.

Amanda was about to accompany her when the footman said:

'There is a gentleman waiting to see you in the Library, Miss.'

Amanda's heart gave a sudden leap. There was only one gentleman, she thought, who could possibly have called to see her. And then she knew that would have been impossible. Wary of a trap, she asked cautiously:

'Who is it? Did he leave his name?'

'It is General Sir Arthur Wellesley, Miss.'

'Oh!' Amanda exclaimed. 'I will see him, of course.'

Without waiting for the footman to lead the way, she ran into the Library, throwing open the door and appearing to the man leaning against the mantelpiece like a sudden breath of spring, with her eyes alight with interest and her fair curls touching the soft, wild-rose bloom of her cheeks.

'You have news for me, Sir Arthur?' Amanda asked and then remembered her manners and said quickly: 'I am sorry. It was rude of me to be so impetuous. I should have greeted you first.'

Sir Arthur Wellesley's eyes twinkled, but his hard face did not relax. He bowed formally and said:

'Last night you asked me to make some enquiries, Miss Burke. I have done so.'

'You have found that Graham Munro is alive?'

'He is, indeed,' General Wellesley replied. 'Not only alive but already a Colonel. I thought I knew the name, and now I have discovered that he is commanding a battalion of the Grenadier Guards.'

'Oh, how splendid!' Amanda said.

'He transferred some years ago when he came into a legacy,' General Wellesley said drily, almost as if he was reading the particulars from a report book. 'Colonel Munro is at present stationed at Wellington Barracks if you should wish to get in touch with him.'

'How very kind of you to find all this out,' Amanda said. 'But, Sir Arthur, there is one more thing I would know.'

'And what is that?' he asked.

'Is . . . is Colonel Munro married?'

Sir Arthur looked surprised. 'No,' he replied after a moment, 'he has never married and is, I understand, something of a misogynist.'

Amanda clasped her hands together.

'That is, indeed, wonderful!' she said. 'Oh, Sir Arthur, I cannot tell you how glad I am to have your news. Thank you for bringing it to me.'

'Does it mean so much to you?' Sir Arthur enquired, somewhat surprised; and Amanda realised, almost with a sense of fun, that he was thinking it strange that she should be so interested in another man while engaged to Lord Ravenscar.

She felt it only polite to set his curiosity at rest.

'It means a lot to a friend who thought that perhaps Colonel Munro was dead,' she said.

'I understand,' Sir Arthur remarked. 'And now, if you will forgive me, Miss Burke, I have an important appointment waiting.'

'You would not care for a glass of wine?' Amanda asked, feeling that good manners expected it of her.

'No, thank you,' Sir Arthur replied abruptly; and she had the feeling that he would not eat or drink in Lord Ravenscar's house, and only because she asked it of him had he forced himself to cross the threshold.

'Thank you again,' Amanda said quickly, as she realised he was going. And then, because she had a sudden intuition about this thin, austere man, she added, 'May I wish you the very best of good fortune in all the splendid things you are about to do!'

He looked astonished.

'What things?'

'I do not quite know,' Amanda answered, 'but I heard people talking last night of repelling the invasion. I somehow felt that you would be in the thick of the fight and that you would defeat Bonaparte.'

'Bonaparte is not a very easy adversary,' he said uncompromisingly. 'But if we ever come to grips with him, Miss Burke, I only hope your predictions come true.'

He bowed to her and left the room and she heard his carriage drive away from the front of the house. Amanda went to the window to see it go and had a sudden glimpse of the General's face, with its large nose etched against the window of his coach, almost as if it were upon a coin.

'Who are you watching so intently?'

Lord Ravenscar's voice behind her made her jump and she turned round to see that he had entered the room behind her and she had not heard him. He was looking very resplendent in a new, plum-coloured coat with velvet facings, and its colour seemed reflected in his face until she realised by a slight unsteadiness of his gait that he had been drinking.

'I came back specially to see you, Amanda,' he said. 'I

have news for you—tremendous news.'

'I am interested to hear what it is, my Lord,' Amanda said nervously, wishing she was not alone in the room and that after Sir Arthur Wellesley had gone she had hurried upstairs.

'I tried to tell you my idea last night,' Lord Ravenscar said, 'but you and Charlotte would not listen to me. So, this morning, I went to Carlton House and had a word with the Prince. He was gracious, very gracious—in fact he promised to be present himself in a most unusual rôle.'

'Present at what?' Amanda asked, bewildered.

Lord Ravenscar did not answer for a moment. His eyes flickered over her and she felt as if he mentally undressed her, and she longed to run away from him. Only pride kept her waiting for an answer to her question. Nervously, one hand crept up to her breast as if she expected that he might deal her a blow.

'His Royal Highness,' Lord Ravenscar said slowly, as if he savoured the words, 'has promised, my dear Amanda, to give you away at our marriage, which will take place immediately!'

11

Amanda gave an audible gasp.

'Immediately, my Lord! What do you mean?'

'Exactly what I say,' Lord Ravenscar replied. 'We shall be married now, tomorrow, the next day— as soon as you have a gown which is presentable and I can make the formal arrangements.'

'But . . : but, my Lord!' Amanda cried. 'Why should there be this unseemly haste? And how can I be married without my father and mother being present? Or, indeed, how can I be married at all at a few moments' notice? What would people say . . . or think, at such speed o . . . over a matter which sh . . . should be deliberately con . . . considered?'

She was fighting for words, gasping a little between them because her agitation seemed to be choking her and it was difficult to express herself. Lord Ravenscar watched her with a faint twist at the corner of his mouth.

'So many excuses; so many questions,' he said at length. 'Fortunately, Amanda, I can answer them all.'

He paused, while Amanda stood watching him. Her eyes, desperate in her white face, were like the terrified eyes of an animal that has been caught in a trap.

'First,' Lord Ravenscar went on, 'let me answer the question about your parents. Of course, I should welcome them at our marriage; and, indeed, I should have sent for them, were it not for something which I believe you will consider of paramount importance.'

'What is that?' Amanda asked in a whisper.

'I heard last night,' Lord Ravenscar answered, 'that the Bishop of Frackenbury has died of an apoplexy. Remembering your devotion to your parents, my dear, and ever mindful of what would please you, this morning, when I was approaching the Prince about our nuptials, I mentioned the vacancy to the episcopal chair, and he has promised to consult with the Archbishop of Canterbury that your father may be appointed.'

'Papa a Bishop!' Amanda exclaimed, astounded.

'The idea surprises you?' Lord Ravenscar asked. 'You will learn in time that when one has influence and friends in the right quarter, nothing is impossible.'

He paused to let the words sink in and then added:

'Nothing—not even a marriage with only twenty-four hours' notice.'

Amanda strove to collect her scattered senses.

'It is kind of you, my Lord, very kind, to suggest such a position for Papa,' she said. 'He will be gratified and I know that as a family we shall be deeply grateful.'

'I feel sure,' Lord Ravenscar interposed, 'that it will, in fact, make your father appreciate the resources of his son-in-law, just as you, my dear, will learn to appreciate the resources of your husband.'

'But . . . but could not we wait until Papa is ordained a Bishop?' Amanda suggested. 'And then perhaps he could marry us.'

'There are other bishops to perform that office,' Lord Ravenscar answered. 'And, although we would appreciate your father's assistance, I feel that at this moment, when his mind will be occupied with the move to Frackenbury and with ecclesiastical matters, it would be unwise to invite him to London.'

He paused, then added briskly:

'Apart from that, there is not time. We shall be married tomorrow at noon and the Prince will not only give you away, but will also provide a breakfast for us at Carlton House.'

'But I . . . I cannot . . . marry you tomorrow,' Amanda cried.

'Why?'

The question was like a pistol shot echoing and re-echoing round the room. Amanda was silent. She had no answer. How could she say now, at this juncture, that she did not love him? And even if she said it, was it likely it would worry him? She had not forgotten how he had told her that she would continue to interest and attract him so long as she did not bore him with her affection.

What else could she say? That she hoped by some wild, improbable miracle the man who had been called '*Monsieur*', who had been suspected by the soldiers of being a French spy, would be able to save her?

'Well?' Lord Ravenscar said. 'Have you no answer to that?'

'Please let us wait a little longer,' Amanda begged with a little pleading gesture which would have melted a heart that was not made of stone. 'There is plenty of time. We have all our lives before us. Please, please, do not let us do anything too hastily.'

'You are a very attractive advocate,' Lord Ravenscar answered, 'but you have not, as the defendant, made out a very logical case for yourself. I had thought that it might be necessary to delay our nuptials for forty-eight hours until Thursday. Now that I have seen you, I know that I can wait no longer than tomorrow. Let me see, it will be the seventh day of May, which I am sure is an auspicious date on which two people can start their life together.'

'I . . . I cannot! I . . . cannot!' Amanda said, her voice hardly above a whisper.

Slowly and deliberately Lord Ravenscar walked towards her. He put his hands under her chin and lifted her face to his. He looked down with hard eyes at the trembling of her soft lips, at her eyes dark with horror and misty with tears.

'So you are afraid of marriage,' he said in a silky voice. 'I think I like women who are afraid. All too soon they cease to flutter like wild birds within one's grasp and are ready to cling to the hands they had feared and to the lips that have conquered them. Go on fighting me, Amanda. Go on hating me. As long as you look as you do now, I shall be your most faithful and obedient servant.'

With an unexpected gesture, Amanda struck his hand away and freed herself. Her eyes, which had been frightened, were suddenly filled with anger.

'How dare you speak to me like that?' she stormed. 'How can you say such things? How can you expect our marriage to be anything but a failure? Marriage should be built on love. Indeed, there should be no question of two people marrying each other unless they are both in love.'

She was thinking of Peter as she spoke, but the amused,

cynical smile on Lord Ravenscar's lips was like a dash of cold water.

'Would you have me believe,' he said, 'that you were in love with me when you promised me your hand in marriage? Was it for my *beaux yeux* that you accepted the bargain I offered you—marriage or that the soldiers should search my park and grounds?'

Amanda was silent. She knew she had no reply to this. He was too perceptive. He had known all along, she thought, that she loved Peter, that she had tried to save him because of her love for him.

'You extracted a promise, but you lied to me,' she said impulsively.

'Did I?' Lord Ravenscar questioned. 'And about what?'

She realised then that she had been indiscreet. He was not to know that she was aware that Peter was alive. Neither was there any point in telling him that she had gone to Oak Dell that night when Peter escaped and had seen the soldiers waiting.

'There is no point in such recriminations,' she said quickly. 'May I have your Lordship's permission to withdraw?'

'That is better,' he said approvingly. 'You are beginning to realise that you cannot argue with me, because I know all the answers. You will also soon learn to appreciate that your duty lies in doing what I wish. We shall be married tomorrow, Amanda, and after that you will no longer be able to evade me.'

'No, I shall have to do as you tell me,' Amanda said with a sudden flash of spirit. 'And, doubtless, in time I shall become like your sister—spiritless, broken and utterly miserable. Haven't you ever asked yourself what her life was like?'

'So she has been confiding in you, has she?' Lord Ravenscar smiled. 'I thought all human impulses had been beaten out of Charlotte.'

'She is your sister,' Amanda replied. 'How can you talk so heartlessly of her sufferings?'

'Charlotte was a fool,' Lord Ravenscar answered. 'She could have managed Standon had she had the wit to do so. Anyway, it was a better marriage for her than the upstart commoner on whom she had set her heart.'

'She might have found happiness with him,' Amanda said softly.

'A cornet in an obscure foot regiment?' Lord Ravenscar enquired scornfully. 'Amanda, you have yet a lot to learn about life. Women always want what they cannot get, just as they always imagine that a different type of life from the one they have chosen would have been preferable.'

He gave a sharp mirthless laugh.

'You will regret that you have not been allowed to run away with a French spy, to share his sufferings for a few months and to watch him swing on the gallows.'

He saw her blanch and added:

'That was undoubtedly his ultimate fortune if a bullet had not ended his miserable life a little sooner than might have been expected. I think you would have found the rôle of widow to a traitor decidedly unpleasant. Instead you will be my wife, and you will find that if you play your part sensibly I shall not be unappreciative.'

He moved towards her again and put out his hand to touch her gown of sprigged muslin trimmed with satin bows.

'Money can enhance a woman's looks,' he said slyly, 'even if she is as pretty as you. Jewellery—and there are some charming baubles amongst my family heirlooms—can frame the loveliness of a white throat.'

His fingers crept upwards and his hand caressed her neck, while she could not suppress the shudder which shook her. He felt it and laughed softly. She tried to move away, but his arm was round her, holding her in a vice from which it was impossible to escape.

'And last of all, Amanda,' he murmured in her ear, 'even the most provocative red lips have to eat. Have you ever tried existing on the bread and water which sustains those who find themselves incarcerated at His Majesty's expense? The menu in the traitors' prison is not a very varied one. I think you will prefer the fare that you will enjoy at my table.'

He bent his head and before she could evade him his lips were on hers. She tried to steel herself against the revulsion of his hungry mouth fastening greedily and almost brutally on the softness of hers. But she felt in that moment that she went down to the very depths of humiliation, into a darkness and a horror from which she not only could not escape, but could never forget.

His hold on her tightened; his lips fastened to hers were like a vice. She felt his passion rising within him like an evil flame; and then, suddenly, he lifted her in his arms.

'Amanda!' he said hoarsely. 'Damme! Why should we wait?'

He was carrying her to a large sofa in the corner of the room; and as she struggled against him, fighting with every ounce of her strength, she knew how small and ineffectual she was and that her resistance was merely exciting him.

'Amanda! Amanda!'

His thick lips were on her eyes, her cheeks, her throat. She felt him lay her down on the sofa, while she fought fruitlessly to regain her feet, knowing as she did so that she was quite powerless. She heard the fichu of her gown tear beneath his hands.

'Please . . . please! Save . . . me!' she cried, and heard her own voice die in her throat as his lips came down on hers once again.

She felt the weight of his body; and then, at that moment, when the room was growing dark and she knew that she must be losing consciousness, there was a sudden interruption.

'Ravenscar! Where are you?' a voice cried from the doorway. Gasping, Amanda found herself free of her attacker. Lord Ravenscar moved slowly from the sofa and, straightening his cravat, turned towards the door.

'Blast you, Wassell!' he ejaculated. 'What the hell do you want?'

'I have news for you,' the voice from the other side of the room said. 'Bad news! 'Tis what we feared. The King will send for Pitt tomorrow.'

'It was inevitable, I suppose,' Lord Ravenscar replied. 'We hoped Addington would be able to carry on.'

'This means that everything will be tightened up,' the newcomer continued as if he had not spoken. 'Pitt's speech in the House last week has roused the whole nation. They insist—nay, they demand—that the war shall be pursued more forcibly.'

With an effort Amanda sat up on the sofa. Lord Ravenscar had his back to her; but she could see that the man he was speaking to was small and middle-aged, with sandy hair and small, shifty eyes fringed with sandy lashes. He looked like a ferret, she thought.

'We shall have to watch our step,' she heard him say in a low voice. 'Pitt is no fool!'

'Why should I worry?' Lord Ravenscar asked in a defiant voice. 'I live here respectably. My marriage is to take place tomorrow and, in her father's absence, the Prince will give away the bride.'

'Tomorrow!' Mr. Wassell exclaimed. 'So it has come to that, has it?'

'It has come to that,' Lord Ravenscar repeated in a light tone.

Amanda rose to her feet, pulling her torn, crumpled fichu around her shoulders. She felt dazed. Her mouth was bruised, her neck and shoulders sore from the strength of Lord Ravenscar's hands.

'We must let him know,' Mr. Wassell said almost beneath his breath, but Amanda caught the words.

Lord Ravenscar turned towards her.

'I must present you to my future bride,' he said. 'Amanda, this is an old friend of mine, Mr. Stanley Wassell. As you can see from his clothes, he is a dandy. When you see him holding the ribbons, you will realise that he is also a Corinthian.'

Amanda dropped a curtsy, conscious of her dishevelled appearance and untidy hair.

'Have I your leave to withdraw, my Lord?' she asked without raising her eyes.

'But of course,' Lord Ravenscar replied. 'Find my sister and tell her that the wedding is to take place tomorrow. I must go at once to the Prince to acquaint him with the fact that in your desire to be my wife we felt it quite unnecessary to wait until the day after tomorrow, which was the later date he suggested.'

He was mocking her, Amanda knew; but she had no answer for him. She could only hurry from the room, her head downcast, feeling that she had been humiliated and degraded in front of Mr. Wassell.

She passed through the door and closed it behind her. She had turned towards the stairs when she heard the door open again and she realised that the latch had not gone home. Without really thinking, because she had been taught as a child to close doors behind her, she turned back and was just about to close the door properly when she heard Mr. Wassell say:

'I have a suspicion that someone is watching you, Ravenscar—a tall, broad-shouldered fellow. Any idea who it could be?'

'Watching me? How do you know?'

'I saw him yesterday following you down St. James's. I was in the bow window at White's. It was dusk and I could not see his face. I did not think much about it, but he was outside Carlton House when you were there this morning with the Prince. You left before me and when I came out later he had gone.'

'A tall, broad-shouldered fellow!' Lord Ravenscar ruminated. 'A dun or Bow Street Runner?'

'No, no, neither of those things,' Mr. Wassell said impatiently. 'A gentleman, by his clothes.'

'It could be!' Lord Ravenscar said thoughtfully. 'But no! It is impossible!'

'Just watch your step,' Mr. Wassell warned.

'I shall,' Lord Ravenscar answered. 'A tall, broad-shouldered fellow, you say!'

Amanda shut the door soundlessly. She realised that she had been eavesdropping. At the same time, she felt as if she had the clue to some strange puzzle; and yet, even so, could not fit it into place.

It was Peter who was watching Lord Ravenscar. She was sure of it. But why? For what reason? She only wished he would confide in her. If only she knew the truth, however bad or however desperate it might be. Even if he were a traitor, she would stand by him if he asked it of her.

She gave a little sob as she ran up the stairs. But when she reached her bedroom, instead of changing her torn gown, she sat down at the writing-desk.

'If I cannot be happy,' she thought wistfully as she drew a piece of writing-paper towards her, 'perhaps I can bring happiness to someone else.'

It took her some time to compose her letter although it was short; and when it was finished she read it through carefully.

Sir,

I have Reason to Believe that I am in possession of Information which may be of great Import to You. I shall be exceeding Grateful if You will make it Convenient to call on me Immediately as I shall be leaving London tomorrow Evening.

I remain, Sir
Yours respectfully,
Amanda Burke.

She signed her name, rang the bell and told the maid that a footman was to convey the letter immediately to Colonel Graham Munro at Wellington Barracks.

'Say it is to be put into his hand with all possible speed,' she said. 'And, Martha!'

'Yes, Miss?'

The housemaid looked at her attentively as Amanda, stammering a little from embarrassment, said:

'There is no n . . . need to tell his Lor . . . Lordship that this letter has been sent.'

'No, Miss. Of course not, Miss. I understand.'

The girl went from the room with a little rustle of her apron. Amanda, with a sigh, began to take off her gown. She threw it on the floor and thought she would never wear it again without that feeling of revulsion and horror that had come over her when Lord Ravenscar touched her.

She shut her eyes for a moment and swayed as she thought of tomorrow night. when he would possess her and make her his own. What could save her now? She could not even tell Peter what was happening If only she could write to him as she had written to Colonel Munro; but he had gone from her, leaving no address.

'Traitor!'

She could hear the scorn in Lord Ravenscar's voice as he had said the word. Was Peter a traitor? Could he really sink to the infamy of betraying his own country? And then suddenly she knew that, if she believed such a thing, she was no better than Lord Ravenscar himself. She could trust Peter, and England could trust him too. No man could look so honest, so straightforward and, at the same time, be treacherous to the very depths of his soul.

'I trust him! I believe in him!'

Amanda said the words aloud; and then, because she suddenly felt stifled in this house that belonged to the man she hated, she flung open the window to let in the spring sunshine and stood hoping her love would wing its way over the house-tops towards Peter, wherever he might be.

'Come to me! Come to me!' she called wordlessly, willing him to realise the horror that had crept up on her and was waiting there ready to pounce.

The sunshine was like a soft hand on her forehead. She longed for the protection of Peter's arms, the feeling of security and peace when she laid her head against his shoulder.

'I want you and I trust you!' she called again in her heart, and it seemed to her as if her whole being went out in a wordless prayer.

It was half-an-hour later before she knocked on Lady Standon's door.

'Come in!'

The words were spoken in that dull, lifeless voice that Amanda knew so well.

She found Lady Standon lying on the chaise-longue by the window. There was a book on her lap, but she was making no attempt to read it.

'I am sorry, Amanda,' she said. 'But I must rest. I have a migraine and my head is aching until I can hardly see. I have, however, taken some physic and in a little while the pain will pass.'

'I am so sorry, Ma'am,' Amanda said. 'Is there anything else I can get you?'

'No, I am better, thank you,' Lady Standon said, with the voice of one who would never be better and who was prepared to endure it.

'I have just seen Lord Ravenscar,' Amanda said. 'He asked me to inform you that he has arranged for my marriage to take place tomorrow.'

'Tomorrow!' Lady Standon exclaimed in surprise. 'That is unexpected news.'

'I begged him to wait,' Amanda said, 'but he will not do so. The Prince is to give me away and the breakfast is to be held at Carlton House.'

'A fine setting for a wedding!' Lady Standon exclaimed. 'Presided over by that dissolute reprobate who has deserted his wife and is rumoured to be morganatically married to Mistress Fitzherbert.'

She spoke with such scorn and feeling that Amanda stared at her in surprise. And then, unexpectedly, Lady Standon reached out her hand and drew Amanda down beside the chaise-longue.

'Amanda,' she said, 'you are too good for this. Run away while there is still time. Do not marry my brother. Do not inflict on yourself a suffering that is worse than death. Leave now while you are still able to do so. Go home! Hide yourself! Do anything rather than go through with this mockery of what marriage should be.'

'I have thought of that,' Amanda answered. 'I have thought of it every moment since I first gave my promise to Lord Ravenscar. It was a bargain I struck with him, a bargain in which I fulfilled my part and I suppose, although he cheated on it, he fulfilled his. Should one, can one, break one's solemn word of honour after it has once been given?'

'I think, when there are exceptional circumstances, one can,' Lady Standon said.

'There is more to it than that,' Amanda replied. 'His Lordship has just informed me that my father is to be made a Bishop—the Bishop of Frackenbury. Can you imagine, Ma'am, what this will mean? He has struggled so long with no money to support and educate us children. My mother, who has been brought up in a very different way, has always hated the privations that the Vicarage has imposed on her and on us. Now she will be free of them. I have seen the Bishop's Palace next to Frackenbury Cathedral. It is a magnificent building. . . .'

Amanda's voice died away and Lady Standon said with a soft voice that she had never used before:

'You poor child! A lamb led to the slaughter!'

'There is nothing I can do,' Amanda went on, 'except pray that perhaps someone will save me—someone whom I love.'

Her voice broke and now the tears came and she put her head down against one of the cushions on the chaise-longue and sobbed.

'Can we not let him know?' Lady Standon asked.

'No, he has given me no address,' Amanda answered. 'If only there was more time!'

'I will pray for you,' Lady Standon remarked. 'There seems nothing else we can do. If only you would be warned by me!'

Amanda raised her head.

'If you had your time over again, Ma'am, would you run away?'

'I would run to the uttermost ends of the earth to save myself from what I went through after I married,' Lady Standon answered. 'I know now, and I can only tell you from experience, Amanda, that position, money, luxury, do not count in the slightest when it comes to a question of love or hate, happiness or degradation. A woman can be happy in a cave with a man she loves and utterly desolate in a palace with a man she detests.'

Lady Standon spoke so positively that a little colour came into her face and just for the moment she seemed young again and almost pretty. And then it seemed as if she relapsed into her perpetual grey nonentity.

'I should not be talking to you like this,' she said in a tone of voice which told Amanda she regretted having broken through her reserve.

'I understand, Ma'am,' Amanda said, 'and I am grateful to you. You have made me feel that someone understands.'

Lady Standon did not answer and Amanda, dropping a curtsy, began to withdraw.

'We will go driving in an hour's time,' Lady Standon said in her ordinary indifferent tone. 'There are many things you will need for your trousseau if the wedding is tomorrow.'

'Yes, Ma'am,' Amanda said dutifully.

She went from the room and closed the door behind her. She was just about to go into her own bedroom, afraid, if she lingered on the stairs, that she might see Lord Ravenscar again, when one of the footmen came up the stairs and advanced towards her.

'Excuse me, Miss, but there is a woman selling lavender at the door. She is just one of the usual street-criers in this district, but she insists that she has a message for you that she will only give into your own hand. I have tried to get her to go away, but she will not budge. She knew your name.'

'I will come and see her,' Amanda answered.

She went into her bedroom and picked up her reticule. Before she left home her father had given her two golden guineas and a small amount of silver.

'You will need to tip the servants, Amanda,' he had said, 'and perhaps to buy some things for yourself in London.'

Amanda had used none of the money. Lady Standon had paid for everything. But now she knew that if the woman had, indeed, got a message, she must reward her.

Could it be from Peter? Her heart warmed at the thought and then she remembered his warning. This might be a trap. This might be yet another of Lady Isabel's efforts to dispose of her.

She followed the footman downstairs to the front door.

'If you will wait here, Miss,' the footman suggested, 'I will fetch the woman. She is down in the area.'

He went outside and Amanda saw him hurrying down the twisting iron steps which led to the basement of the house. There were two footmen on duty in the hall and she felt safe enough while they were near her. There was no carriage outside and very few people in the square.

This could not be a trap, she thought: but all the same she was a little tense and on edge. After last night she suspected anyone and everyone.

The footman came back up the area steps followed by a large, fat, elderly woman, a shawl over her shoulders and a hat trimmed with tatty feathers on her head. She carried a basket filled with small sprigs of lavender.

'Here she is, Miss,' the footman said to Amanda, and then to the woman: 'This is Miss Burke. And if it's only money you're after, you will get short shrift after all the tales you have been telling.'

'I don't want yer money, ye young jackanapes,' the woman answered with a broad Cockney accent. 'Go and put yer powdered 'ead under the tap and cool it orf.'

She turned to Amanda with an ingratiating whine.

'I've brought yer some lavender, pretty lady. Special lavender from a friend.' She picked a bunch out of her basket and as Amanda took it from her, she felt something thick round the stalks. ' 'E said to give it right into yer 'and, dearie,' she said in a whisper which only Amanda could hear. ' 'Andsome young man 'e was, and 'e told me, so as yer'd know it was from 'im, to say it came towards yer with wings. Them was 'is very words—wings.'

Amanda held the lavender tightly in her hand.

'Thank you very much,' she said. 'I am very pleased to have this.'

She felt in her reticule and drew out a florin.

' 'E's paid me already, lady,' the lavender woman said honestly.

'Never mind, I should like to give you this for your trouble,' Amanda answered.

She felt that if she obeyed her instincts she would give the woman a guinea. It was so wonderful to hear from Peter and know that he was thinking of her.

She turned from the door and ran across the hall and up the stairs. As she went, she heard the woman's high cry of:

'Lavender! Buy my sweet lavender!'

She ran into her room, closed and locked the door behind her. With trembling fingers she undid a screw of paper from the stalks of the lavender. There was no address and no beginning or end to the note. It only said, in strong, upright writing which Amanda felt was characteristic of him:

I must see you. Meet me tonight in the little arbour at the far end of the garden. I shall wait until dawn.

12

Lady Standon was indulging in a wild orgy of extravagance. Amanda could hardly believe her eyes as they went from shop to shop, ordering not one but a dozen gowns, not two or three bonnets but twenty or thirty.

The list of their purchases grew and grew and Lady Standon was deaf to any suggestions Amanda might make as to having more than enough or of finding such a colossal wardrobe an embarrassment.

It was as if Lady Standon relieved her own feelings against her brother and against the marriage by piling up the cost. Furs, shoes, shawls and sashes were added to the total, until Amanda gave up the unequal contest of trying to remember what had been bought.

Finally she said wearily as they stopped at yet another Bond Street shop:

'I am fatigued, Ma'am. Could we not return to Grosvenor Square?'

She thought for a moment that Lady Standon seemed relieved; but almost as if she steeled herself to spend more money, she replied:

'We will see what they have here, but this shall be the last.'

Slowly, Amanda followed her into the soft carpeted, low-ceilinged shop with its discreetly veiled window. As had happened a dozen times before, a smiling proprietress glided forward with an expression of sheer delight to exclaim:

'My Ladies! Your Ladyship! You are indeed welcome!'

The word had already gone round up and down Bond Street. Amanda thought, that there were extravagant spenders in their midst. She followed Lady Standon to a brocade and gilt sofa while the proprietress ran to open cupboards and bring out gowns made of material which, she told them in a lowered voice, had been smuggled only that very week from across the Channel.

Amanda could well believe it. England might be at war with France. but the ladies of St. James's still demanded the Lyons velvet, the gauzes, the lamés and the muslins with their unmistakable Parisian stamp, and the gold and silver ribbons which were unobtainable from any other country in the world.

'They say the First Consul's wife, Madame Bonaparte, has ordered a gown exactly like this,' the proprietress was saying. 'Look at those ribbons, *Mesdames*, and the embroidery round the hem. Only Paris could give a gown with such an air of distinction, such *chic*.'

'How much is it?' Lady Standon asked indifferently.

The proprietress named a sum which even after the formidable sums they had already spent made Amanda give a little gasp.

'We will take it,' Lady Standon said.

'Ma'am . . .' Amanda whispered, only to be thrust aside with a firm:

'We will take it, Amanda. It looks as if it will fit you. What alterations are required can be made immediately.'

'Let me show you some other gowns,' the proprietress said in a kind of ecstasy, running to the wardrobes and bringing down an assortment of beautiful clothes which seemed to echo the very colours of the rainbow itself.

Amanda rose and walked across the shop to where, at the far end, she could see an amusing collection of dolls dressed in the latest fashion. It was no use arguing with Lady Standon, she thought; and if she wished to spend her brother's money in such a manner, she must do as she wished.

Amanda had already resolved that a large number of the gowns should go to Harriet. There might even be one that could be altered for her mother, and certainly there were several that could, in time, be cut down to fit Caroline.

She wondered if they were thinking of her at this moment. She wondered how soon they would get Lord Ravenscar's letter to say she was to be married immediately. It might arrive tomorrow or the day after—at any rate, too late for them to do anything about it even if they wished to do so.

In a sudden despondency she thought that they might have forgotten about her in the excitement of planning their move to Frackenbury. At the moment they would be thinking that their destination was to the house reserved for the Dean. Soon they would know it was to the Palace.

She was staring at the dolls on the counter without seeing them and, suddenly, from the back of the shop, where she gathered the dressing-rooms were situated, a familiar figure swept out.

It was Lady Isabel, wearing a hat trimmed with feathers and a gown cut in the very latest fashion. It revealed the full beauty of her figure and gave her a sinuous, rather serpentine grace as she moved towards the door.

Amanda was standing a little to one side and for a moment Lady Isabel did not see her. Suddenly an expression of astonishment spread over her face and Amanda realised, also in surprise, that she had not been told what had happened. After a perceptible pause Lady Isabel found her voice.

'How did you escape?'

The question came bursting from between her red lips. It was obvious that she had not considered the full implication of her words.

Amanda met the dark, vindictive eyes coolly and without embarrassment. For the first time since she had come to London she was in control of the situation. For the first time she was not afraid or even embarrassed by what was happening.

'I fail to understand you, my Lady,' she said quietly. 'Why am I supposed to have escaped? And from where?'

She saw a kind of convulsion contort Lady Isabel's face. It was obvious that she had not expected such a reply any more than she had expected to see Amanda herself.

'Damn you!' she said furiously. 'Someone shall pay for this!'

She turned towards the shop assistant who was hovering anxiously in her wake.

'Cancel those gowns,' she said, her voice like the snarl of an angry dog. 'Cancel everything I have purchased here this afternoon.'

'But, my Lady . . . my Lady . . .' the shop assistant cried out; but Lady Isabel paid no heed to her.

Once again she was glaring at Amanda and her fingers were clenched almost as if she would deal her a blow. Then through gritted teeth she said:

'May you, too, rot in the hell into which you have cast me,' and sweeping from the shop she left behind her an atmosphere of tumultuous discomfort.

Quite suddenly Amanda felt she could bear no more. If Lady Isabel was in hell, then she, herself, knew only too clearly what hell awaited her on the morrow. She crossed to Lady Standon's side.

'I pray you, Ma'am, to finish all this another time. I am indisposed.'

As if Lady Standon realised that Amanda had reached the end of her tether, she rose instantly.

'You can get Miss Burke's measurements from Madame Beauclaire, next door,' she said. 'We have already made several purchases there.'

'That will be easily arranged, my Lady. Thank you for your patronage. It has been a pleasure to serve you and Miss Burke.'

They stepped into Lord Ravenscar's coach which was waiting outside and Amanda sank back against the cushions. She knew that her own emotions in the encounter with Lady Isabel had depleted her to the point of exhaustion. Harriet would have laughed at her for being so frail, but she knew that there was nothing more tiring than the misery and anxiety from which she had been suffering ever since Lord Ravenscar had told her that they were to be married the following morning.

The only comfort was Peter's note, lying now against her heart and making her feel that the hours were creeping by with tortoise-like slowness until they could meet that evening. At least she could tell him. At least he would know what was afoot. She hardly dared to hope that he would find some way to save her, and yet she dared not anticipate that he might not.

Lady Standon, wearing her habitual expression of sadness and disinterest, appeared to have nothing to say and they drove back to Grosvenor Square in silence. It was, by now, getting on for five o'clock and Amanda began counting the hours until she would dare to creep downstairs and go to find Peter in the garden.

The horses drew up outside Ravenscar House. A footman hurried to roll the red carpet across the pavement and Lady Standon stepped from the coach. As she rose to follow her, Amanda dropped her reticule. She groped on the floor to pick it up, and when finally she had found a handkerchief which had fallen from it Lady Standon had already passed into the house and therefore did not hear the Major-domo say:

'There is a gentleman to see you, Miss. He would not give his name, but he said you had asked him to call.'

'Yes, of course,' Amanda replied. 'I was expecting him.'

'I put him in the Music Room, Miss. I thought you would not wish to be disturbed if his Lordship returned.'

'That was very thoughtful of you,' Amanda said. 'Thank you.'

She walked into the hall and the Major-domo led her down a passage to the Music Room, a room which opened on to the back of the house and was, Amanda imagined, little used.

She entered the room and a tall, thin, middle-aged man in the uniform of the Grenadier Guards rose from the chair in which he had been seated. He had a stern, lined face that might, Amanda thought, have been good-looking in his youth. Now she felt that he was rather frightening, a man of deep reserves, who gave her an abrupt, rather diffident bow as he said, almost in a tone of surprise:

'You are Miss Burke?'

'Yes! Good afternoon!' Amanda said politely, dropping a small curtsy. 'I am Amanda Burke and you, I believe, are Colonel Graham Munro?'

'That is my name. You wrote to me.'

'It was very kind of you to come so quickly,' Amanda said. 'Will you not be seated?'

'I have a suspicion that you wrote to me about young Rupert Burke, who was in my regiment,' the Colonel said. 'I have been trying to get in touch with his family, but I believed that they lived in Yorkshire or the north of England. I think I should tell you at once that he is dead. He was killed beside me in India at . . .'

Amanda put up her hand.

'No, no, Sir, you are mistaken. I did not write to you on account of myself. Indeed, the name is quite a common one and I have no knowledge of any Rupert Burke or of any relation who might have been serving with you in India.'

'I am sorry,' Colonel Munro said. 'I could not imagine why you should wish to see me unless it was on behalf of Rupert Burke.'

'I think in my letter I said that my reason concerned you,' Amanda said.

'Me?' Colonel Munro said stiffly. 'I think that is unlikely. I have not been in this country. I have been in India for fifteen years. There is little here that can concern me.'

'On the contrary, there is someone whom I think once concerned you very deeply,' Amanda said. 'Her name was Charlotte!'

'I think, Miss Burke,' he said tersely, 'that you have brought me here under false pretences. There is therefore nothing further that we need say to each other.'

Colonel Munro rose to his feet.

He gave her the same stiff, almost gauche little bow that he had given her on their first acquaintance.

'Good day, Ma'am,' he said firmly and walked towards the door.

Amanda watched him go with a sense of dismay, and then she said quietly but very clearly:

'Can your pride really let you behave in such a manner? Have you no interest, no curiosity about the woman you once loved and who loved you so desperately that her whole life has been not only ruined, but made an agony of unhappiness because she could not be with you? She may be dead, she may be suffering; and yet you are not even interested to ask how she is.'

As she had begun to speak, he had stopped with his back to her. Now he turned round and asked:

'Is she dead?'

Amanda gave a little sigh of relief.

'So you do care enough to ask that question,' she said.

'My feelings have nothing to do with this matter,' Colonel Munro said. 'I do not know who you are or why you are interfering in my private affairs, but since you seem to know so much I must make myself clear.'

He gave a dry cough before he continued.

'I once, as you rightly suppose, knew someone called Charlotte. I had an affection for her which I imagined was reciprocated. I was mistaken. She married someone else.'

There was a bitterness in his voice which told Amanda so much that he left unsaid. It was with a note almost of thankfulness in her voice that she said:

'So you have remembered her. In fact you still care for her. Have you ever asked yourself why she married someone else?'

'That was obvious,' Colonel Munro said.

'Obvious in what way?' Amanda questioned. 'Because Lord Standon was richer and more distinguished? Because he was old—old enough to be her father? Because she was coerced, threatened and forced into marriage with a man whose morals disgusted her and who, when she failed to satisfy him in other ways, beat her into submission?'

She saw Colonel Munro's lips tighten and his fingers clench together in the palm of his hand. Slowly he retraced his steps until he stood beside her on the hearth-rug.

'Who has told you all this?' he asked.

'I happen to know exactly what did happen,' Amanda answered. 'How your letters to each other were intercepted. And I know, too, that if you had been strong, if you had forced your way into the house to find her, she would have run away with you right there and then, without a thought for the consequences.'

'How could I do that?' Colonel Munro said. 'I was penniless. How could Charlotte have lived on the pay of a cornet? How could she have endured the hardships of the only life I had to offer her?'

'She would have found it far easier than the life she had to endure with a man she hated,' Amanda answered.

'Perhaps I was a fool,' he replied. 'But there seemed nothing I could do but accept her decision that we should part.'

'It was not her decision,' Amanda corrected, 'but her brother's.'

'Ravenscar?' The Colonel raised his eyebrows. 'So he was at the bottom of this.'

He looked around him almost apprehensively.

'Whose house am I in now?'

'Lord Ravenscar's,' Amanda said.

'Then I must leave,' he ejaculated. 'I will not remain under that fellow's roof.'

'You will not meet him,' Amanda said soothingly. 'But before you leave there is something I should like to give you, a memento of the past, something that I feel you will treasure.'

'Something of Charlotte's?' he said, his voice suddenly deep and a little gruff. 'I should like that.'

'Then wait here. I will not be above two or three minutes,' Amanda said. 'You will not go, will you?'

'No, I promise you,' he answered.

She ran from the room, leaving him gazing into the fire, an expression of deep melancholy and regret on his face. She ran up the stairs with a speed that she and Harriet would employ when they were escaping from unwelcome guests, or hurrying home when they had been playing and thought that they would be late for the evening meal.

Breathlessly she reached Lady Standon's door, knocked, then opened it.

'Oh, Ma'am,' she said urgently. 'Would you come to the Music Room. There is a man there in deep distress and I feel that only you can help him.'

Lady Standon was seated by her dressing-table and had just removed the bonnet she had worn to go out shopping. She rose now and said in tones of perplexity:

'A man in deep distress, Amanda? Who is he and why has he come here?'

'He came to see me,' Amanda replied. 'There is no time to explain, but please come. I feel that only you can help him.'

'Of course, if you ask me,' Lady Standon replied. 'Is he ill? Shall I take my hearts-horn with me? Have you told the servants to bring some wine?'

'I do not think those remedies will be of the least use,' Amanda replied as she hurried down the stairs with Lady Standon following her. 'I think when you see him you will understand what he wants. But please hurry.'

She glanced, as she spoke, apprehensively towards the front door, realising how disastrous it would be if Lord Ravenscar chose this moment to enter the house and ask them where they were going. But there was no one about and they reached the Music Room in safety.

Amanda opened the door. The Colonel was where she had left him, staring into the flames. He raised his head as she entered and then his gaze travelled from her to the woman who came in behind her.

Lady Standon had advanced several paces into the room before she recognised him. Then she stopped and it seemed to Amanda as if two people had turned to stone before her very eyes. For a long, long moment they stood looking at each other, and then, with a little cry that was quite indescribable, Lady Standon ran forward.

'Graham! Oh, Graham!'

She reached his side and her hands went out to touch his chest, as if to reassure herself that he was really there.

'Graham! Graham!' she repeated, and there was so much poignancy and pathos in her voice that Amanda felt the tears come into her eyes.

And then it seemed as if a transformation took place and Lady Standon was gone and in her stead stood a girl—a girl with shining eyes and parted lips, a girl with colour in her pale cheeks and an air of youth and excitement about her which swept away the years and all the misery they had carried in their trail.

'Graham, it is really you!'

The words were like a psalm of praise and thanksgiving, and Colonel Munro's face, as he looked down at her, was transfigured too.

'Charlotte!' he said. 'You have not altered. You are just the same.'

Amanda slipped away and shut the door behind her. The tears were running down her cheeks, tears of happiness because two other people had found happiness, and tears of envy because she knew that they had the only thing that mattered in the world, while she had nothing.

After a moment she wiped her tears, and walking down the hall to where the two footmen on duty stood beside the front door, she said:

'Lady Standon is in the Music Room. She does not wish to be disturbed and no one is to go in there. Is that understood?'

'Very good, Miss,' one of the footmen replied.

Amanda went slowly up the stairs to her room. Whatever else happened, she thought, she had at least made two people happy, she had at least saved Lady Standon from the empty years of regret and misery which she had believed were all that was left to her.

She had not been in her room long before Lady Standon came running in, her face aglow and looking, Amanda thought, as if she was little more than her elder sister. Amanda jumped up at her entrance and Lady Standon flung her arms around her and pressed her cheek against hers.

'Thank you! Thank you, Amanda!' she said. 'You have made us so happy. Neither of us can begin to show our gratitude for all that you have done.'

'Why has Colonel Munro gone so quickly?' Amanda enquired.

'Graham will not stay in this house,' Lady Standon said. 'After the way my brother has behaved to me and to him, he cannot bear even to breathe the same air as Hugo. But tomorrow everything will be different. He is coming to take me away. He has gone now to get a marriage licence. There will be no question now of having to ask Hugo's permission, or anyone else's.'

She gave a little sigh of ecstasy before she continued:

'Graham wanted me to go with him tonight and find a priest to marry us, but I told him that I could not leave you. But the moment you are wed I need never enter this house or speak to my brother again.'

'You hate him so much?' Amanda asked.

'I detest him for what he has done to me,' Lady Standon replied. 'When I think of the fifteen years wasted when Graham and I could have been together! It does not matter what I suffered. It is the fact that those years were lost and we can never have them again.'

'Perhaps without them you would not have appreciated each other so greatly,' Amanda suggested.

'There is that about it,' Lady Standon agreed almost humbly. And then with a smile which was like the sun breaking through a cloud, she said: 'Oh, Amanda, to think that he has loved me all these years. There has never been another woman in his life.'

'Sir Arthur Wellesley said he was a misogynist,' Amanda told her. 'Does that not mean a man who does not like women?'

'I think it the wrong word to describe Graham,' Lady Standon smiled. 'He says there has only been one woman in his life and he could never find room for another.'

She stretched her arms suddenly wide.

'Amanda! Amanda! I am so happy! I thought I should never know again what happiness meant. I thought I was old and withered and without feelings of any sort. Instead —thanks to you—I am young again. I am happy and in love. I want nothing and no one save Graham, and he wants me.'

'I am glad,' Amanda said.

She could not help her voice sounding a little flat, and as if her newly awakened happiness had made her perceptive, Lady Standon put her arms round her again.

'If only things could come right for you, too, my dear,' she murmured.

A knock on the door made them both start.

'Who is it?' Amanda asked.

'His Lordship's compliments and he wants Lady Standon and Miss Burke to join him in the Salon.'

'We must go to him,' Lady Standon said quickly. 'And, Amanda, pray keep him engaged in conversation. Do not let him look at me too closely or he will guess something has happened. If he should prevent Graham and me from being together for a second time, I think I should kill him with my own bare hands.'

'I will do my best,' Amanda promised.

They crossed the landing to the Salon where they found Lord Ravenscar waiting.

'I have some last-minute instructions to give you both,' he said. 'I cannot dine here tonight because I have arranged a dinner party at Wattier's. The privilege, my dear Amanda, of every bridegroom is to have a last-night fling with his friends before he sacrifices his freedom.'

'I understand, my Lord,' Amanda replied demurely.

'I have just come from the Prince,' Lord Ravenscar went on. 'He fancies that he has a slight cold and you know how careful he is with his health. It has therefore been decided that the marriage shall take place not in the Grosvenor Chapel, as we intended, but in the Chinese Drawing Room at Carlton House. The Archbishop of Canterbury will officiate.'

'The Archbishop!' Amanda exclaimed.

'Yes, indeed,' Lord Ravenscar said. 'We shall be well and

truly tied to each other, my dear.'

Amanda said nothing, but looking at her downcast eyes, he added:

'You will be glad to hear, of course, that the Archbishop has approved your father's appointment to the bishopric of Frackenbury. I am at this moment sending a notice to the *Gazette* that the marriage has taken place between the 8th Baron Ravenscar and Amanda, eldest daughter of the Bishop of Frackenbury and Mrs. Burke.'

'Papa a Bishop!' Amanda exclaimed. 'How proud he will be!'

'And you? Are you proud or grateful?' Lord Ravenscar enquired.

'Naturally I am both, my Lord,' she replied.

'I am glad to hear that,' Lord Ravenscar said in a tone of voice which made her sure that he was mocking her.

A footman appeared at the door.

'What is it?' Lord Ravenscar enquired.

'A man has arrived with a basket of birds, m'Lord. He said you were expecting him.'

'Ah, yes! It is Whistler, my bird man.' Lord Ravenscar said. 'This is another little addition to tomorrow's ceremony which I feel will please you, Amanda. It is an old tradition—and one which is often forgotten—that the bride should release some white doves immediately after her marriage has taken place. I suggested it to His Royal Highness, who was delighted at the idea. It is those sort of little things which please him. So I told Whistler—who has provided me with those very pretty little creatures that you see in my aviary—to procure for me every dove that is possible. He has been prompt in executing the order I gave him. Let us go down and see them.'

'I think it is a charming idea,' Amanda said.

'And what do you think, Charlotte?' Lord Ravenscar asked, as if he suddenly realised that his sister had been standing there taking no part in the conversation.

'I only wonder what happens to the poor creatures after they are released,' Lady Standon replied in a voice which Amanda knew she was deliberately making dull and colourless. 'I am told that birds with gay plumage are often pecked to death by other birds.'

'I do not think that is true of doves,' Amanda said. 'We

had some pet ones at home when we were children and they were quite unharmed. In fact, all the other birds did was to come down and eat their food.'

'Charlotte is full of ill omens,' Lord Ravenscar said lightly. 'Come, Amanda, we will see what Whistler has brought us.'

They went downstairs towards the room which housed the aviary. When they reached the hall, Amanda realised that Lady Standon was not following them; but she was not unduly apprehensive because she knew that she and Lord Ravenscar would not be alone—Mr. Whistler would be there with his doves.

As they crossed the hall the grandfather clock struck the hour of six. Lord Ravenscar drew his watch from his pocket.

'I cannot be more than a few minutes,' he said. 'I have got to change and my party begins at half after seven.'

'You must not be late, must you?' Amanda said ingenuously.

The hours between six and midnight passed more slowly than any hours Amanda had known in the whole of her life. Every two minutes she glanced at the clock on the mantelpiece and half-a-dozen times, thinking that it must have stopped, she ran out from her bedroom to look over the well of the stairs into the hall, only to find the big grandfather clock said exactly the same time as hers.

When Lord Ravenscar had gone off to his dinner party and Amanda had returned to Lady Standon's room, they both decided to dine in bed.

'I just want to lie and think about Graham,' Lady Standon said quite simply. 'I do not want to talk; I do not want to see anyone. I just want to be alone and think how happy I am.'

'I can understand that,' Amanda answered. 'And I, too, would like to be alone.'

She had dinner in bed because she knew that the maid who brought in her tray would relay the news downstairs. When finally the tray was removed and she had told the girl she was going to sleep, she got up and dressed quickly.

She was vain enough to wear one of her new gowns in which to meet Peter. It was a very simple one; but the soft, expensive material and the low-cut bodice made her feel both sophisticated and beautiful. She did her hair with special care. Even so, she was ready and waiting at least two hours before there was any chance of Peter being in the garden.

Finally, as the hands of the clock crept slowly towards midnight, Amanda picked up a shawl and put it round her shoulders. Then, very, very softly, she turned the handle of her door.

The house was in complete silence except for the ticking of the clock in the hall, but she knew there would be a footman on duty by the front door. She tiptoed across the landing and went down another, less important, flight of stairs which led to the back of the house.

She had already ascertained that the easiest way into the garden would be from a small ante-room leading out of the Music Room. Here there was a French window and the room itself was seldom used.

It was dark in the passages for most of the servants had gone to bed, but Amanda found her way, and when at length she came into the ante-room looking on to the garden she found that a pale moon struggled from behind the clouds and gave her enough light for her to see the French window and how to open it.

She pulled back the bolts and was frightened because they made a slight noise. She turned the key in the lock and to her relief the window swung open. She slipped out, moving on to the little terrace, then down the stone steps towards the fountain. And then, hurrying as quickly as she could away from the house, she went through the formal garden to where, at the far end, she could see the arbour.

It had been built to create from the house the illusion of an elegant building; but it was nothing, in fact, but a few pillars supported against a high wall. There was, however, room inside for a bench, and the domed roof cast a shadow which meant that anyone inside the arbour was, at this time of night at any rate, invisible.

Amanda reached it and entered a little apprehensively. For the first time since she had received Peter's note she was afraid that this was some trap of Lady Isabel's and that he, himself, had not invited her there.

And then, as she passed between the pillars, she felt his arms go round her and with a little exclamation of relief she found herself close to his heart.

'My darling! My little love! I was afraid you would not come,' he exclaimed.

'And I was afraid you would not be here,' she answered. 'How did you know I needed you so desperately?'

'I felt it,' he answered. 'Something told me that you wanted me.'

'I was crying out for you,' she said. 'Sending my heart winging towards you, as you told me to do. And you heard. You really did hear.'

'When your heart beats, mine does too,' he answered. 'What has happened?'

He did not kiss her, but drew her down beside him on the bench. She could only just see the outline of his head and his broad shoulders. But she felt as if the tragedy in her eyes and on her lips must pierce the darkness so that he could see the full horror of it.

'I . . . I am to be . . married tomorrow,' she faltered.

She felt as if her words struck Peter like a blow. He seemed to reel under the very impact of them. And then in a voice that was strangled in his throat, he said:

'Oh, my God! What can I do? How can I save you?'

13

Amanda stood while the expressions of admiration buzzed around her.

‘ ’Tis exquisite!’

‘Madam will make a beautiful bride!’

She hardly heard the compliments, conscious only of a heaviness within her breast and a feeling of constriction in her throat. Her hands were cold, and the face that looked back at her from the mirror seemed heavy and listless, except for the eyes which were dark with apprehension.

Could it really be happening? she asked herself. Could her wedding day really have arrived? She knew that hope was dying hard within her. She had believed so firmly that by now, at any rate, something would have occurred—some miracle to save her. But all the time at the back of her mind—just as the roar of the sea had been a background to her childhood—she could hear Peter’s voice saying:

‘My God! What can I do? How can I save you?’

She had felt then as if the bottom had fallen out of her world; and now she could still listen to the desperate tragedy in his voice and feel the tension of his fingers as his hands gripped hers.

After he had spoken they had sat in silence and she had known that she was past tears, past pleading, past, in some extraordinary way, even the terror which she had known on other occasions when she had thought she must lose Peter. Now it seemed as if the inevitable had happened, that she must accept the situation for what it was.

She had looked out on the small paved garden and beyond it to the great house rising upwards towards the sky. All this would be hers and she knew that she would relinquish it willingly to be with Peter, even if it meant living in a mud hut or sailing away to some unknown land.

After a long time he had bent his head and buried his face in the palms of her hands.

'I am failing you, Amanda,' he said in a broken voice. 'I am failing the one person I love utterly and completely.'

'It is not your fault,' she said softly, her heart torn by the agony of his tone.

'If only I could have one little thing to help me,' Peter said. 'One clue! One pointer! It seems as if I am up against a blank wall.'

'I have begged Lord Ravenscar to wait,' Amanda said, 'but he was insistent that we should be married tomorrow. But why, Peter? Why must there be this unseemly haste?'

'I think I can answer that question,' Peter replied. 'Lady Isabel has sent post-haste to the north for her cousin, the Duke of Eastminster. He has not been in London for some years, but he used to be a very close friend and confidant of the Prince in his young days and still has influence with His Royal Highness. Lady Isabel believes that he will champion her because she insists that Lord Ravenscar has compromised her. A word from the Prince and his Lordship would be obliged to marry her.'

'So that is the reason,' Amanda said.

'That is what I have heard,' Peter replied.

'And how soon can the Duke be in London?' Amanda enquired.

Peter shrugged his shoulders.

'It is unlikely that he could be here before another forty-eight hours and then it will be too late.'

Amanda could hardly believe the words and yet they both knew they had been spoken. She felt Peter make a sudden movement as if he stiffened himself and threw back his shoulders.

'You are not married yet,' he said. 'You have got to try and help me. Think, Amanda! Think of who has been to the house since you have been there. Think of every single person who has visited Lord Ravenscar. Do not miss one out. Tell me their names.'

'There have really been very few,' Amanda said wonderingly. 'Lord Ravenscar has been with the Prince most of the time. There was, of course, the dinner party, but after he had told me you were dead I did not hear anyone's name. It all seemed to take place like a strange nightmare in which I was there and yet I had no connection with anyone else.'

'Forget the dinner party. Who else has called?' Peter asked.

'There has been Mr. Wassell,' Armanda replied.

'Yes, I know about Wassell. I have seen him go in and out,' Peter said. 'An unpleasant chap and someone I would not trust in any way. But he is a particularly intimate crony of Lord Ravenscar and there is nothing we can learn from him or about him.'

'I think that is really all,' Amanda said, desperately searching her mind. 'Lady Isabel came one day, but you will remember I told you about that. And, of course, there was the bird man this evening.'

'The bird man?'

Peter's question was sharp.

'Whistler was what Lord Ravenscar called him. He buys the exotic birds for his aviary; but I think perhaps he is not entirely straight, because tonight, when he brought the doves for the wedding . . . Oh, I forgot to tell you that I am to release two baskets of doves from the balcony at Carlton House after the ceremony has taken place. Lord Ravenscar says it is an old custom of his family.'

'You said that Whistler was not entirely straight. What makes you say that?' Peter enquired.

'Well, tonight, when he brought the doves and Lord Ravenscar showed them to me,' Amanda answered, 'I could see that they were not all doves in the basket. Two or three of them were pigeons, but their feathers had been dyed white.'

'Pigeons!'

She heard, with surprise, Peter almost shout the word. Then he had jumped to his feet and dragged Amanda up with him.

'*Mon Dieu!* What a fool I have been!' he cried. 'Amanda! Amanda! You have given me what I asked for!'

He threw his arms about her and held her close.

'Pray Heaven I am in time, my darling,' he said; and then, before she could ask what this strange elation meant, he had run from the shadow of the arbour and she saw him climb up the lattice-work which covered the wall.

He reached the top. For a moment he was silhouetted

against the sky and he raised his hand to her in salute before he vanished down the other side.

She stood staring after him, perplexed and amazed. What had she said that could cause such a commotion? How could the mention of pigeons change his mood of despondency to one of action and urgency?

Slowly she went back to the house and up to her bedroom. For a little while she felt that perhaps she had, indeed, given Peter the clue he required. And then, as the long hours of night dragged past, a dark depression settled on her again. She could only hear his voice saying: 'My God! What can I do? How can I save you?'

Morning brought sunshine through her windows and an obvious air of excitement amongst the maids who brought her breakfast, drew her bath and prepared the clothes she was to wear at her wedding.

A hairdresser had been engaged to arrange her hair, and, when he had finished, there was the ceremony of stepping into her wedding gown. There were, by this time, half-a-dozen women in her room—Mrs. Hewitt, the two housemaids, the dressmaker and her assistant who had come to give a last-minute touch to the gown, and, finally, Lady Standon.

It was difficult to recognise the gloomy and indifferent middle-aged woman who had chaperoned her in the young, smiling person who entered her bedroom dressed in the height of fashion in a gown that she must have sent for as soon as the shops opened.

She bent to kiss Amanda and there was an expression of tenderness and sympathy in her face which had never been there before. Because the servants were present, there was nothing that they could say to each other; but Amanda knew that Lady Standon understood what she was feeling and somehow it eased her misery a little.

When the wedding gown was in its place Mrs. Hewitt went to the door and the Major-domo entered with a large jewel-case in his hand.

'His Lordship's compliments,' he said to Amanda, 'and he has sent you the famous diamond tiara to hold your veil in place and a diamond necklace which he hopes you will honour him by wearing.'

Amanda glanced indifferently at the magnificent tiara,

which was made in the shape of a wreath of flowers. The hairdresser fixed it on her head; and then Lady Standon clasped around her neck the necklace which went with it. Again the expressions of admiration and excitement buzzed round the room, but Amanda did not listen to them.

A sudden knock at the door made her turn swiftly, hoping against hope that it might be a message or something which would prevent her going to the marriage ceremony. But a second later she heard Lord Ravenscar's voice.

'Amanda, I want to speak to you,' he said. 'Come into the Salon.'

'If it please your Lordship.'

Amanda spoke without thinking and she heard one of the housemaids murmur:

' 'Tis unlucky. The bridegroom should not see his bride before the ceremony.'

Mrs. Hewitt hushed her into silence as she lifted the train of the wedding gown and Amanda walked slowly from the bed-chamber across the landing and into the Salon. Lord Ravenscar was looking magnificent, no one could deny him that, for he was wearing the full dress uniform of the Hussars, of which he was the Honorary Colonel-in-Chief. On it blazed his medals and decorations which combined with the gold lace on his coat, his plumed hat and ornamental sword to make one forget the lines of dissipation on his face and the cynical twist of his lips.

But Amanda saw only the look in his eyes that she dreaded. He looked her over and she felt the fire of his passion rise, dark and disturbing, in the glance he gave her.

'Your Lordship is satisfied?'

It was Mrs. Hewitt who dared to ask the question, and Lord Ravenscar replied with a smile:

'Very satisfied, Mrs. Hewitt. She is enchanting; a bride whom any man might find desirable.'

There was a note in his voice which told Amanda all too clearly that he had some idea of her feelings. He knew her heart was given to someone else; and yet, in his bestiality, it merely excited him, merely made him desire her the more.

'I came to tell you Amanda,' he said, 'that I am now leaving for Carlton House. The carriage to convey you and my sister will be waiting outside in exactly five minutes. You must not be late. The Prince dislikes being kept waiting, especially when he has a cold.'

'I am ready, as your Lordship can see,' Amanda said in tones of one who goes to the guillotine.

'And impatient, no doubt,' Lord Ravenscar said mockingly. 'I can see the eagerness with which you wish to rush into my open arms. Ah, Amanda! This afternoon we leave London on our honeymoon.'

'Our honeymoon! I had not thought of that,' Amanda exclaimed.

'Everything is planned,' Lord Ravenscar said. 'But it is to be a surprise. I can promise you, Amanda, many surprises in our life together. This will be the first of them.'

He raised her cold and trembling fingers to his lips. She felt the hot passion of his mouth burn against her skin and she parted her lips to say she could not do it, she could not go through with it. But the words would not come. They were stifled in her throat, and as she strove to speak a voice from the doorway said:

'May I enter?'

Lord Ravenscar released Amanda's hand.

'Oh, it is you, Wassell! I was wondering what the devil had happened to you.'

'I was delayed in the Club,' Mr. Wassell explained.

He came into the Salon and Amanda was able to see that he was dressed in the most dandified manner, his high cravat reaching almost up to his ears, his yellow coat seeming a parody of the fashion set by the more distinguished and important dandies of St. James's.

'There is news . . .' he began.

'News! What news?' Lord Ravenscar asked quickly.

'Napoleon Bonaparte is today being crowned Emperor of France,' Mr. Wassell replied in the solemn voice of one who makes an important announcement.

'Emperor of France!' Lord Ravenscar exclaimed. 'Gad, but the fellow is invincible!'

There was a queer glint in his eyes as he spoke. Then from the doorway where she had been watching but taking no part in what had been taking place, Lady Standon said:

'No one can call Bonaparte invincible until he has conquered England. The invasion barges are still waiting in Dieppe harbour.'

'And the summer still lies ahead of us, Charlotte,' Lord Ravenscar said.

'It is too late,' Lady Standon retorted. 'I am told that he has missed the opportunity.'

'And who, may I ask, has given you his considered opinion on this subject?' Lord Ravenscar enquired.

Lady Standon did not answer, and Amanda, interposing because she was afraid that Lord Ravenscar might enquire deeper into why Lady Standon's interests were suddenly aroused in military matters, said quickly:

'Will this mean anything to us—to the country I mean—that General Bonaparte should become Emperor?'

'I must go to Carlton House and find out,' Lord Ravenscar replied. 'I shall be awaiting your arrival, my dear Amanda, with more than the customary trepidation of a lovelorn bridegroom.'

He was mocking her again, Amanda thought; and yet, at the same time, she knew that the news Mr. Wassell had brought, for some obscure reason, had pleased him. He went from the room in what she guessed to be a high good humour. She heard his voice, with a note of excitement in it, as he went down the stairs.

Five minutes later she and Lady Standon were on their way to Carlton House. They did not speak much. There was little either of them could say. Amanda knew that Lady Standon was counting the hours until the wedding was over so that she could join the man she loved. Lady Standon knew, in her turn, that Amanda was dreading every second which took her nearer to a marriage which she loathed and detested and which could bring her only fear and disgust. And yet what could either of them do about it?

The coach, drawn by four horses with its outriders in claret and gold, swept through Berkeley Square into Piccadilly and turned down St. James's Street. Peering through her veil Amanda scanned the passers-by, hoping that she might have a glimpse of Peter standing by the roadside or amongst the crowds which had congregated outside Carlton House. Surely, if he could not save her, he would be there so that she could see him, could have one last glance at him.

Why, why, she asked herself, had he hurried away last night without even giving her a farewell kiss, without holding her against his heart and telling her that he loved her, even if it were for the last time?

The coach stopped. She knew that her last hope had gone.

'God bless you,' Lady Standon said.

'Here's luck!' someone called from the crowd and a piece of white heather fell at Amanda's feet.

She did not stoop to pick it up. She knew it could bring her no luck. Surely, surely, something would happen now, at this moment as she stepped down from the coach, as she paused while the flunkeys lifted out her veil and arranged it behind her. But there were only a few half-hearted cheers from the onlookers.

Slowly Amanda turned and walked through the hall and began the slow climb up the great marble staircase. Now it seemed that all feeling had left her. She was just a body from which all life had been extinguished, just a puppet that must move forward towards extinction and leave behind everything that had made life worth living.

She reached the top of the stairs and there, waiting for her, was the Prince's private secretary.

'You are exactly on time, Miss Burke,' he said primly. 'His Royal Highness is waiting for you.'

He led her into the Chinese Drawing Room and she saw that a large company of distinguished personages was assembled there. The Prince, resplendent in a coat of deep rose-pink velvet and ablaze with decorations, was standing in the centre of the room under the lighted chandelier. Beyond him, at an improvised altar, stood the Archbishop in his vestments.

Amanda swept to the ground in a deep curtsy before the Prince.

'Welcome to the bride!' he said extending his hand, and she knew that he was enjoying this little charade in which he himself was able to play a part.

With pomp and dignity the Prince gave her his arm and they moved slowly up the room to where Amanda could see Lord Ravenscar was already waiting. The Prince was deliberately slow and Amanda felt as if it took an hour, at least, to traverse the length of the Chinese Drawing Room.

And now Lord Ravenscar was on her other side. She saw his eyes boring their way into hers; she saw the smile on his thick lips and wished only that she might die.

The Archbishop began the service. Amanda heard him say the words with which she had been familiar ever since she was a child.

'Who gives this woman to this man?'

'I do!'

The Prince made the two words sound dramatic, and then the next part of the service had begun.

Amanda shut her eyes. If only she could faint or die, she thought. If only an earthquake would take place and the ground open and swallow her up. But none of these things happened.

'Say this after me,' the Archbishop said. 'I, Hugo Alexander . . .'

'I, Hugo Alexander . . .'

'Take thee, Amanda Mary . . .'

'Take thee, Amanda Mary . . .'

'To be my wedded wife . . .'

'To be my wedded wife . . .'

'For better for worse . . .'

It was over, Amanda thought; now there was no longer even the faintest glimmer of hope. She was married to a man she hated with every drop of blood in her whole body.

'I hate him! I hate him!' She almost said the words aloud, and then knew it was her turn.

'Say this after me. I, Amanda Mary . . .'

'I, Amanda Mary . . .'

'Stop!'

A voice from the door behind them, peremptory and commanding, seemed to echo round the room.

'Stop this ceremony!'

The words made everyone turn their heads; and in a sudden silence, which was almost like the gasp of indrawn breath, Amanda saw that Peter stood there—Peter with a strange, commanding expression on his face that she had never seen before—and following him, escorted by two

Bow Street Runners, were two men; one of them she recognised as Whistler, the other was a seaman wearing the high fishing-boots of his trade.

In the general stupefaction it was the Prince who found his voice first.

'St. Just!' he exclaimed. 'What are you doing here?'

Peter advanced swiftly until he stood facing the Prince, then he bowed.

'I must crave Your Royal Highness's pardon for this intrusion,' he said, 'but it is a matter of the utmost urgency, a matter which concerns Your Royal Highness's safety as well as that of His Majesty's subjects.'

'My safety!' the Prince exclaimed. 'What is all this? And who let you in?'

'I must ask Your Royal Highness to listen to me for one moment,' Peter said. 'When you sent me into exile for defamatory words and unproved accusations against a member of your household and your friend Lord Ravenscar, I did not cease to try and prove the point of my assertions.'

'I do not see why we should listen to this now,' the Prince said petulantly. 'You were exiled, St. Just, from this country and I cannot perceive how you can have come here and into this very room without being arrested.'

'That is what I have come to explain to Your Royal Highness, and because the plot against England is taking place under this very roof I must ask your indulgence.'

'Under this very roof!' The Prince stared around. 'How can such a thing be possible?'

'That is what I am ready to tell you,' Peter said.

He made a gesture and the Runners pushed forward the seaman.

'I should like Your Royal Highness,' he went on, 'to listen to this man. He is the Master of a fishing boat, *The Lucy Jane,* which fishes habitually in the Channel and the North Sea. He will inform you that he was paid what seemed to him a very large sum of money to pick up at various intervals parcels from another fishing boat which he met at night at a certain point on the compass. Is that true?'

'Aye, Sir, it be true enough,' the fisherman said surlily.

'Now tell His Royal Highness what was the nationality

of the boat from which you collected your parcels at regular intervals.'

'Twere a French boat,' the man said.

A sudden buzz went round the room. The wedding guests pressed forward. Lord Ravenscar, who had seemed to Amanda to be stunned into silence, now interrupted.

'Surely, Your Highness,' he said, 'it will be possible to finish the ceremony before we go into these extraordinary details?'

The Prince waved him to one side.

'No, no,' he said. 'I want to hear what St. Just has to tell us.'

'A parcel from a French ship,' Peter repeated in case someone had not got the point. 'And what was in that parcel?'

'There didna seem no 'arm in it, Yer Royal 'ighness,' the seaman said. 'No 'arm at all.'

'What was in the parcel?' Peter repeated.

''Twere pigeons. Just birds goin' back ter their rightful owner was what Oi was a-told.'

'Pigeons!' Peter said. 'And these were delivered when you reached harbour to this man here, were they not?'

'Yes, Sir.'

Peter turned to the man called Whistler.

'These pigeons were brought to you, were they not?' Peter enquired.

'Yes, Sir.'

'And what did you do with them?'

'They were mine, m'Lord. They were only returned to me by some friends who had collected them.'

'No one had ordered you to send them out or to receive them back in this peculiar manner?'

Whistler hesitated. There was obviously some conflict going on within him. Beads of sweat appeared on his forehead and he glanced towards Lord Ravenscar, hesitated, then said firmly:

'No, Sir, it was entirely my own idea.'

'I am glad you are so rich, Mr. Whistler,' Peter said sarcastically. 'Ten guineas for each parcel delivered to you in this manner from France is a large sum of money for a man in your position to pay.'

'Ten guineas!' someone ejaculated in the company.

'You would, of course, recognise your pigeons when you saw them again?' Peter continued. 'Good! That is what I wanted to know.'

He turned towards the doorway and said to two footmen who were standing there:

'Bring in the doves if you please.'

There was a gasp amongst the crowd as a large hamper decorated with white wedding bows was carried into the centre of the room.

'I do not understand!' the Prince exclaimed.

'I am about to explain, Your Royal Highness,' Peter replied. 'These doves have been supplied for the wedding ceremony. They are to be released, as I think Your Royal Highness knows, from the balcony by the bride herself. They spent last night in Lord Ravenscar's house in Grosvenor Square. Now there are amongst them, I believe, some birds which do not conform to the characteristics of the dove. These birds, moreover, carry round their legs secrets of this country which would be of inestimable value to the newly crowned Emperor of France!'

'By Gad! Carrier pigeons!' someone ejaculated.

'Exactly,' Peter said. 'Now I do not intend to open the basket myself—there are people who might say I was prejudiced. And so I would ask someone to examine the birds; someone who will know how valuable the secrets are which are being flown out of this country.'

He looked round to the wedding guests.

'General Sir Arthur Wellesley!' he said. 'And Admiral of the Fleet Lord Cornwallis! Would you be kind enough?'

The two men stepped forward; and then, as they did so, there was a sudden exclamation.

'Damn you!' a voice said by Amanda's side.

She turned to see the expression of fury on Lord Ravenscar's face, she saw him draw his sword.

'Out of my way!' he said. 'The first man to touch me will get this through his chest!'

He started to walk through the guests, the naked steel in his hand. Everyone shrank back with expressions of surprise and alarm.

'Ravenscar! What the devil are you doing?' the Prince ejaculated.

Peter sprang forward, and, taking an astonished Ambassador by surprise, drew his sword from its scabbard before he realised what was happening.

'This man is mine!' Peter cried. 'On guard, Ravenscar!'

Lord Ravenscar turned towards him and his blade flashed out. Now there were cries on all sides.

'In front of the Prince!'

'Seize them!'

But before anything could be done the Prince held up his hand.

'No, leave them alone,' he commanded. 'St. Just is entitled to his revenge.'

Someone moved the hamper to one side. The Bow Street Runners took Whistler and the seaman to a far corner of the room. And now the two men were lunging at each other with a desperate fury which told the onlookers this was no game of skill but a fight to the death.

Lord Ravenscar's teeth were bared. He looked cruel, evil and somehow deadly as he bore down upon the younger man, fighting with a brilliance which was undeniable and with a fury which left everyone in no doubt at all that he realised, too, this was a fight to the death.

Amanda could only stand and find the prayers for Peter's safety trembling on her lips. At this interruption in the marriage service she had felt her heart leap suffocatingly. She felt as if it would spring from her very breast towards him. He had come! He had saved her!

She had known at the first sound of his voice, and when she had seen him standing there, that she had been mad not to trust him, not to know that whatever happened he would not fail her. And now she knew that he was in deadly peril.

She heard people murmuring around her; heard someone say:

'Ravenscar has always been an expert in a duel. He has killed two men to my knowledge.'

'Oh, God, save him!' Amanda whispered, her eyes on Peter.

There was no doubt that he was being hard pressed. At the same time, he had youth on his side. He was, for the moment, playing for safety—retreating—and advancing only when Lord Ravenscar had made a supreme effort and missed him; keeping always a little of himself in reserve; tiring out the older man.

And now, suddenly, he seemed to go into the attack. He drove Lord Ravenscar down the room, drove him through the anteroom and on to the landing outside the grand staircase. The older man was fighting every inch of the way, but Peter had the upper hand.

The clang of steel was the only sound to be heard as the guests, following behind the Prince, pressed through the room, the light from the candles glittering on their jewels and decorations and on their tense faces as they watched and waited.

Peter made a sudden lunge forward. Lord Ravenscar had tried to parry him and failed. The blade passed through his shoulder. The blow carried him backwards to the very top of the staircase, his feet slipped beneath him and he fell. Heavily he rolled over and over, down step after step, to sprawl finally in a broken, twisted heap at the foot of them in the Marble Hall.

Peter stood looking down at him. There was blood on the blade of the sword, but he did not move. Someone ran down the stairs to Lord Ravenscar's side. It was the Prince's own physician. He examined him and then said quietly:

'His neck is broken.'

Peter turned towards the Prince.

'So perish all traitors, Your Royal Highness!'

The Prince made a gesture with his hands.

'Take him away! Take him away!' he said testily. 'Follow me, St. Just.'

He turned and walked back into the drawing-room. Amanda was standing where the assembled crowd had left her, in front of the altar. She had not followed because she dared not, because she knew that the only thing she could do at this moment was to pray for Peter.

Now, when she saw him returning at the Prince's side, she stifled a little cry and her hands went to her breast while her eyes were shining. He looked across at her and there was a smile on his lips.

The Prince stood between them and now, with one of the dramatic gestures which those with whom he was familiar knew so well, said:

'My Lords and Ladies! We must thank the Marquis St. Just for uncovering this dastardly plot against our country and for unmasking this traitor who was hidden in our midst. We must also beg the Marquis to forgive the aspersions against his fair name which were most unfairly proclaimed by the aforesaid traitor. We not only apologise to you, my Lord Marquis, but ask you to forget the exile that was imposed upon you in all good faith, and to return to take up your life amongst us so that we may enjoy your friendship as in former days.'

Peter bowed.

'I thank Your Royal Highness for your most kind and generous words.'

'What is more,' the Prince continued. 'As under the law of the land the properties and wealth of a traitor are confiscated by the Crown, it seems to me only just and fair that these effects of Lord Ravenscar's should pass into the possession of the Marquis whose own property was seized at the time of his exile. There will be no difficulty on that score, I am quite certain; and you, my Lord Chancellor, will no doubt see that the transfer is performed with all possible speed.'

The Lord Chancellor bowed.

'It shall be as Your Royal Highness commands,' he said.

'And now we have made amends, St. Just,' the Prince continued, 'can we have your assurance that you have, indeed, forgiven all the defamatory things that were said against you?'

'Your Royal Highness not only has my word for it,' Peter said, 'but you have my assurance that my sword and life shall be at your disposal and that of my adopted country, England.'

'Then there is nothing more that can be said,' the Prince said with a smile, holding out his hand.

'There is, however, one favour I would ask, if Your Royal Highness would grant it,' Peter replied.

'It is yours, yours,' the Prince said quickly. 'You have but to ask.'

'It is that the marriage ceremony might continue,' Peter said, 'with just a change of bridegroom.'

'The marriage ceremony! What is this?' the Prince asked, looking quickly at Amanda.

'Miss Burke and I have loved each other since we first met,' Peter explained.

'Indeed! Well, we must ask the Archbishop what he has to say about this!' the Prince exclaimed. 'But it would, indeed, be a pity to waste the wedding breakfast!'

'If this is what Miss Burke wishes,' the Archbishop said, 'I am only too pleased to marry Pierre St. Just, son of my old friend who met his death on the guillotine. Pierre has lived in this country, as Your Royal Highness knows, since he was a young boy. He managed to escape from the Terror. He is a Protestant by religion, for his family were resident in Normandy, and I can imagine no way of rewarding him more effectively than by making him happy in the holy bonds of matrimony.'

'Come along then,' the Prince said genially. 'Let us get on with it, my Lord Archbishop.'

Peter walked towards Amanda and held out his hand to her. There was nothing they could say to each other. Everything was too wonderful, too glorious and golden at this moment. She felt her fingers cling to his; she felt the strength of him holding her up and sustaining her. Her eyes were shining like stars in her pale face as she looked into his eyes and saw there an expression of love and tenderness beyond anything she had deemed possible.

Afterwards there would be many questions she would want to ask him: Why he had not told her who he was? Why he had not trusted her with his suspicion that Lord Ravenscar was a traitor? Why he had ever allowed himself to be exiled without refuting the charges against him?

But now the only thing that mattered was the fact that Peter was alive and that she was free—free to belong to him. She felt her love rise up within her like a flame. She felt her whole body tremble with the excitement and ecstasy of the thrill that swept over her because she knew that in a few seconds she would be his wife and belong to him for ever.

'I love you, Amanda!'

His words were only a whisper for her ear alone.

'I love you too.'

There was no need to say the words aloud The movement of her lips told him all he needed to know. He took her hand and led her forward.

'My Lord Archbishop, will you please marry us?' he said, and it seemed to Amanda at that moment as if the room was filled with the wings of angels and with the music of some Heavenly choir.

This was the man of her heart. This was the man to whom she had given her whole love, holding back nothing. They were to be one—one united, indivisible against the world, joined together by a love which would defeat time and space and last for eternity.